P9-DDC-427

"The farther west I travel, the more... open I feel. Less closed in."

Logan couldn't help but smile. "That's how I feel when I'm flying."

"You're a pilot?"

"Private jets. Experimental sometimes—but mostly redesigns." Until he got his promotion. Then his assignments would become way more interesting.

"A test pilot," Blossom said. "No wonder you don't seem that happy to be here."

He looked outside the barn at that big blue sky. "Got me," he said.

"I think I know how you feel. Flying high must seem like being a bird. I suppose if I reached California, I'd feel positively free." She didn't sound that convinced. "Or maybe," she added with that look again, "I'll just run out of road."

He didn't want to care, but still he had to ask.

"Blossom, what are you running from?"

Dear Reader,

How much fun can a writer have? I loved fitting all the pieces together for *The Reluctant Rancher*. As a bonus, I got to write about cowboys—always a favorite!

In his "real life," Logan Hunter is a test pilot who needs an upcoming promotion with higher pay so he can fight for custody of his young son. But when the grandfather who raised Logan gets hurt on the family ranch, Logan becomes a temporary cowboy again.

He's not looking for love. And Blossom Kennedy, the caregiver he hires to help out, is clearly on the run. She won't stay long and neither will he. But, of course, love has its own plans for these two.

I hope you'll enjoy this ride on the Circle H ranch, where the buffalo still roam. And there's more good news: *The Reluctant Rancher* is the first book in my new miniseries, Kansas Cowboys.

Happy reading!

Leigh

HEARTWARMING

The Reluctant Rancher

———

USA TODAY Bestselling Author

Leigh Riker

HARLEQUIN® HEARTWARMING™

If you purchased this book without a cover you should be aware that this book is stolen property. It was reported as "unsold and destroyed" to the publisher, and neither the author nor the publisher has received any payment for this "stripped book."

Recycling programs
for this product may
not exist in your area.

ISBN-13: 978-0-373-36808-2

The Reluctant Rancher

Copyright © 2016 by Leigh Riker

All rights reserved. Except for use in any review, the reproduction or utilization of this work in whole or in part in any form by any electronic, mechanical or other means, now known or hereinafter invented, including xerography, photocopying and recording, or in any information storage or retrieval system, is forbidden without the written permission of the publisher, Harlequin Enterprises Limited, 225 Duncan Mill Road, Don Mills, Ontario M3B 3K9, Canada.

This is a work of fiction. Names, characters, places and incidents are either the product of the author's imagination or are used fictitiously, and any resemblance to actual persons, living or dead, business establishments, events or locales is entirely coincidental.

This edition published by arrangement with Harlequin Books S.A.

For questions and comments about the quality of this book, please contact us at CustomerService@Harlequin.com.

® and TM are trademarks of Harlequin Enterprises Limited or its corporate affiliates. Trademarks indicated with ® are registered in the United States Patent and Trademark Office, the Canadian Intellectual Property Office and in other countries.

Printed in U.S.A.

www.Harlequin.com

Leigh Riker, like many dedicated readers, grew up with her nose in a book. This award-winning, *USA TODAY* bestselling author still can't imagine a better way to spend her time than to curl up with a good romance novel—unless it is to write one! She's a member of the Authors Guild, Novelists, Inc. and Romance Writers of America. When not writing, she's either in the garden, watching movies funny and sad, or traveling (for research purposes, of course). With added "help" from her mischievous Maine coon cat, she's now at home working on a new novel. She loves to hear from readers. You can find Leigh on her website, leighriker.com, on Facebook at leighrikerauthor and on Twitter, @lbrwriter.

Books by Leigh Riker

Harlequin Heartwarming

Lost and Found Family
Man of the Family
If I Loved You

Harlequin Intrigue

Agent-in-Charge
Double Take

Harlequin Next

Change of Life

Red Dress Ink

Strapless

Visit the Author Profile page
at Harlequin.com for more titles.

To
Aidan, Kaitlyn, Jackson and Lily,
my youngest loves...

CHAPTER ONE

"This one had better be good," he said.

Because being a cowboy—or a nursemaid—wasn't in Logan Hunter's plan.

His black Stetson cocked at an angle, he narrowed his eyes at the distant plume of dust rising off the dirt access lane to the ranch. The Circle H was cut off—literally, in bad weather—from the road by half a mile. One reason he didn't want to be here, especially in spring when he knew the rains would come. Staring across the wide expanse of land, which looked as flat as an old mare's shank, he studied the fast-approaching car.

Logan wished he were in a car and headed the other way. Three years after the nasty divorce that had turned him into a hard man, he was still dealing with the fallout when his grandfather got hurt. He was more than willing to come back here and help Sam—he'd raised Logan and his brother after all—but April was the busy season. He couldn't run the ranch and care for Sam at the same time. He needed more help. Fast.

Certainly his brother hadn't stepped up to the plate. Sawyer hadn't even answered his calls. Everything was up to Logan, at least for now.

Still watching the lane, he scooped up the tortoiseshell kitten that had kept twining around his feet. Cradling the little cat, Logan propped a shoulder against the front porch post and listened to her purr. He was a sucker for animals, with one exception.

Bison.

Why couldn't his granddad run cattle like everybody else?

The car barreled into focus, gathering speed the closer it came, as if someone was chasing the driver. The broken-down sedan crunched to a stop in the gravel by the front steps, and Logan envisioned another frustrating go-round with the Mother Comfort Home Health Care Agency's latest candidate. The male caregiver he'd asked for was a rare commodity in the middle of Kansas, so he'd been told.

He didn't want excuses. The driver's door opened and disappointment swamped him. Logan didn't want another woman in the house—in his life either. Then the dust cloud settled and he really saw her. As she climbed out of the car, the denim ball cap she wore snagged on the door frame. The hat flopped off into the dirt, and a riot of russet curls spilled free. That bright hair bobbed everywhere. Hidden behind huge sunglasses, her eyes could be any color, but her chin hitched upward in her heart-shaped face and his stomach clenched.

He might have been a fool at twenty-three, but at thirty-two he knew better.

The woman's clothing was something else. Baggy top, baggy pants, both in dark colors, which shouldn't have made her look attractive, but did.

She pulled off her glasses. Her eyes were brown, like the plain grass in winter, yet he saw something deep within them. Despair? Fear? He couldn't tell.

But her voice held firm. "Mr. Hunter?"

"Yep." From his casual stance against the post, he gave her his best strong, silent cowboy stare. "You're looking at him."

She took a breath. "I thought I'd never get here."

"So did I." Idly, he stroked the kitten. He'd

waited most of the afternoon for this newest applicant.

She glanced behind her at the long drive. "Well. This *is* Kansas." Suddenly, she grinned up at him from the bottom step. "I feel like I'm in *The Wizard of Oz* before the tornado whisked Dorothy away. Not much out here, is there?"

"Not much." Logan had almost flinched. He didn't need any reminders of the ranch's isolation.

"I was sure I was lost. Even your driveway goes on forever." She shot another look over her shoulder. Who was she expecting to see?

Logan exaggerated a drawl. "Well, that's the thing about Kansas. Straight roads. You can just keep goin'. Even fall asleep if you want, then wake yourself up when you get here—or there."

Her smile faded. Worrying her lower lip, she took a step backward toward her car. Logan couldn't blame her. He wanted to run, too, and never come back. This was the place where he'd lost his parents, then his wife, his marriage. And, nearly, his child.

"So," she said, "this must be the Circle H."

"That's what the sign says."

She tilted her head to study him. "That sign

at the end of your road is hanging by a thread. It wouldn't take a minute to put it back up."

"That part of your job description?"

"No," she said, looking away. "I imagine it's part of yours."

"Look, we have ten thousand acres here. Miles and miles of fence line. Two men quit this morning, the cook three days ago." Thanks to Sam's grumpiness. "Things keep going this way, we won't need a sign except one that says For Sale." Her mouth fell open. "On top of that—"

"Logan, where are you?"

It was uncanny timing. His grandfather's voice blasted from his upstairs bedroom down the steps and through the screen door onto the porch. It happened about ten times a day. He'd always been difficult, but since his accident…

Sam was making a real racket now. Banging on his tray, probably, with the spoon he'd thrown at Logan earlier because he didn't like canned stew for lunch. Stroking the kitten he still held, he stood frozen. If Sam continued to be the worst patient in medical history, Logan might never be able to get any work done. Or leave. He *had* to hire help. Right now anyone would do.

"Coming!" he called and then studied the woman. "You still want this job?"

She returned his hard stare. "I'm not sure yet. But I do *need* it."

Well, at least she'd made herself clear. He couldn't keep from asking.

"That bad?"

She bent to pick up her ball cap. "Even worse."

Logan took another look. None of his business. Whatever had caused that haunted expression deep in her warm brown eyes, he shouldn't care. Still, he could recognize the same look he often saw in his own mirror. Trapped, it said. So maybe she could help out for a few days until he found a man to replace her.

"Come on. We'll find out what Sam wants," he said. "He'll size you up then we'll decide." He added, "Call me Logan."

She sent the little cat a smile, not him. "Blossom Kennedy."

Logan peeled away from the porch post, set the kitten down with a gentle pat on her rump and watched her tumble down the steps then scamper away toward the barn. Feeling Blossom Kennedy's gaze on him, he resettled his Stetson and headed inside.

Blossom followed.

"I'm told the senior Mr. Hunter is sweet," she said, as if to convince herself that everyone on the Circle H didn't have the disposition of a billy goat.

Logan couldn't help a wolfish grin. "Let's see how long you think that."

BECAUSE SHE HAD no other choice, Blossom trailed Logan Hunter up the steps to the second floor of the sprawling house. Really, with that dark hair and those broad shoulders, he was something to look at. Too bad she wasn't interested, even for the brief time it would take him to fire her. And oh, she'd seen that intent in his dark blue eyes.

The man himself was like a bruise: black hat, midnight eyes, blue jeans and ebony boots. Her first sight of him, holding that kitten, hadn't matched what she'd been told by the woman at the agency. Or rather, warned about. She bit back a sigh.

Considering her life experience so far, she should hate men. This one wasn't very friendly, even if his shoulders did look just right for leaning on. But Blossom wouldn't lean, or cry. That was behind her now. She would try to become a stronger person who relied on herself.

"Has your father been sick long?" she asked, wondering why he'd called Sam by his first name. The agency hadn't given her any details. All the woman had said was that the owner of the Circle H needed in-home care.

"He's my grandfather—stepgrandfather, actually. When my folks died, my grandmother was already a widow herself. This ranch—which my dad had run for her—belonged to my family. Then she married Sam and he took over. They raised me here on the Circle H. Sam adopted me." He kept going up the steps. "He's not sick. He broke his leg in three places." Logan sighed. "He cracked his skull. And to complicate matters, he had an intra-cranial bleed."

Logan didn't trip over the big word, which made her unsteady stomach churn. Maybe she should have thought twice before signing on with the Mother Comfort agency, which had admittedly been a last resort. As she'd heard often enough, she was no homemaker. She was surely no nurse. Frankly, she didn't know what she was. Out of money and stranded in the nearby town of Barren, Blossom had largely faked her experience on the agency application.

"He came home from the hospital a few days ago," Logan went on, "but his memory's not so good. He gets confused."

Predictably, her heart melted. "Poor man."

"Don't feel sorry for him. He *needed* his head examined."

At his dry tone, Blossom couldn't resist. She made a face at Logan's back. If she didn't need this job so badly, she wouldn't work for a man who didn't have so much as a soft spot for his own grandfather. Or was he smiling? She couldn't see his expression.

They'd just reached the top of the stairs when a crash sounded, and Logan lit off down the hall. He flung open the door of the end room and sent his black hat sailing onto the nearest chair, where it settled perfectly, like a lasso around a calf's neck.

"Still alive, I see," he said, his tone gruff. "You're not safe even from yourself."

Blossom followed him into the room, a sinking feeling in her uneasy stomach. Maybe she'd bitten off more here than she could chew—as usual.

An older man who didn't fit her idea of an invalid, except for the large cast on his right leg, sat in the middle of the hardwood floor rubbing his head. "Didn't you hear me call?" Whipcord lean, he looked like a much younger person than she'd envisioned, and his dark hair had only a few broad streaks of gray. He peered around Logan, who had knelt in front of him. "Who've you got there? You finally get some sense and answer that ad I picked out for you in the paper?"

"No," he said. "She's from the agency."

"The Department of Agriculture? Well, I've got something to say to—"

"Not the government, the health care people." His voice had gentled, the same way he'd treated the kitten.

"I don't need health care," his grandfather said.

Logan searched his limbs, probably for more fractures, then his head for lumps. He stared into his grandfather's eyes. "What's your name?"

"Samuel…uh, Hunter."

Logan didn't look happy with the hesitant answer. "I can't leave you alone for fifteen minutes. You know how dizzy you get when you try to stand up. Where did you think you were going?" He tugged lightly on his arm.

"Come on, now. I've got you. Let's get you back in bed."

"I'm dizzy because I *was* in bed. All day," Sam said, still studying Blossom. "I told you those ads would pay off."

"Forget the singles ads."

Sam snorted. "I may have smashed my head, but you don't know the first thing that's good for you. One bad experience, you don't stay off the horse—"

"Are we talking about you or me now?"

Sam sagged onto the bed, his face white. He gazed at Blossom again. "Come over here, girl. Let me get a better look at you. My eyes don't work so good these days, but I sure do like what I can see, which is two of you."

Startled, she stepped closer to the bed. In her view he was a dear, all right. Crusty as the outside of a loaf of country bread, but with a soft center that she favored in bread and in people for that matter. Was that why she'd been called a pushover? She glanced out the window, past the lace curtains blowing in the breeze, to make sure the coast was still clear.

"You've had a bad time," she said.

He grinned. "Not that bad, it turns out. I sure know how to pick 'em."

"Sam," Logan muttered.

"We're going to get on just fine," he continued as if Logan hadn't spoken. His blue eyes twinkled. "What kind of cook are you?"

"A…reluctant one." She wanted to stay, to help, but she couldn't fib anymore. She'd used up her quota on the agency application.

Blossom waited for Logan to take her arm and steer her down the stairs to her car right that moment, but instead, he sighed then let Sam continue the interview.

"Can you keep house?"

"If I have to." She added, "I try." That was one thing you could say about her.

Sam smiled. "A clean rag, some lemon oil… there's nothing to it."

"You never cleaned house in your life," Logan pointed out.

"And we have a laundry setup on the back porch."

"No, it's in the basement." Logan was standing by the door now.

"I guess I can figure out a washing machine," she said, giving in to a smile, "as long as it's not the old-fashioned wringer kind or a washboard. And takes quarters."

Sam cackled. "You got a good sense of humor. I like that." He glanced at Logan. "This house could use a few laughs." His sharp gaze pinned her like a butterfly to a mounting board. "How old are you?"

"Twenty-nine last month."

He sank back against his pillows. "You want babies?"

Logan shifted his weight. "All right, Sam. Time for you to sleep."

"I don't need a nap. I'm ready for supper." He paused. "As long as it's not more canned stew—and I don't want some TV dinner tonight either. No one ever called me picky but…" He pointed at her. "While you're at it, make me some decent lemonade."

"If life hands you lemons…" she said, which was the story of her life.

Blossom actually believed the old saying, but she'd think about the disaster she'd made of things so far, and about her dubious future, later.

She was already half in love with Logan's grandfather. Better still, the isolated Circle H offered a temporary hiding place.

"WHAT IS THIS stuff I'm supposed to eat?"

Logan stared at the yellow glop on his plate. After calling the Mother Comfort agency to say Blossom could stay temporarily but to keep looking for a male replacement, he'd left her to Sam for the rest of the day. Because bison rarely had trouble giving birth, Logan had watched half a dozen cows safely deliver the first spring babies in six far-off pockets of the ranch. He'd brooded the whole time.

That haunted look in Blossom's eyes was enough to bring a man to his knees. Determined to suppress the disturbing thought, he'd ridden home near sundown hoping for some peace of mind and a hot, home-cooked meal. Not too much to ask, was it?

He could hardly blame Sam for complaining about the stew. Logan had fixed too many skimpy frozen dinners in the past few days, too many cans of mediocre chili. He'd had to admit it would be nice not to have to rustle up something himself.

Now he couldn't identify anything on his plate except the rice, if that's what it was, under all that goop. The two cowhands who lived at the Circle H were eating dinner here tonight. Another pair had gone home to their families, and another couple worked only as needed. Seated at the long plank table that, to his surprise, was set with his mother's best china, Willy and Tobias made curious sounds.

"Madras curry," Blossom finally said from behind a pitcher of flowers at the opposite end of the table, her head bent over her dish, her russet curls shining in the overhead light. She wouldn't look him in the eye, which seemed to be a habit of hers whenever things weren't going well.

"You mean like a plaid shirt?"

"It's a province in India."

Logan didn't consider himself to be an ignorant man. But in his regular job as a test pilot he flew mostly local flights around Wichita and it had been a long time since geography class. Still, he'd also served time in the military and now watched *Jeopardy* some nights to keep aware of the world beyond this place.

"I know where India is," he said at last, glancing at the two cowboys, who were trying not to laugh. They kept sneaking looks at Blossom, too, but for some reason he didn't want them to notice her like that.

"You know about Madras, do you, Willy?"

"Sure. I've ate curry. Before that restaurant in town with the bead curtains closed last year."

Willy, a rough-hewn six foot four with dishwater blond hair and hands like shovels, hadn't lifted his fork. Any other night he would have been done by now, his plate all but licked clean. Logan had assumed Willy was a meat-

and-potatoes man like him. He was clearly lying to please Blossom Kennedy.

She raised her head. "Try it," she told Logan. "It won't kill you."

Tobias, the other cowhand, eyed his plate.

"Your cooking come with a guarantee, Miss Blossom?"

She half smiled. "I guarantee it'll fill your stomach."

"Good enough," Tobias said, then dug in to his food.

His balding crown glowed like a pearl on his lowered head. Both men were eating now. What about Sam? Logan cocked one ear but heard only silence from the second floor. It wasn't like his grandfather to remain so quiet. Frowning, he pushed rice around. "Did Sam eat this?"

"Without a word," she informed him.

"You don't say."

"Yes. I am saying, Mr. Hunter." So they were back to that again. Two bright flags of color appeared on her cheeks, but her voice stayed soft as if she was afraid of offending him too much. "I should think, after the day's work you put in out there—" she waved toward the darkened window "—you'd eat anything that didn't move, especially when you didn't have to heat it yourself." Despite the brave words, her eyes held that uncertain look again. "If you don't like it, there's sliced turkey in the refrigerator, a ripe tomato and some bread. You can make yourself a sandwich."

Or go hungry, her tone implied. Like a traitor, his stomach grumbled. At the sound, Willy snickered and Logan glared at him. His men hunched over their plates, forks flying. Tobias even smacked his lips. If he said one word, Logan would fire him. Or think about it anyway. He'd taken enough jabs in the past three years since his divorce. He wouldn't be laughed at.

He picked up his fork and took a tentative bite then another. If he didn't look at the stuff, he could get it down at least. With an audible gulp, he swallowed. Fire hit his throat, and he grabbed his water, which Blossom had served in his mother's wedding crystal. Logan emptied the glass, certain steam was coming from his ears.

"What's in here?" he managed, eyes watering.

"Curry powder, of course. The hot kind, too."

Logan glanced around the table but didn't see the same reaction from Tobias or Willy.

Both men were shoveling in food as if they'd skipped breakfast and lunch, which Logan knew they hadn't. Wait a minute. Had Blossom given him an extra dose of curry powder?

"What makes it so yellow?" It looked almost orange.

"The turmeric—it's one of the spices—and some saffron, too."

"I thought that was a color."

"It's also a spice, from which the color got its name. It comes from the stigmas of crocuses."

He grunted, not wanting to be impressed by her knowledge. *Stigmas?* He didn't want to be eating flowers.

"Where'd you learn to make curry? In fact, where'd you find any curry powder? I doubt it was in the pantry here."

"My father was in the service. We moved around a lot. I brought this curry powder with me," she said. "It was a special order from overseas."

"I bet."

He leaned on his forearms, eyes fixed on a point just north of his plate so he wouldn't have to look at what passed for his meal tonight, or at Blossom. Those frozen TV dinners had been the best part of his week after all.

Miss World Traveler was different, all right. Maybe that explained her weird, shapeless clothes.

After his throat stopped burning, Logan managed to finish the curry. He imagined a woman like Blossom Kennedy must love tofu.

Her red curls had grown even springier from the humidity in the kitchen, but he didn't want to think about her hair right now. Or anytime. He needed to make it clear that he was the boss here. "Next time—if it wouldn't be too much to ask—I'd like a nice thick steak, some home fries and a pile of green beans." He sent her a thin smile. "I'm partial to green. Never cared much for yellow."

All she said was "You'll learn to love it."

Logan tried to shut out the choked-off laughter from the two cowhands. A couple of comedians. He'd deal with Tobias and Willy later. But he wondered what had put that haunted look in Blossom's eyes and, never mind her other travels, why she was clearly on the run.

CHAPTER TWO

LATER THAT NIGHT Blossom surveyed her temporary bedroom. She'd made it through dinner, even held her own with Logan Hunter, although it would be an understatement to say her new boss wasn't impressed by her cooking. She'd tried to make the meal special with lacy place mats and the few flowers she'd found in the neglected garden, but it had been Willy and Tobias who kept up the conversation.

At least she'd managed to wash the dishes without breaking any of Logan's best family china.

By the half-open window she plopped down in an old rocking chair. Its wooden arms were worn to a smooth patina that soon warmed under her hands, and the nighttime breeze smelled of grass and animals. Blossom breathed deep. The aroma was better than perfume to her. She'd never had a home like this, but oh, more than anything she wanted one. *Her* bedroom. The chintz curtains weren't her style, nor was the fading forget-me-not wallpaper, but tonight she had a job—if only she could do it to Logan's satisfaction. Something she'd never been able to do with Ken.

Blossom put a hand over her heart, making sure the treasure she'd put there was still safely tucked away. She should feel peaceful tonight, but of course she didn't. As clear and sharp as broken glass, she recalled how quickly Ken had changed from the attentive boyfriend who said he loved her into the coldhearted fiancé who seemed to hate her.

Not all men, she kept telling herself, had his mercurial temper. Just the ones she'd known. She hadn't seen that in Logan—yet—but then men like Ken and her father never showed their true colors until it was too late.

Blossom slipped a hand under her oversize shirt to touch the small picture she'd hidden in her bra. Carefully, she withdrew it then held it near the light to study the creased, blurred sonogram image in black-and-white, trying to make out a tiny hand here, a foot there.

She saw no need to tell Logan about her baby. If she could keep from getting fired for even one week, she would take her pay and hit the road again.

Every week, every mile down the road from Pennsylvania to Kansas, every awful job she'd taken to stay alive and protect her unborn baby, took her that much farther from Ken. She had to keep going.

She held the picture to her chest and began to hum, as if the baby she carried was already here in this safer place, his or her sweet, warm body against hers.

Blossom shut her eyes. Tonight she was in a nice, if a bit old-fashioned, room in a wide-windowed, airy house in the middle of nowhere. A house that only needed a woman's touch—even hers—to feel homey again. Once she got the hang of it, this job wouldn't be half-bad. And while she was here, Blossom meant to do it well. As well as she could anyway.

Comforting herself, she rocked and sang.

About a little baby…and a mother who'd buy her a mockingbird.

In the dark Logan listened to the soft melody that drifted from the upstairs window. He pushed the front porch glider with one sock-covered foot. For years it had had the same creak, even before his parents had died, and even when his grandmother was still alive, but he wouldn't oil it. Neither would Sam. Everything in this house had its own special sound by now, and he didn't see any reason to paint the metal swing while he was here either. A few rust spots sure wouldn't ruin his faded work jeans. No problem.

But Blossom? She had trouble—big trouble—written all over her. And that was a problem he didn't need.

Hours after he'd choked down that too-hot curry, he was still seeing her at his grandmother's table tonight using his mother's things. She'd looked more at home there on her first night than any of Mother Comfort's other candidates would have in a dozen years. No, she'd looked relieved.

Sure, she was pretty enough—although he'd never been drawn to redheads before—but what really got to him was that lost look about her. And if he kept seeing her as an appealing woman, a woman in need, rather than an employee...

Logan wasn't looking for love. Blossom, on the other hand, looked as if she'd found it then lost it somehow and wouldn't be the same until it was in her grasp again.

He had enough to worry about. One day he'd been in Wichita about to flight-test a sweet new jet, vying for the promotion he badly needed—the one with better pay that would allow him to fight his ex-wife for joint custody of their now six-year-old son. The next morning he'd been back on the Kansas plains, a temporary cowboy again.

The soft tune floated down to him once more from the window, and the glider jerked to a stop. He should be inside going over the ranch accounts, because no way could Sam do them right now. With his mind on some other planet, he couldn't be trusted to make any decisions. Instead, Logan had been sitting out here alone in the blackness with a sweet song for company, thinking sad thoughts about his broken marriage and the child he seldom saw.

Upstairs Blossom was buying a diamond ring for some baby she sang to.

He wouldn't fall for Blossom Kennedy. If she thought he'd missed the travel plans that shone in her eyes, she was mistaken. She wouldn't stay long.

Neither would he.

"Girl, set yourself down a spell. You haven't stopped moving all morning."

Sam's blue eyes sparkled, all the more vibrant in his pinched white face as he lay back against the fresh sheets Blossom had just put on his bed. She elevated Sam's head on a stack of pillows and tucked an old but hand-sewn quilt around him. Dull sunlight streamed through his bedroom windows, which were filmed with dust, and Blossom made a mental note to wash them.

"Rest," she said. "Your grandson won't thank me for making you more tired this morning than you were when I got here yesterday."

Sam grunted. "What I'm tired of is being in this bed."

"Logan is right. The more you rest, the quicker you'll heal."

"What's that?" he said. "Another old wives' saying?"

She smiled. "I don't know any old wives."

Sam snorted. "That was good lemonade you made for dinner last night. Tart but just sweet enough." He grinned. "Too bad my pucker was wasted. Some woman missed the best kiss of her life."

Blossom laughed. "You're bad." Gathering up his used sheets, she walked to the door. He looked pale to her, and although his running conversation had been sprinkled with corny jokes while she cleaned his room, she sensed he wasn't quite himself. Blossom could read moods as fast as any high-speed computer could crunch numbers. "You take a short nap and when you wake up, I'll have lunch ready."

He straightened. "More of your curry?"

"There's none left." She raised her eyebrows. "The other men took care of that. And you," she added. Last night Sam had eaten two helpings.

"Not Logan," he guessed.

"He finished his dinner, too, but he wasn't happy about it."

"Fussy eater. Always has been." Sam shook his head then seemed to think better of it. He rubbed one hand over his forehead. "That boy didn't eat anything but grilled cheese sandwiches until he was ten years old. Then came beef—when I still ran cattle like his daddy and grandpa before me. Even then, he still wouldn't touch anything that didn't start out bawling, on four hooves, right here on the Circle H." He paused. "Far as I'm concerned, my bison now are better than beef. They yield less fat and more protein. But Logan won't even try the meat."

We'll see about that. "He needs to expand his horizons."

Sam's expression turned wistful. "I wish I could have seen him choke down that curry. I heard Tobias and Willy laughing all the way up here."

Blossom didn't miss his underlying message.

"You can join us for dinner as soon as that dizziness goes away. I'll save your place at the head of the table."

He fell back against the pillows again, as if the spinning in his brain had gotten worse, and Blossom felt her heart clench.

"I am kind of tired," he admitted. "Too much thinkin' yesterday. I'll rest my eyes to get ready for lunch. Don't tell me what it is. Surprise me."

Blossom had no idea what to serve, or if Logan and his men would come back to the house for the noon meal. Maybe she should ask him to approve her menu—as soon as she made one. With a last glance at Sam, who had turned his face away, she stepped out into the hall.

"Olivia?" The unfamiliar name stopped her, the bundle of sheets in her arms. "Thanks. Makes a man proud to have a daughter-in-law like you.

Now, if you and Logan can just set your minds to giving me a few more great-grandkids…"

He trailed off and Blossom's heart sank. He'd mistaken her for his daughter-in-law. Yesterday he'd thought she'd come to the ranch in answer to some singles ad. When Logan had asked him his name, Sam had stopped to think. He was clearly disoriented, at least part of the time, but she wouldn't make things worse by pointing that out and upsetting him.

"We're working on it" was all she said.

With her cheeks feeling flushed, Blossom carried the old bedding down the stairs, through the front parlor and the dining room, and on into the kitchen. She dropped the pile down the laundry chute.

More great-grandkids, Sam had said, which implied there was at least one already. Blossom hadn't seen any children and certainly no wife for Logan. So where was *Olivia*?

None of that was her concern. As long as Sam got well enough so he could leave his bed, she'd feel she'd done her job here. It was the least she could do in return for finding this brief refuge at the Circle H.

The sunny morning and the vast expanse of land isolating her here on the ranch lifted her spirits. If she could find Logan, she'd ask about the lunch menu she didn't have yet. While she was at it, she'd tell him about the incident with Sam.

LOGAN WAS IN a corral on the far side of the barn, trying to keep from getting his head kicked in like Sam. He'd rather be mucking stalls because, oddly, that chore was his favorite—if he had one here. As a kid he'd sure spent enough time at it. Logan had lived on the Circle H from birth until he left to join the service. With a pitchfork in his hand, he still liked to let his mind drift, to pretend he was really where he wanted to be, back flying a jet. Sometimes he even whistled to himself as he worked. But if he couldn't cut short the brief leave of absence he'd taken from his job, this unplanned stay on the ranch could threaten his pending promotion. He wasn't whistling now. No pitchfork either.

"Stand still," Logan told the shaggy bison bull calf he'd been trying to doctor for an infection. The stubborn weanling had turned over a bucket of warm water, splashing Logan's boots. He'd just bent over the bull's hoof again, one foreleg trapped between his thighs to steady it, when Blossom suddenly appeared. The startled bison knocked Logan on his backside in the dirt.

"Hey!" he yelled, when he knew better than to shout or move fast around the touchy bison. Struggling for breath, Logan picked himself up, dusted himself off and glared at Blossom over the corral fence. "You live on a ranch, you learn to be careful. Hear me?"

Blossom froze like some ice sculpture. "I'm sorry. I didn't mean—"

Oh, no. There was that lowered head again, and her gaze had shifted away.

"It's okay," he said in a softer tone. "No harm done."

Or would the new ache in his hip turn into something worse by nightfall? Getting hurt on a ranch with danger all around was par for the course.

"These bison are ornery critters, easily spooked," he said.

Wide-eyed and white-faced, Blossom stood stock-still by the rail. He had started toward her, afraid she might faint, when from behind the bull rushed past him, almost flattening Logan again. For one second he thought it meant to crash through the fence and run right over her. Instead, it thrust its broad, runny nose at her through the boards with a low-ing sound like a whiny toddler. It hadn't liked being separated from its mother, and the cow was pacing back and forth along the side of the corral that edged the far pasture.

To her credit, Blossom didn't scream.

She held one hand to the gap between the boards and let the bison sniff her.

"What a cute boy you are," she crooned, as if she were still singing that lullaby from last night.

Logan was so surprised he was speechless. "I wouldn't say 'cute,'" he finally said. "He nearly stomped me into the ground. I don't mean to criticize, Blossom, but these animals aren't pets. And they don't normally like people much."

He'd already rescued the tortoiseshell kitten from the bison's hooves twice today. The fool cat followed him everywhere. Logan had been forced to shut her in the tack room. Maybe for Blossom's own safety he should lock her in there, too.

But he couldn't seem to move. "I'll be," he said.

That bison calf looked all moon-eyed.

He sure seemed to like Blossom.

Logan couldn't take his eyes off her either. "I'd ease away from that fence before the calf takes a mind to hurt you. You never can tell what they're going to do. And even this one is stronger than you might think. Ask my grandfather if you don't believe me."

"He only wants a little affection," she said.

Did she mean the calf, or Sam?

"Still, I wouldn't—"

He didn't get the rest out. The bull calf shoved its huge shaggy head into the stout fence—and splintered several planks. Before Logan could react, the bison pushed his whole upper body toward Blossom.

"Whoa, Nellie!" he yelled. "Blossom, head for the barn." The much bigger bison cow was bawling her head off now. "I'll open the gate to the pasture so he can rejoin his mama."

Logan didn't wait to see whether Blossom followed his order. As soon as the far gate opened, the calf whirled around then thundered toward freedom.

With a sigh of relief that no one had been killed, Logan went after Blossom. He found her standing in the barn aisle, talking to one of the horses in its stall. Cyclone, the big black colt Sam had bought months ago.

"Watch it. He nips," Logan told her, though *bite* was more appropriate.

Horse or bison, they were tame only as long

as they wanted to be. Strange, how unafraid she seemed of these animals when one look from Logan could make her shy away as if she were about to bolt.

"I'm sorry about—out there," she said. "You're okay?"

"Fine." He hoped she hadn't noticed him limping across the barnyard.

"Nellie?" She quirked an eyebrow. "That's his name?"

Logan blinked. "No, this is Cyclone."

"I meant the little buffalo."

He did a double take. "Blossom, we don't name these bison." He suspected Sam sometimes did, and so had he during his 4-H years of raising beef calves for the summer fair, but Logan refused to personalize them now. By fall some of the herd would become pricey burgers—something he didn't like to think about—on the menu at a fancy restaurant in Dallas, LA or Chicago.

And Logan would be back in Wichita. Flying again. He wasn't about to make any more personal connections to this place.

"Maybe you should name them." Her mouth tightened. "Instead, you shouted at him, scared him."

Logan shook his head. "He could've killed you—and you feel sorry for him?"

"Yes. What did *you* do to him? It wasn't just me. It must have been something to make him want to knock you over like that."

Her tone told him he'd only confirmed her worst opinion of him. The knowledge should keep him clear of any involvement he might be tempted into, but she was easy to look at, and in that moment the sweet smell of her shampoo teased his nose with the clean, fresh scent of outdoors.

"He has a hoof abscess. I was treating it. He didn't want me to." That pretty much summed things up.

"You're wrong."

He rubbed his neck. "You have to show an animal like that who's the boss. He's wild, Blossom—dangerous." He paused. "How do you think Sam wound up in bed with that busted leg and his head all mixed up?"

"Not from a baby like him," she insisted.

"*You're* wrong." He repeated her accusation. "Sam got between that same calf and his mama. She flung him like a rag doll up against a tree. By the time he landed, he was in a world of hurt." He paused. "The bruises were just the start. I don't want you to end up the same."

Now it was Blossom who blinked. "Well. Thank you for your concern."

As if no one else had ever cared about her.

Exasperated, Logan planted both hands on his hips. Heedless of his warning, she had slipped her hand through the bars to pet Cyclone's neck. The colt all but purred like a cat. "He has a lot of promise but no common sense," Logan said.

"He's like the bison baby. He'll never learn to be gentle if he's…"

"Mistreated?" The word had just popped into his head.

"Punished."

"You've got to be kidding. I'm the bad guy here?"

He turned away. And nearly tripped over the tortoiseshell kitten. How had she gotten out of the tack room?

He eyed Blossom. "You again?"

"I was looking for you. I heard her crying. So I let her out."

Logan picked up the cat, who instantly nestled into the crook of his neck. "Just so you know. I didn't touch that calf except to help him. I'd never touch this horse in anger."

"They won't respond to threats either."

"Ah," Logan muttered. "I see. You decided to work on this ranch, so you stopped at some bookstore on the way and bought a copy of *The Horse Whisperer*. Or *The Cat Whisperer*. No, there's probably a *Bison Whisperer*, too." Putting the kitten down, he gave Blossom a pointed look. "I have news for you. Sometimes—like when you're about to get kicked—that touchy-feely stuff doesn't work, city girl."

Still shaken from his near brush with serious injury, he tried to stare her down. Finally, she glanced away, her gaze following the kitten as she meandered down the barn aisle. From the bend of Blossom's slender neck, he realized she must consider herself akin to the bison calf. *Mistreated.* Was that the expression he kept seeing in her eyes?

He knew little about her. He wanted it to stay that way.

The kitten disappeared around the corner, probably headed for a hay bale and a nap. And Blossom was gazing past Logan, out the barn doors. She stared at the long driveway, as she often did.

"You're right," she said. "I'm sorry I put you in danger. I am a city girl."

He tried to lighten the moment. "Let me guess. New York? Boston?"

"Philly," she admitted. "City of Brotherly Love."

Logan nearly missed her subtle change of tone. She'd seemed so cheerful earlier, yesterday, too, and even at dinner last night. He didn't want to see that other look in her eyes or hear the trembling words that spoke of some deep hurt. He had enough troubles of his own and all the responsibility he could handle.

She took a breath. "The farther west I travel, the more…open I feel. Less closed in somehow."

He couldn't help but smile. "That's how I feel when I'm flying."

"You're a pilot?"

"Private jets. Experimental sometimes—but mostly redesigns." Until he got his promotion. Then his assignments would become way more interesting.

"A test pilot," she said. "No wonder you don't seem that happy to be here."

He looked outside the barn at that big blue sky. "Got me," he said.

"I think I know how you feel. Flying high must seem like being a bird. I suppose if I reached California, I'd feel positively free."

She didn't sound that convinced. "Or maybe," she added with that look again, "I'll just run out of road."

He didn't want to care, but still he had to ask.

"Blossom, what are you running from?"

CHAPTER THREE

ON HER WAY back to the house, Blossom shook so hard her teeth clacked together. But she forced herself not to run. She could sense Logan staring at her from the barn doorway, but she wouldn't let him see that he'd frightened her. Reminded her of why she was running.

She hated feeling afraid.

There was no need to be scared. She'd finally found a place where she wouldn't startle awake each night to find herself in yet another cheap motel room. Lying in the dark, listening to the rush of traffic on the road, clutching a musty blanket to her throat, her other hand on her stomach, waiting for that sharp pounding at the flimsy door.

Mornings had rarely been better. Over breakfast whenever she could afford a meal, Blossom planned the next leg of what she liked to think of as her journey to freedom. In the past month she'd changed cars three times, paying cash so Ken couldn't track the transaction. Each "bargain" buy had cost less than the last, and she'd bought from people who didn't worry about such minor things as a title transfer, but she'd kept moving even when she was cold, hungry, out of hope, out of money...and always afraid.

Shivering in her loose chinos and big shirt, she climbed the back steps to the house. She'd changed her style, too, thrown away the bright clothes she preferred and all the designer labels Ken had bought her. She didn't want to be noticed anymore like some shiny trophy, didn't want to be "seen."

Then why this heart-pounding sense of alarm now, this leaden feel to her limbs?

In the kitchen she dropped onto a chair, still cold and shaking and in darkness even though the room was bathed in sunlight. She should be thankful. Today she wasn't on some back road to avoid the highways, praying her old sedan would make it to the next stop.

She propped her elbows on the kitchen table, buried her face in her hands. Yet she was afraid and Logan had seen through her.

And with that, she was back in Philly again in Ken's condo with the bathroom door lock that didn't work when she needed it most...

remembering all the things she couldn't seem to do right, no matter how she tried to forget.

The memories shrieked through her mind like tires on wet pavement, like her life was then, skidding out of control...

"YOU WOULDN'T LAST a day without me."

Looming over her, Ken shook a paper in Blossom's face. Through a tangle of curls she stared up at him, wondering what she'd done this time. Every night before he came home from work, she hurried around the condo, changing the king-size sheets, taking care to make crisp hospital corners that were folded and tucked in just so, as her father and Ken had taught her to do, then checking the pots on his fancy stove to make sure she didn't let their meal burn or boil over and create another mess.

"I haven't done anything!" she insisted.

"You can't even remember to pay a parking ticket. This citation was written a month ago—and you hid it in my *glove compartment!"*

Oh, God. She'd forgotten. She'd borrowed Ken's car while hers was at the Lexus dealer's to be washed and waxed. She'd gone to a doctor's appointment, which he didn't know about.

Ever since she'd used the home pregnancy-test kit, Blossom couldn't seem to find the right time to tell him.

"Ken, I'll pay it tomorrow."

"Do you know how important I am in this burg? You'll pay it now! Before word gets around that I'm engaged to a scatterbrain."

Blossom frowned. Who would tell anyone about the ticket but him? But then, as he'd said often enough, Ken did have a reputation to safeguard. He was a successful real estate developer. He knew everyone—and everyone knew him. It was Blossom who'd become invisible without quite knowing how it happened.

As if he'd fired a starting gun for a race, she streaked for the living room, her entire being focused on the checkbook in his desk drawer. She needed to fix this, to make Ken smile again. He was right. She'd been careless, and not for the first time. She was stupid, useless, worthless...

She was halfway across the room when he jerked her around.

"In person. You get down to the police station. Now." His hands tightened on her upper arms, his face red.

She didn't dare to meet his gaze. He'd also

taught her not to look directly at him, which he saw as some kind of challenge to his authority. "Ken, I'd have to go to the courthouse instead. I had ten days to pay by mail but that's already passed."

"Then do it. Now," he repeated. "Didn't you hear me?"

He would have shaken her, but Blossom managed to free herself from his painful grasp. Keeping pace with her, he pushed her toward the front door. "How long do you think you'd survive on your own without me to fix your messes? Huh?"

Her shoulders slumped. What had she done to make their relationship so miserable? She wanted to curl inside herself, to disappear. How could she feel this bad when, as he often reminded her, she was lucky to live in this luxury high-rise with a wraparound terrace and a view of the whole city? All of Philadelphia at her feet, he liked to say. But she could no longer remember even a simple dinner or special occasion that didn't end up spoiled— Christmas, her birthday, the anniversary of the day they'd met, their engagement—she couldn't remember a kind word or a loving touch, only her relentless wrongdoing, his sudden outbursts, the screaming nerves inside her.

And now she had another life to worry about.
Above all, to protect. No, she couldn't tell him.
For her baby's sake, she needed to escape.

PUSHING THE PAINFUL memories aside, Blossom brushed stray curls off her cheeks. She hugged herself tight and stared out the kitchen window. Logan's voice had been harsh for an instant just like Ken's. *Hear me?* they'd both said. Why be surprised? She knew men—her father, too—and what they were capable of, how easily they could cause hurt.

She wasn't about to let that happen now, not with her baby to consider. The day after Ken had gone crazy about the parking ticket, Blossom had run. Such a simple thing shouldn't have mattered, but for her it had been the last straw.

She straightened, remembering it was time for lunch. She'd meant to ask Logan what to fix and tell him about Sam's confusion. Again, she'd done the wrong thing with the bull calf. But he'd also said, *I don't want you to end up the same.* To be hurt.

A brief sense of calm settled over her. Yes, the Circle H provided a good place to hide, and for a moment today Logan had seemed to care about her, which might just be the most frightening thing of all. She wouldn't trust him. Yet his very strength, that hard edge that let him shout at a bison baby—he'd corrected her about the proper term—might ironically protect her, if it came to that.

If Ken found her here before she could run.

BLOSSOM WAS CLEARING the breakfast dishes from the table the next morning when she glanced out the window and felt her heart stop. A sleek silver pickup was pulling up near the back door. It didn't look familiar, which shouldn't surprise her. She didn't know anyone here, and the only vehicles she recognized belonged to Logan or the half-dozen ranch hands the Circle H employed. But could it be a rental?

Her legs went weak. Her pulse thudded. Had Ken found her already? A door slammed. A second later she heard footsteps coming up onto the porch. It couldn't be, yet…

She hadn't seen Logan since breakfast. They'd said only a few words to each other since yesterday. Except for Sam upstairs in bed now, she was alone in the house. Helpless. Her sedan was parked out front. Where were her keys? Blossom fumbled through her pockets—and with a cry of relief found them. Could she reach her car in time?

Before she could think to run in that direction, the back door flew open, and a small blond boy in jeans and cowboy boots burst into the kitchen.

Blossom sagged against the nearest counter. The truck didn't belong to Ken. Besides, he'd likely rent a flashy sedan. Still, she tensed again at the deep voice that came from behind the boy.

"Nicholas Hunter, slow down." A man whose hair was a shade darker than the child's had obviously tried to make his voice sound scolding but he couldn't hide a grin. "Sorry," he told Blossom with a tip of his straw cowboy hat. "He gets a bit excited about the Circle H." He held out a hand. "I'm Grey Wilson, a neighbor."

"Blossom." Without adding her last name, she glanced at the little boy, who was scaling the counter to reach a high cupboard. "Is he…?"

"Safe?" Grey snagged an arm around the boy's waist. "Never. At least to hear his mama tell it. Nick, get down."

He wriggled but Grey held fast.

"Be careful now—you'll fall and break something. Like Grandpa Sam."

"My arm?" Nick landed on the floor with a giggle. "A kid at school fell out of a tree. He has a cool cast and everybody drew on it. It's really green."

The back door opened again. A smile tugging at his mouth, his eyes alight, Logan stepped inside. He must have recognized Grey's truck. But then Logan saw Nick and stiffened. He pulled off his Stetson and eyed Grey with a familiar, less than welcoming expression.

"Uh-oh," Grey murmured. "Looks like somebody got up on the wrong side of the bunk." He added, "We can't stay long but I brought you a present."

"You mean me?" With a hopeful look, Nick glanced at Logan. "*I'm* a present?" He took a step then stopped, and his gaze fell. "Hi, Daddy," he said.

Logan cleared his throat before he reached out a hand to ruffle Nick's hair. "Hi, buddy." He frowned at Grey over Nick's head. "This'll make his mother real happy."

So this was Logan's son, the great-grandchild Sam had referenced yesterday, confusing her with Olivia. Not that anyone would readily see a strong family resemblance, except for their eyes, between father and son. Logan's hair was dark; Nick's was lighter. She imagined Olivia, who must be Logan's ex-wife, was blond, too.

"Mommy doesn't know we're here," Nick said.

Grey groaned. "Nick, I thought you and I agreed that sometimes we men have to stick together. Little secrets don't harm anyone."

His mouth tight, Logan strode over to the coffeemaker. "Don't tell him that." The dark brew had been sitting in the pot for hours while he fed horses and did other morning chores, but its bitterness and acidity didn't seem to bother him. He gulped down half a mugful in one long swallow.

"What?" Grey looked wounded. "I bring your kid to see you and all I get's a lesson in manners?"

"No, in ethics."

Nick's sunny smile had dimmed. He sent Blossom a shy look then rummaged through a fruit bowl on the counter for a banana. She tensed even more. She didn't expect to be noticed—she was just one of the hired help here—but no wonder poor Nick looked more than uncomfortable. Logan's reaction had unsettled her, too. He was all but standing at attention now. Avoiding another glance at Nick.

This was no surprise, in a way, to Blossom. Her father had never been one to fold her in a warm embrace or to make her laugh at some silly joke. She'd been grateful whenever he simply ignored her. A best-case scenario for Blossom. But she'd seen the quick flash of joy in Nick's eyes then the way he'd retreated, as if knowing his hug wouldn't be welcome. And that his daddy wouldn't respond except for that light pass of a hand over Nick's hair.

Logan turned to Blossom. "My ex-brother-in-law," he said with a gesture at Grey. "Blossom's taking care of Sam."

"Howdy, ma'am."

"I'm learning on the job," she said.

After that, there was an awkward silence. Blossom didn't think about herself, but she couldn't take another second of Nick's disappointment or Logan's coolness. She'd had enough of that in her time. And at Nick's age, she had still craved her father's love.

She held out a hand. "Nick, would you like to come with me? I need to gather some eggs."

With a whoop of delight, Nick grasped her fingers then pulled her out the back door away from the two men in the kitchen. Blossom could understand that. How many times had her father rejected her, or hastened to correct something she'd done wrong? Ken had taken that to another level.

This was not a happy situation either. Apparently, she and the bison baby weren't the only ones who irritated Logan.

Why feel drawn to a man she couldn't trust and might easily fear? A man who didn't seem to connect with his own son?

"WHAT THE HELL'S wrong with you?" Grey asked as soon as the back door had closed behind Blossom and Nicky.

Frowning, Logan didn't answer. His throat felt too tight to speak, and what could he say? He wanted to be angry with Grey because he'd had no warning of this visit—a rare thing these days. Instead of a heads-up, he'd walked from the barn to the house and into this kitchen, and there was Nicky. Right where he'd belonged until a few years ago.

As a baby in his high chair, a toddler running around under Libby's feet, a chattering three-year-old who'd let everyone in the house know his opinions, he'd giggled and cried in this very room and even thrown temper tantrums, kicking his legs on the floor as if he were determined to be in charge of all the adults. He'd banged a spoon against his tray at the end of this table, flinging oatmeal everywhere.

Logan was still in shock. He watched Grey pull out a chair at the table. He'd been blindsided, yet at the same time…he didn't often get to see Nicky. Grey sat, eyeing him with disapproval, which Logan supposed he deserved.

"I thought you'd be happy to see him without Olivia riding herd on him."

Logan couldn't fault her for trying to coddle Nicky or to keep him safe, even keep him away from Logan, after what had happened. In her view he hadn't been much of a father, and Logan couldn't disagree.

"I *am* happy to see him." *Except it hurts more each time I do.* Logan was missing out on Nicky's growing up. His son changed by the day, it seemed, and a few minutes ago a real kid, not the newborn baby or toddler imp he remembered, had walked into the house. "But Olivia—Libby's—gonna be madder than a bull in a rodeo ring when she finds out you shanghaied Nicky and brought him over here. You know how she feels about the Circle H." *About me.*

But what if she hadn't come to hate the ranch, and him? To blame him? Maybe they'd still be rubbing along, raising their son in Wichita together as they'd planned. Instead, Logan's time with Nicky had become increasingly rare. He'd tried to tell himself maybe that was for the best. For now. He didn't want to confuse Nicky any more than he must already be after the divorce.

Grey stretched out his legs and stared down at his boots. "It's time she changed her mind. But I'm the first to admit, my sister can be as stubborn as a too-big calf trying to get born."

As stubborn as me. That had been one problem between them.

"She won't change her mind."

"Then you'll have to change yours. Logan, the divorce papers got signed, what, three years ago? Nick's not a baby anymore. He needs his daddy, too."

"Libby got custody," he said. And because of the reason she'd left him, Logan hadn't given her much of a fight. He'd regretted that ever since. Once his promotion came through—which meant getting back to Wichita as soon as possible—he'd be able to afford a lawyer, sue for joint custody this time. Settle the matter at last.

"You have visitation rights. Why don't you use 'em more often?"

He looked away. "Well, she doesn't make that easy. If Nicky doesn't have a school event, a kids' party, anywhere else he has to be, then he's sick or it's a school night or something else. He hasn't been to my place in Wichita in almost a year. Besides, I won't be here long this time."

Grey shook his head. "You might try reestablishing a relationship with your kid before he leaves home at eighteen."

"That wouldn't please Libby either." And he wouldn't share his plans with Grey, who might tip her off before he was ready to take her back to court. "I won't see Nicky used in a game of ping-pong between us."

Grey pushed back from the table. "How long are you two going to battle because of that crazy storm? It's not as if there isn't at least one blizzard every winter or a flood out here in spring sometimes, and you always made it through." His jaw hardened. "I can't believe you're still blaming yourself. Even the emergency crews couldn't get through."

"Tell me something I don't know." Logan would never forget the helplessness he'd felt then, the fear. Never again. Not on his watch.

When the rains had hit, Nicky was already sick. Then he'd spiked a high fever. *You have to get him to the hospital*, Libby had pleaded with him by phone because Logan had been in Wichita. And the long driveway to the ranch, always a washout in such storms, was impassible. Trapped at the house...

"He had pneumonia, it turned out. Nicky could have *died*."

"But he didn't," Grey pointed out. "How many times do I need to tell you and Libby he's a tough little kid?" With a faint smile, he gestured. "You should have seen him climb that cupboard today." He paused. "He was after his dinosaur mug in the upper cabinet. He doesn't have the same bad memories you and Libby do of this place, Logan."

She'd left the Circle H a few days later, just gathered up all her things and Nicky's, his toys and games, and moved out. Her first stop had been Grey's adjacent ranch, which sat at the crossroads much closer to the main road. It didn't have the same long driveway the Circle H did, but she hadn't stayed there long either before she'd rented a house in town.

"What do you want from me? I'm paying support. I meet my obligation every month—and risk my neck to do it, not that I don't love flying," he added. He wished it was that simple. "Libby hasn't lacked for anything. Neither has Nicky."

"Well, that's where you're wrong."

Logan merely gazed at him.

The pain inside squeezed, hard again. "Know what she told me the last time we spoke? She said Nicky has her, and Nicky has you. And that's all he needs. She doesn't want him here, Grey, and she doesn't want me…there."

"In town or at my ranch? I own Wilson Cattle. I'm the boss there, not Libby—even when she still has a family share." He shifted. "Man, you and I go back a long way, and my sister doesn't tell me who my friends are. You're welcome anytime. You know that."

Logan stared at the floor, his throat closed. *You and Nicky are welcome here, too*, he wanted to say, but the words wouldn't come out.

Grey stood up. "I guess you both like it this way then, huh? You know what? This reminds me of my own childhood. I was shuttled between my parents after their divorce like some bag of laundry—a piece of property."

"I know, Grey. I don't like this either."

He blew out a breath. "I'm sorry I stopped

by. You were right. All I've done is give Nick a hundred questions to keep asking, and now I'll have Libby yelling at me."

"Grey."

His friend held up a hand as if to ask for a truce. And changed the subject.

"By the way. That pretty woman in this kitchen when we got here—Blossom-something?" He raised an eyebrow. "If you ignore those ratty clothes and the startled deer-in-the-headlights look, she's—I mean, what's that all about?"

"I wouldn't know." So Grey had seen the fearfulness in Blossom, too. Her appeal.

"Maybe you should find out."

"Maybe neither of us will be here that long."

Grey ignored him. "Does Sam like her?"

"Yeah." That was putting it mildly. "He's called down the stairs for her every five minutes since she got here. He raves about her, but I don't want him getting too attached."

"You like her?"

Logan didn't have to answer. The back door banged open, and Nicky charged in with Blossom in pursuit. Her cheeks looked pink and she wore a bent yellow daffodil in the top button of her floppy denim shirt. Nicky's eyes were as big as the headlights on Logan's huge pickup.

"Daddy! Uncle Grey! Come quick!" Tossing the words over his shoulder, Nicky ran out again. "Hurry, a kitty…we gotta save 'im!"

Blossom disappeared, too, the screen door slamming behind her.

"Well?" But Grey was already headed outside, as if Logan's help wasn't something he could count on. The decision on his character seemed unanimous. "You coming or not?"

CHAPTER FOUR

"Is he hurt bad, Bloss'm?"

"I don't know, sweetie. I hope your daddy will."

They were on their knees in the barn aisle beside the tortoiseshell kitten, the one she'd seen with Logan that first day. Now as he entered with Grey, Nick clapped both hands over his ears to shut out the cat's cries of distress.

Blossom had put the kitten in an old bushel basket—the kind used to haul peaches or apples—with a scrap of horse blanket she'd found in the tack room, but she hadn't assessed the kitten's injuries.

"Okay, what happened?" Logan asked.

Nick hung over the basket. "It fell."

If she didn't miss her guess, he was more than halfway to crying. Blossom was surprised he'd held out this long. Now if only his father didn't make things worse…

Bending down, Logan flicked the blanket aside. The chubby kitten gazed up at him as if in mute appeal, golden eyes blinking a clear message, *Please help me.*

Logan sat back on his heels. "Nicky, maybe you should wait in the house."

"I wanna stay here. And make 'im better."

Blossom gave in to a weak smile. Logan's son had his strong will.

Logan looked up at Grey. "Get me some warm water and a clean rag," he said, "please," then watched Grey go into the tack room.

"Did this kitty break its leg?" Nick asked. "Like Grandpa?"

Blossom said, "The kitten was limp when we found her, unconscious."

"I think she had the wind knocked out of her. That ever happen to you, Nicky?" Logan asked the question without looking at his son. "Happened to me just yesterday."

"But you're okay now?"

"Sure." He laid the cat in his palm and examined her thoroughly from her head to her four tiny paws. They had pink pads and looked as tender as a newborn baby's feet would be. "Nothing broken so far." He glanced at Blossom. "You weren't here when it happened?"

Nick answered. "No, me and Bloss'm were in the garden. We picked flowers but there weren't very many. Then she saw clovers coming up in the yard and we picked them, too. I wanted to give 'em to my horses. Here," he added, "not at Uncle Grey's. But when we got to the barn…" He swiped at his first tears.

Logan touched the cat's rear leg, and the kitten yowled then bit him. Logan jerked back. His mouth opened but nothing came out. He must have thought better of uttering an oath in front of his son. But when he held up his injured finger, Nick recoiled.

"Blood! Yuck."

Blossom drew him against her side, hiding his face against the slight swell of her stomach that would soon become impossible to disguise no matter how loose her clothes were.

Logan straightened. "She has a nasty gash on her rear leg, but we'll fix that right up. Don't worry, Nicky."

Blossom supposed the sight of blood was nothing new to a rancher—even a reluctant one—who delivered calves and such, but to Nick it seemed a major catastrophe. He was turning whiter by the second.

Grey reappeared with the pan of water. "Crisis under control?"

Logan indicated the kitten. "I have some patching up to do. Nicky may be better off with you."

"Come on, then, little cowboy," Grey said, his eyes soft. "Let's check on your grandpa before I take you home to see what your mama's up to."

"But I wanna see the kitten get better!"

Blossom saw a strange expression cross Logan's face.

He cleared his throat. "You go ahead, buddy. Do as I tell you."

Nick's face was tear streaked, dirt smeared, and her heart turned over. How could Logan bear to be separated from this child? She knew she could never be apart from her baby the way Logan was.

She met Nick's gaze. "I'll help your daddy with the kitten. All right?"

He thought a moment. "Will you call me at my uncle Grey's house when she's better? It's the Wilson Cattle Company," he added solemnly, as if Blossom wouldn't know where to find him.

"Of course I will."

Nick flung both arms around her neck and buried his face against Blossom's throat. Then as quickly as he'd hugged her, he turned and ran down the aisle to his uncle.

"Grey." Logan's voice echoed through the barn. "I'll take good care of him for you."

Logan nodded but that was all. Seeming unaware of Blossom, he watched the two walk toward the house, a look on his face that she could only term anguished.

Logan's relationship with Nick puzzled her. Right now she could see the rigid set of his shoulders, the hard line of his jaw as if he were gritting his teeth.

Logan had finally stopped staring after Nick and Grey. "Let's take her into the tack room," he said.

The small area was lined with saddle racks and bridle hooks. In one corner a pile of patterned blankets smelled faintly of damp wool.

Blossom might know little about homemaking or caregiving, but she knew nothing about ranch life. Yesterday she'd startled the bison calf into knocking Logan off his feet. Interested today in the neglected garden behind the house, she'd forgotten to collect the eggs with Nick.

While she cuddled the kitten to her chest, Logan gathered supplies.

"This cat just used up one of her nine lives." He set the pan of water down on a tack trunk. A small bottle poked from his rear jeans pocket.

"I've never owned a pet. My father didn't

like animals, probably because he couldn't always control them. I thought cats landed on their feet."

"Their instincts are good, and their reflexes, but they can get hurt bad—killed—if they fall a shorter distance. They don't have time or enough space on the way down to twist their bodies and land upright. Like a gymnast. Don't know where she fell from, but she must have bounced off those hay bales in the aisle. They cushioned her landing or she wouldn't be talking to us now. The impact or something she hit on the way down must have split her leg open."

Blossom sat on the trunk and held the kitten even closer as if to protect her the way she had Nick. And would her own child.

"Where's her mother? She seems young to be on her own."

"Gone."

Her heart lurched. "She's an orphan?"

"No, her mama drifted off a few weeks ago, probably looking for love again." He half smiled. "Barn cats are fickle." Logan squatted in front of Blossom. "Turn her around so I can see what I'm doing."

He dipped a clean cloth in water and dabbed at her rear leg. The cat howled but Blossom held her steady. His midnight-blue gaze intent on the task, Logan made a second pass at the wound then prized the bottle from his rear pocket.

Blossom watched him work. "These past few days have been something. You should have DVM after your name." *Doctor of veterinary medicine.*

"Running a ranch demands all kinds of skills. Mine are a bit rusty."

Blossom didn't have talents. He hadn't liked the Greek gyro she'd made yesterday for lunch. And she'd never asked him about the menu.

After pouring disinfectant on the wound, he glanced up.

"What do you think?"

"Looks good."

"She'd heal better with a few stitches, though. Let me get a needle."

When he returned, her stomach felt queasy at the thought of sewing flesh.

She studied Logan's bent head as he shaved off some fur, blocking her view of the kitten on her lap. She held on, gently, yet for dear life, watching his lean face mere inches from her stomach. The man had great cheekbones. She had to fight the foolish urge to comb her fingers through his dark hair, to touch his shadowed jawline.

His very concentration moved her, sent an unexpected rush of longing through her. Must be hormones, she thought. Pregnancy unbalanced a woman's emotions big-time. So did Logan's tenderness.

She didn't realize the job was done until he sat back on his heels and flexed his shoulders.

He studied Blossom. "Okay? You look a little green."

"I would never make a good nurse," she said.

"You did fine." He stroked the kitten, his fingers brushing Blossom's hand. "We've done our part, little girl. Now we just need to..." He stood then glanced around. "Let's use one of these horse blankets to make her a bed. She can rest here in the tack room. Then she won't be tempted to run around."

"I'll bring her some water."

"I'll fix kitten chow for her later." He looked at Blossom and broke the mood between them as abruptly as Ken might have done. "Don't you have to cook dinner? And see to Sam?"

But this time Blossom wasn't fooled.

"Logan." It was the first time she'd used his given name and he stiffened, as if he expected some blow. She knew all about that. Still holding the kitten, she rose to face him. His gruffness with Sam, his sternness with her about the bison calf and the horse, his seeming indifference to Nick, were only a pose. To protect himself? Yet he'd also taken great care to shelter his son from the kitten's wounds. He'd spoken gently to him just the way he'd softened his voice with Sam that first day. "You're a fraud," she said, "but in a good way."

Lightly, she put a hand on his shoulder then lifted up on her toes to kiss his cheek so quickly her lips barely touched his face before she drew away. She'd misjudged him. His afternoon beard had felt like sandpaper, its texture so rough beneath her softer lips.

Blossom's mind had gone numb. But her stomach had settled.

His muscled strength was something to rely on yet to be wary of.

Still, underneath beat the heart of a good man. She knew that now.

Too bad she couldn't trust him.

BLOSSOM DIDN'T COME to the table for dinner that night. Logan ate alone. From upstairs he could hear her talking to Sam, eating with him instead.

Willy and Tobias were nowhere to be seen. Logan had had words with the two cowhands—bison hands, he ought to say—that first night after dinner, and both of them had been avoiding him ever since. He'd never seen two men volunteer faster to ride fence today to keep out of his way. Probably they were at the bunkhouse heating up a big can of spaghetti or ravioli. He hadn't meant to sound harsh. But their teasing, their looks at Blossom had gotten to him and he'd lost his temper.

His mood was always precarious when he was at the ranch. He couldn't seem to forget he'd nearly lost Nicky here. He had lost Libby, not that his marriage had ever been one made in heaven. She felt the same, he supposed.

He dug into the casserole Blossom had served before she slipped away upstairs. No steak again tonight. Mac and cheese? At least there was no way she could ruin that. The way he criticized her cooking, no wonder she preferred his grandfather's company. Even though he and Blossom had gotten along pretty well earlier in the barn while he sewed up the kitten, and she'd surprised him with that quick kiss, she'd pulled back right after.

His face still burned. But it was their conversation he missed now.

When the landline rang, he jumped up from his seat. Any interruption from his train of thought, even a telemarketing call at dinnertime, would be almost welcome.

"Circle H," he answered, ready to hang up at the latest sales pitch.

"Hey, brother." To his amazement, Sawyer had finally called him back, and Logan fought another familiar twist of loss inside. How long had it been since they were in the same place at the same time? Since they'd talked the way they used to?

"I've been trying to get through to you for the better part of a week."

As usual, Sawyer sounded unconcerned. "What's up?"

"Sam busted his leg. Bad," Logan said. "He was in the hospital for a few days, had surgery and now he's confined to his room. Picture that." He explained about the bleed and concussion that had rattled Sam's brain and messed with his sense of balance. "Where are you?"

"Here and there."

Logan rolled his eyes. Sawyer was always vague. About everything. It had been too long since they were boys, growing up on the Circle H after their dad and mom had died, learning from Sam how to be men. They'd been even closer than most brothers, inseparable as kids.

"You might think about coming back now and then." He couldn't bring himself to say *home*. The two of them hadn't seen each other since Logan had married Libby.

"I'm sure you can handle things."

"That's it?" He had the sense Sawyer was about to hang up first.

"You're the big brother. You're in Kansas. I'm not."

"I'm older by less than five minutes," he reminded Sawyer. "We could really use some help here, Tom." Sawyer didn't laugh at the old nickname he'd been taunted with as a kid. It was as if he'd put their past behind him and moved on, determined to make a life for himself anywhere else. He'd cut all ties—which wasn't that different from Logan's plans. Yet he was the one here now. "I thought you liked horses and cows and getting your boots dirty."

"Don't own a pair of boots anymore."

"Sawyer. Look." He glanced at his plate of cold macaroni and cheese and wondered why Blossom was still upstairs. "I'm almost at the end of my rope. Sam's not easy to keep down—you ought to know that—and I should be in Wichita. I'm up for a promotion there."

"Hope you get it."

"If I don't show up soon, they'll give it to someone else." His worst rival.

"You're the big captain of the skies. Took off first chance you got. You left me holding the bag then, Logan. You think I've forgotten that?"

"No," he admitted. He'd come back after the service to marry Libby, and Sawyer had left. "But this is now."

"I bet Sam hasn't even mentioned my name. Sorry," he said, not sounding sorry at all. "I'm busy with…whatever I'm busy with, so the answer's no." He paused. "Hire somebody."

"I did. She's temporary—and she's a caregiver, not a cowhand."

"Neither am I."

"Sawyer—"

"Don't," he said. "I can't."

"You mean you won't help."

"Right back at you. And don't try that 'we're twins' bit with me, okay? I haven't had a spooky twinge about you in years. I don't know when you're sick or you're in trouble at the stick of some jet. You don't know when I'm—" He broke off. "Ah, hell. Good that you're still walking around. Tell Sam I said hey."

"Sawyer…"

But the phone had gone dead in his hand.

"Is something wrong?" Blossom said from the kitchen doorway.

Yeah, there was. He just didn't know what where his brother was concerned. Sawyer had been hiding something. *I'm busy with… whatever I'm busy with.* He turned to find Blossom holding a tray of dirty dishes and cutlery. If he wasn't mad at Sawyer, even worried about him, he would have grinned. Sam had cleaned his plate again. He really liked Blossom's cooking.

"My brother," he finally said. "We don't have much in common these days."

"Is he coming home?"

"Because of Sam?" When she nodded, he said, "Nope. He's *busy.*"

She looked shocked. "Too busy to visit his injured grandfather?"

"So he says."

"I don't think I'd like him, then." Taking care not to come too close to Logan, she lugged the tray to the sink. He offered to take it from her, but she only stepped aside with a murmured "I've got it." She pursed her lips as she began to rinse the dishes. "My dad was a difficult man, but if we needed him, he tried to be there." She paused. "The trouble with that, he was often deployed somewhere—and couldn't come."

"Families can be tough."

"Tell me." Blossom loaded the dishwasher and smiled over one shoulder. "But I have good news. I let Sam sit in a chair tonight to eat dinner and when I helped him up, he barely stumbled."

"Let us pray," Logan said, although he couldn't see Sam taking over the ranch again any time soon. Which made him all the more frustrated with Sawyer. At the least they could have taken turns on the Circle H—and Logan wouldn't have to risk his promotion. His chance to fight for shared custody of Nicky.

"How's the kitten doing?" he asked.

He'd seen Blossom hurry out to the barn several times since that afternoon. Although he'd fed the kitten, even stuck around to scratch her under the chin and talk a bit, Blossom acted as if the cat was in an ICU and needed constant care.

She blushed. "You saw me."

"She doing all right, in your professional opinion?"

"Fine," she said. "You did a good job with her stitches."

"They won't win her any beauty contests, but they'll work."

Blossom hesitated. "We should probably take her to the vet's anyway," she said. "I mean I could. Tomorrow. If that's okay with you."

"No need," he said. "Unless it's an emergency—which this isn't—or something we can't treat, we don't bother the vet. Saves the ranch money, too. But I do have to go into town tomorrow." Then Logan heard himself say, "You want to go with me? While I'm at the ag store for supplies, you can buy groceries and whatever else you'd like. I know the ranch can seem a lonely place for a woman."

She didn't answer at first. He shouldn't have said anything.

Logan passed her the detergent for the dishwasher.

Maybe he hadn't made himself clear. She needed to know he wasn't putting any moves on her, just offering her a ride into Barren.

"About earlier today in the barn—"

"I shouldn't have kissed your cheek," she said, then in the next breath, "Yes. I'd like to go to town with you tomorrow."

His insides unwound. "Okay, then. We'll leave around nine."

"I'll fix breakfast," she said. "A nice omelet."

Logan nearly groaned aloud. At the table the mac and cheese, never his favorite, had congealed on his plate. He doubted her version of a Western omelet, which he normally liked, would be either.

"Let me buy you an early lunch instead," he told her.

CHAPTER FIVE

LOGAN LEANED AGAINST the side of his truck and checked his watch again. Blossom was late. Then he glanced up and saw her coming from the barn.

"Sorry," she said with a little duck of her head and no eye contact.

Ah, he thought. "The kitten."

It was obvious by now that she'd formed an attachment to the little cat.

"I checked on her when I fed the horses at six," he said with a smile. "We need to coordinate our schedules."

Without another word Blossom climbed into the truck. She sat as far away from him as possible, pressed against the passenger door. In the driver's seat Logan hit the locks, and she startled, almost lifting off her perch.

"Can't have you falling out into the road," he said, shifting into gear. They were soon down the long drive and onto the main road, and Logan breathed his usual sigh of relief.

The ranch always made him feel as if he were locked up in solitary confinement. It was one reason he'd asked Blossom to join him today. He imagined she might feel the same.

Logan didn't want to examine the other reason.

Yet as he drove toward town, his gaze kept straying to her. He could still feel that briefest touch of her lips to his face yesterday. To Blossom it had meant nothing, he supposed, no more than a friendly gesture—as if to say she knew how hard Nicky's surprise visit had been for him—but it had been a while since a woman had touched him even like that.

He ran through an imaginary preflight checklist to refocus his thoughts and tried to keep his eyes on the road instead of on Blossom.

Neither spoke until they were at the edge of town.

"The kitten needs a name," she said.

He could tell she'd been turning that subject over in her mind the whole way, as if she'd decided it was the only safe topic they might discuss. "Thought we agreed. We don't name the animals."

"I bet Sam does."

"Yeah, well," he conceded. "But barn cats are different."

"I know. They don't always stay around. Maybe they would," she added, "if they did have names. If they felt a part of the ranch instead of just coming and going."

Like me, he thought.

Logan glanced at her again—and nearly rear-ended the car in front of him on Main Street. The big flashy SUV likely belonged to a spring tourist who didn't know it sometimes snowed here even in April or one of the wealthy out-of-towners who'd settled in Barren in one of those monstrous log homes on ten-acre "ranches" that made them feel like true Westerners.

"Are you really talking about the cats?"

She blinked. "Excuse me?"

"Philadelphia," he said, swinging the truck into an angled parking spot that had just opened up halfway down the street. "You left home. For some reason."

"I wanted to see the world," she said, but Logan didn't believe her. According to Blossom herself, she'd already seen plenty of it.

In front of the ag store, he cut the engine. "All right, we'll save that for later. I'm going in here to order supplies, get some feed. The market's right across the street. When you're done with the groceries, I can roll over to pick you up."

"How long?"

"An hour, maybe? Like a lot of guys I tend to get lost in the aisles, trying out this gadget and that." His mind should be on getting back to Wichita, not on farm equipment or a woman he had no business even thinking about except, he reminded himself, as an employee.

Or maybe he was just delaying their return to the ranch.

And the isolation that always reminded him of losing the people he loved.

"I might have another errand to do," she said.

"Take your time."

It took Blossom a while to reach the far end of Main Street, not because the street was that long but because she kept stopping to look in store windows. And to bask in the spring sunshine, letting the still-cool air blow through her hair.

She glanced back toward the agriculture store. Logan had disappeared inside.

The little town of Barren was a far cry from

Philly—it was no more than this one street and a few surrounding blocks, from what she'd seen—and most of the area's population probably lived on ranches like the Circle H. That suited Blossom just fine. She was anonymous here, another bonus.

A smile crossed her lips. She couldn't imagine Ken here in his fancy suit that had cost thousands of dollars, his silk ties and custom-made white shirts, not to mention his pricey shoes. He'd stick out all right. The local dress code seemed to be jeans and boots and, of course, the ubiquitous cowboy hat.

Logan hadn't worn one today, but then he didn't seem to consider himself a cowboy. A jet pilot, he'd told her, and his job was as far from ranching as she was from Philadelphia and Ken. No wonder Logan looked uncomfortable on the Circle H.

In front of a pet store, she gazed at the window display. A red dog collar studded with silver adorned the neck of a stuffed black-and-white border collie. A herding dog. Blossom had seen several of them at the Circle H but only from a distance. *We don't name the animals.* They weren't family pets any more than the little no-name kitten was, at least in Logan's view.

Unable to resist, Blossom stepped inside the store. From the cat department in the rear, she bought a couple of toys—a mouse with catnip inside, a fishing-pole type thing with feathers at the end—then a dish with a goldfish design and, finally, a small pink beaded collar with a bell to warn the birds.

Outside again, she strolled along the paved walkway, humming to herself.

A few doors down, a children's apparel shop looked too enticing to be passed by, even when she shouldn't keep Logan waiting. He'd said not to hurry, but Ken had been good at laying traps like that to spring on her without warning.

Carrying her pet-store bag, she went in.

"Good morning." A clerk came forward. "May I help you find something?"

"Oh, no. Thank you. Is it all right if I just look around?"

The woman smiled. "Of course. Take your time," she said as Logan had.

Blossom wasn't used to dallying. With her father she didn't dare, and when Ken said jump, she'd asked how high—at least in her mind. Her daily routine in Philly had come to be very structured and, ultimately, confining. She'd even quit her first job there to have more time at "home" to meet Ken's demanding standards, and it wasn't often—or hadn't been until now—that she could simply enjoy part of a morning doing what she liked.

The clerk, who trailed her through the shop, clearly wanted to chat. She had no other customers. Or did she expect Blossom to shoplift from one of the displays? In the next instant she had her answer.

"Do you live here?" the woman asked. "I haven't seen you before."

And in small towns, people noticed. She'd gathered that right away from a few curious glances she'd gotten on the street. Blossom would bet the woman knew everyone around here by name.

"I'm passing through," she admitted with a twinge of regret. What if she'd grown up in a town like this one on a ranch like the Circle H? In a house she could truly call her own?

She explored a rack of oh-so-small baby clothes mostly in blue then, moving on, a set of cream-colored shelves that held silver mugs, little spoons and picture frames. The baby in one photograph made her heart turn over. "What a sweet face," she said to the clerk, who was still hovering nearby.

"That's my niece, actually. I wanted to show

off this frame in a more personal way. Usually, my stock comes with inserted photos of complete strangers who stare out at me all day. Barren is a close-knit town. People like to make a connection. Isn't she cute? If you're not looking for baby boy things, we have some adorable new dresses over there on the far wall." She waited only a second before asking, "Are you having a little girl?"

As if by instinct, Blossom's hand went to her stomach. Was she showing already? She hadn't thought so. It wouldn't do for word to get around town that she was pregnant. Certainly, she hadn't told Logan. Or even Sam. Her job at the Circle H seemed precarious enough. She'd be here only a short time, and she'd seen Logan with Nick. She doubted he'd welcome the idea of a baby there.

"No, I'm not," she said. "I, um, have a friend who is."

The clerk raised one eyebrow but said nothing.

"Let me show you."

As the woman pulled out one after another of the most beautiful baby dresses, Blossom all but melted into a puddle on the floor.

She fingered the embroidered hem of a too-cute-for-words gingham sundress. "Pink still seems to be very popular."

"Purple, too," the clerk agreed. "Or should I say lavender?"

But it was the tiniest things that called to Blossom. She drifted toward a white basket heaped with layette items from receiving blankets to booties before her gaze fell on an artfully stacked pile of baby hats on the same table.

"The hospital in Kansas City orders these for the newborns," the clerk told her. "Parents like them for home, too. We have some really nice ones."

Blossom picked up a multicolored cap in pink and blue and yellow that covered all the bases. To her delight it had an interwoven cowboy/cowgirl motif. "Maybe my friend would like this."

"I'm sure she would. That's one of our new designs."

Blossom couldn't leave the store without buying something, having taken up the sales associate's time, and the tiny cap warmed her heart. It didn't cost that much, which seemed to disappoint the saleswoman but suited Blossom's budget, and Ken wasn't here to tell her she didn't need it.

Moments later she was on the sidewalk again with another bag to carry.

At the end of the street she hurried into the Mother Comfort Home Health Care Agency, her original destination.

"Hi, Blossom." At the reception desk in the front room, an attractive dark-haired woman had been typing on the computer. When she glanced up, a slight frown crossed her face. "Everything all right on the Circle H?"

Not really. She'd stepped over a boundary with Logan yesterday because of that kiss, and on the way into town she hadn't known what to say to him. "Fine," she said, struggling to remember the woman's name. A few days ago she'd helped Blossom fill out her application.

"I had a terrible time finding someone for Logan. I'm glad you filled the bill."

"I'm not sure about that but—" She didn't go any further. "I wanted to ask about my pay. I wasn't sure of the arrangement."

The woman's frown deepened. "The agency collects the money from a client, we take our commission for placing you, then cut a check." She paused. "It's not Friday so I can't pay you yet for the week. But don't worry. The Hunters always meet their bills and if they didn't—"

"I'm not worried." Which was a lie for a

different reason. "But…could I get cash instead?"

"That's not our usual policy." She hesitated again. "If it's inconvenient for you to come to town again, we could do direct deposit at your bank."

Blossom's pulse skipped. That was even worse. There was no way she'd open a bank account. She wouldn't give Ken a trail to follow. She'd already made one slip soon after she left Philadelphia. "Not cash then?"

"I can check with my accountant." She gave Blossom an encouraging smile. "Or I could mail the check to you."

"No, I'll come in on Friday." If she lasted that long before she had to move on again.

Shifting her packages, Blossom finally remembered the woman's name was Shadow. Her brown gaze was very direct. "Is there a problem, Blossom?"

"No, of course not. I like the Circle H," she said, which was true. "I was just wondering. Please ask your accountant."

Her heart was still thumping by the time she finally finished the grocery shopping. The ranch cupboards and pantry, the huge double freezer, held plenty of food so she didn't need much, but a few items had been missing for the dinner she planned to make tonight. Assuming she could think straight by then. A check? Up until now she'd worked for cash doing odd jobs or waiting tables whenever she ran out of money.

But at the baby store the clerk had noticed she was a stranger and seemed suspicious of her at first—and even more of Blossom's claim that she wasn't pregnant. Then Shadow had wondered about her need for cash.

As he'd promised, Logan was waiting for her outside the grocery store.

He hopped out of the truck to load her bags into the open bed beside some big sacks of feed.

"I'm sorry I took so long." She glanced at his face to see if he'd meant what he said earlier or might erupt at any second because she'd taken her time.

"No problem. You hungry?"

Her stomach was in knots. "I could eat something," she said because Logan looked so eager, and it was already his lunchtime, if not hers. "But I should get this food in the fridge."

He peered into the bags, not noticing the Baby Things logo. She'd stuck the small bags into a larger one from the market. "Not that much cold stuff here. It'll be okay while we eat." They got back in the truck. "How does fast food sound, then?"

"Perfect."

Blossom expected him to pick up some burgers and fries then head straight back to the ranch. Instead, after their stop at a local drive-through at the edge of town, Logan suddenly pulled off into a nearby parking area beside a swift-flowing stream.

"Let's eat here. The sun is out, it's one of the first decent days after winter and the temperature's warming up—at least for an hour or so. In Kansas the weather can change on a dime. Come on," he said, already halfway out of the truck. "The groceries can wait a bit longer."

Blossom followed him, though she wasn't sure it was such a good idea. In the barn yesterday she'd glimpsed another side of Logan, and this morning he'd been nothing but kind, so she wasn't afraid of being alone with him.

As long as he didn't ask her too many questions.

CHAPTER SIX

LOGAN WAS IN no hurry to get back to the ranch.

He'd decided to stop while they ate and make a little small talk to take his mind off things. He hadn't been exactly charming when Blossom first stepped foot on the Circle H, and yesterday, when he saw Nicky, he'd acted even worse. He had to be careful not to let her see his interest in her—an interest he had no right to indulge—but he needed to take a breather before they drove back to the ranch and the gates closed behind him like a steel prison door.

The small roadside park had one table under a large cottonwood tree, so he set out their meal then sat beside Blossom on the bench. He wolfed down one cheeseburger then started on another. When he glanced sideways, he saw she hadn't taken a bite of her grilled chicken sandwich.

"You okay?" It was becoming a habit to ask how she felt.

"Yes." She was staring at the water. "I'm enjoying the view."

He had to admit, there was a lot to like. The clear stream rushed past. Birds chirped and twittered among the trees. Sunshine slanted through the branches, gilding Blossom's face with a soft gold, and the air smelled of flowers. Wild ones, probably, this time of year.

"It's beautiful here," she said.

"And you're not eating."

She took a small bite, as if to please him, which didn't please him.

"What did you do in town?" he asked.

"I bought groceries." He already knew that. "And window-shopped."

When she didn't say any more, he dug into his fries. Good, greasy food to fill a man's stomach. He still hadn't gotten that steak.

"The shops in Barren are pretty small," he said. "Not like the stores in Philadelphia I bet."

She sipped her soda. "I wasn't much of a shopper, but Barren is a nice town."

"I never thought of it as 'nice,'" he said, smiling. Just as a bison calf wasn't that cute to him. Yet Blossom appreciated both.

"You really don't like it here."

"Point for you," he said. "The ranch, though,

that's where the tough memories are." He slanted her another look. "I imagine you've got some bad ones, too. Or am I wrong?"

"A few" was all she said. "Do you like Wichita better?"

"I like my job. I always wanted to fly, ever since I was a kid." He finished the fries then wadded up the wrapper. "We used to go to the air show in KC every year—when my folks were still alive—and I guess that's where I caught the 'bug.'" He paused, remembering. "In part because of my dad, too. He loved planes and passed that on to me. Too bad he didn't live long enough. He would have been proud."

"What happened to him?"

Logan looked away. "I was almost eight then, the day before my birthday. He and my mom had gone to a cattle auction near Denver—this was before Sam ran bison. He wasn't in the picture yet. They started for home early not to miss my party the next day. Dad had bought me a new horse, the first I ever owned, and my grandma later told me he'd wanted to see my face when he led it out of the barn in front of all my friends. But on their way home, the weather turned bad. The roads iced over and then the snows came. By the time they were halfway, it had become a true blizzard."

"They were in a car crash?"

He nodded. "With the roads like that… I'm pretty sure my mom begged him to pull off for the night. He could be stubborn, though. Like me sometimes," he added. "Anyway. Some guy coming the other way hit them head-on." Logan swallowed hard. "They were both killed. I've always thought—if he'd listened to her, or they hadn't gone to that auction…but they were also far from the nearest town or a hospital. There was no LifeFlight helicopter. If there had been…" He trailed off. "Maybe that's one reason I became a pilot. Didn't help with Nicky, though. Years later, a flood at the ranch put me right back in that other time… Frankly, I've never been one for birthday parties ever since." He pressed his lips tight then let out a breath. He didn't usually spill his guts like this.

Time for a change of subject.

"You ever see the Blue Angels?"

"No. My dad was army."

He grimaced. "Ouch. Well, we can't all fly, but those navy guys were my heroes. Man, their precision, even the closest they get wingtip to wingtip until you're sure they'll collide, the deafening sound of that team just overhead as if you could reach out and touch them, the power of those engines screaming past…" He felt his face heat. "I sound like that eight-year-old kid. I guess I still am."

"I'm sorry about your parents, Logan. So you took flying lessons once you were old enough?"

He forced a grin. "Nah. Decided to skip all that. Bought my pilot's license from some website—and off I went, into the wild blue yonder. Learning on the job." She'd said that to Grey the other day.

Her lips twitched. "You're joking."

He laughed. "Yeah. I am. I hope you don't mind my teasing."

She tilted her head. "I like it. I haven't seen you really laugh before."

"Every now and then," he said then sobered. "Seriously. I did take lessons—a Christmas present one year from Sam." His grandfather had wanted him—and Sawyer—to stay at the Circle H, but he wouldn't deny Logan his dream. "Then I joined the military right after high school graduation. I wasn't Blue Angels material, as it turned out, but I did all right."

"Were you in combat?"

"From the air," he said. "All that experience

got me my civilian license and a college education, thanks to my veteran's benefits. After I got my BA in engineering, and had married Libby, I spent more time at the ranch while I looked for a job in Wichita. I'm working my way up there."

"I bet you're good."

Warmth flowed through him. "Why do you say that?"

"I've seen you with the ranch hands—Willy and Tobias?—and you're a natural leader. You maintain discipline."

"Which you know something about." It was a guess but not by much. She'd spoken of her father before.

Blossom admitted, "My dad ran a tight ship—or rather, house."

"And your mother?"

Her gaze faltered. "She ran it for him when he wasn't there. She was like his next in command. He's retired now and they live in Alabama. Still, I think having to be so careful and precise over the years has finally worn her down."

"What about you?"

"I never quite measured up," she said, "and maybe that was my way of rebelling." She almost grinned. "Maybe that's why I keep making dinners you don't want to eat."

But he couldn't let the subject go at that. "After you left home—?"

"I got a job, then shared an apartment in Philly." She didn't go on.

To give her time, Logan gathered up his trash. Was there a man in the picture? He dumped his bag and wrappers in the nearby garbage can then turned back to Blossom. She was still sitting there, her meal half-eaten, her hands twisting in her lap.

Today he'd seen a strange, and worrisome, combination. On the one hand, she was bold and funny and...dear, his grandmother would have said. On the other, she was sometimes like a stray dog that'd been kicked too often, abandoned in an animal shelter, cowering in a corner.

His hands fisted. A guy, he thought. Logan might have made a hash of his marriage and lost Nicky for now, but he'd never even thought of harming Libby. Or any woman. As any decent man would, especially one raised on Western values, all at once he wanted to protect her, too.

"I know about your father. Did someone else hurt you, Blossom?"

Her eyes looked wide, and almost teary. She put her hands together on the tabletop, like a child in school, and shrugged.

"You're safe here," he said at last.

But Blossom shook her head. "You told me yourself you don't think the Circle H is that safe."

Logan didn't voice his next thought.

I didn't mean the ranch. I meant with me.

THAT NIGHT BLOSSOM stayed in the barn until she thought Logan would be upstairs in his room. He went to bed early and got up before dawn. It shamed her that she'd let Ken—let anyone—turn her into a woman who jumped at the slightest sound. A woman who ran. She'd been so tempted to spill the rest of her story that afternoon, even to beg for Logan's help with Ken if it came to that.

She'd enjoyed their impromptu lunch way too much. She'd liked being on neutral territory where they weren't simply boss and employee, talking with him, being teased without the words turning into something else, proving all over again that there was something wrong with her.

Now Blossom sat on a trunk in the tack

room with the overhead lights off, holding the tortoiseshell kitten.

"No-Name," she murmured. "That's as good as any, I guess."

Blossom had eaten dinner with Sam again. She'd scrubbed the pots and pans while Logan checked on the horses for the night, then when he came back to the house she'd headed outside, grateful that, for a change, he hadn't seemed to dislike his meal even though he'd eaten burgers for lunch, as well.

How had he guessed she didn't feel safe?

She got up and carried the kitten over to the wall mirror where there was just enough light from the barn aisle through the open door to see by. She held the little creature close against her chest then studied their reflections. Blossom's too-big eyes held the familiar hint of fear, which apparently she couldn't hide. A pale face. The reddish hair she should have dyed brown or even black as a disguise and which Blossom had always hated. It stood out now like a beacon. The baggy clothes.

She didn't look appealing. She knew Logan was still calling Mother Comfort about her replacement. Of course he would. She'd heard him on the phone in the ranch office just before dinner when she passed by with Sam's tray.

So why had he said what he did? *You're safe here.* Why did she keep seeing such unexpected warmth in Logan's gaze?

She was still peering at herself in the glass when Willy walked in.

He jumped back. "Jeez. Didn't know anyone was in here. Scared me."

"I'm sorry." Blossom turned toward him. "I was showing this kitten her image in the mirror."

He laughed. Without turning on the lights, he came deeper into the room.

Blossom tensed. She'd only seen him once or twice since dinner on her first night at the ranch. He and Tobias had been making themselves scarce. Either that, or they had so much work to do that they were always out on the range.

Willy took off his hat. "Pardon, ma'am, but I need to clean my saddle."

She turned toward the door. "Oh. Then I'll just—"

"No need to run off. Plenty of room here for both of us. And—" he nodded at the kitten "—that one."

"I'm calling her No-Name."

Willy snorted. "Logan'll love that, but you're wasting your time. She'll take off one of these days just like her mama. I can't keep 'em straight."

Logan thought so, too. "I don't think she'll leave."

He shrugged. "Suit yourself." Willy rummaged in a trunk for a can of saddle soap. "A man don't clean his equipment," he said, "he's lookin' for trouble."

"I don't know anything about horses."

He pulled his saddle from a rack. "You stay here, you will. Springtime it can flood, bad sometimes. That driveway to the road gets covered deep enough, the only way out of here—or in—is on horseback. You should learn to ride."

"Really?"

"Logan can tell you."

He'd mentioned a flood at lunch and Blossom wanted to ask more, but she didn't. She probably wouldn't stay long enough for it to matter, and she didn't like the way Willy looked at her. His sly expression, his crafty eyes made her nervous, and he was so big he seemed to fill the small room. She began to edge toward the door behind her.

"Sit down," Willy said without looking up. "Watch me work."

Still holding No-Name, she sat. Her pulse pounded. She was clearly overreacting. *Did someone else hurt you?*

Logan had easily read her wariness of men. Was it that obvious? Ken had done that to her. But not every man was out to destroy her spirit, she tried to tell herself.

"What made you decide to become a cowboy, Willy?"

He rubbed soap into the leather. "Nothin' else I ever wanted to do," he said. "Kind of like Logan in reverse. He couldn't wait to get off this ranch." He snickered. "Now he's back, not for any reason of his own—and I have to tell you, I wish old Sam would get better. He's ornery but at least he loves this place. Logan'll be off to fly planes first chance he gets." He nodded. "Hot Shot, that's what I call *him*."

"Not to his face," Blossom said, remembering the way Logan had reprimanded Willy at the dinner table that first night.

He laughed again, harder this time.

"Don't you just know it. He and his brother are twins, you know, but only in how they look. Sawyer loved the ranch, like Sam. Don't really know why he left after all. Hasn't been back in quite a time."

"Twins?"

"Can't tell one from the other."

"Identical," she said. And how weird would that be, seeing two Logan Hunters at once? "His brother didn't want to take over from Sam? Work with him till he retired?"

"As a kid, he'd trailed Sam everywhere—so I heard. A cowboy from the heart. That was before my time here, and it was Tobias who told me, but the legend grows." He glanced at Blossom through dark lashes. "Nobody quite knows what Sawyer does now, or where he does it."

Logan and Sawyer. Blossom smoothed a hand over her abdomen. What would it be like to have twins? Had she just felt a faint flutter of movement?

Willy's gaze had followed the motion. "Your stomach sour?"

"I feel fine." She rose from the trunk and laid the kitten gently in her bed.

"Don't hurry away."

Willy rose from the other tack trunk, the can of saddle soap in his hand.

"I really should go," she said.

With the speed of one of the ranch's border

collies, he blocked her way. "I fill you in on the big man—and you want to leave? I must be wrong," he said.

"Wrong?"

"I could have sworn I saw something with you two. So, a word of warning—don't get your hopes up."

"I wasn't," Blossom said weakly as her lunch with Logan flashed through her mind. "He's my employer, that's all."

Willy leaned one thick, brawny arm on the door frame just above her head. "Maybe we *employees* should stick together."

With a quick shove, Blossom ducked out under his arm. She plucked the kitten from her cozy nest of blankets. She wouldn't leave No-Name here. She didn't like, or trust, Willy.

"You and me," he went on, tracking her out the door. "We could go to the Grange Hall on Saturday night." He did a little dance step, holding out his arms.

Blossom didn't answer. With his crude laugh ringing in her ears, she rushed into the aisle then raced from the barn to the house and up to her room.

She wouldn't be alone with Willy again.

Or even Logan. Today, eating lunch by the stream had been a mistake.

Hadn't she learned her lesson with Ken? She really couldn't trust any man.

IN THE LIVING ROOM, Logan flicked the remote control to shut off the TV. He'd tried to watch three different shows—a documentary on terrorism, a silly sitcom, the first period of a basketball game—but none of them had registered. He couldn't get Blossom out of his head.

What had he been thinking that afternoon? Watching the sun set fire to the rich red of her hair? Bumping shoulders beside her on the picnic bench? Getting to know her, at least a little better than he had before? Worrying about her, when he shouldn't even try—or want—to get close to her.

Hours ago he'd snatched his cell phone from the end table. A minute later he'd had Shadow Moran on the line. He was still mulling over their conversation, too.

"Hey, handsome," she'd said. "Does this call have to do with Blossom?"

"What makes you think that?"

"Well, I am the face of the Mother Comfort Home Health Care Agency."

"And I may have made a mistake."

At the other end of the line, Shadow huffed out a breath. "Logan, I'm getting a definite set of mixed messages here. From all sides. First, you drive me half-crazy trying to find a caregiver for Sam. There are no male caregivers in this whole county, which I tried to tell you a hundred times. Then Blossom Kennedy walks into my office—and you hire her. There still isn't a man to replace her. That is your question tonight, isn't it? Hers too, maybe." She paused. "Blossom came to see me earlier."

"She did?"

"Just before noon. She was carrying a couple of bags so I guess she'd been shopping, but there was clearly something else on her mind. I don't think she even remembered my name at first. And to me, she looked a bit jumpy. That was nothing out of the ordinary," Shadow went on. "She looked the same way when she first filled out her application. Today she asked me for cash pay instead of a check. Did you fire her, and she just didn't want to say so?"

"Not me. Sam's happy with her." He wouldn't include himself. Maybe this explained Blossom's stiffness during lunch. "I admit, we had a few words when she first got here and I still want someone more suitable, stronger, experienced—" Not as appealing, he thought.

"Does she do a good job?"

"Fair enough. Not much of a cook," he said, "or at least not real food, but she tries. You think she's getting ready to leave?" He'd still worry about her if she wasn't around, but he wouldn't have to see her every day, hear her move around in her bedroom each night across the hall. Caution himself to keep his mind where it should be—on getting back to Wichita.

"Leave?" Shadow maintained a brief silence. "*Run* would be my word for it."

"Huh. I agree." Logan voiced his earlier thought. "I think she's in trouble, Shadow. I've thought so from the start. We talked today, too, and now after what you're saying, I'm sure she is."

"She didn't want a check and she didn't want me to deposit her pay in the bank. Sounds like trouble to me. What do we do?"

Blossom's visit to the agency changed things. It brought out his protective instincts again, suddenly stronger than his need to avoid any type of relationship.

"I'm sure not pushing a woman on the run out into the night. She obviously needs the money she's earning here at the Circle H. And," he added, "a place to hide."

"You want me to stop looking, then? For her replacement?"

Silence on his part for another moment.

"No," he finally said. "But keep me posted."

CHAPTER SEVEN

AT THE SOUND of a car pulling up to the barn's open doorway, Logan dropped Cyclone's right rear leg, which he'd been holding between his thighs while he dealt with his hoof. Then he saw the woman who stepped out of the familiar new-model sedan—most likely paid for with his alimony check. And mentally braced himself.

Wearing a crisp gray suit, Olivia Wilson Hunter marched down the barn aisle with murder in her beautiful blue eyes. A coral cami or whatever it was called peeked out between the lapels of her jacket. Stopping in front of him, almost in his face, she slapped both hands on her hips. "Did I give permission for Nick to come over here?"

"I don't know. Did you?" He gave her a grim smile then set aside the rasp he'd been using to file a rough spot on the colt's hoof that could make him lame. "We don't live together anymore, Olivia—*Libby*. I haven't seen you in weeks. I can't read your mind."

"Grey knows better," she said, taking care to avoid coming too near the colt. "I could kill him for that."

"If you didn't love your brother," Logan pointed out. How did she know about Grey and Nicky's visit? Grey surely wouldn't have told her. "I had no idea they were coming to visit until I walked into the kitchen—and saw Nicky. Grey had just pulled him down from climbing the cabinet."

"Climbing?"

Uh-oh. Wrong thing to say. Libby watched their son like a hawk until Nicky must be afraid to take a step.

He hadn't meant to goad her. Watching Libby's face turn pale always reminded him of the flood, his wife's panic and his own failure. She had pleaded with him then for help. She wasn't pleading now.

"*I'm* in charge of his well-being—"

"The judge agrees with you."

"And if I ever catch Grey bringing him here again without my say-so—"

Logan's mouth tightened. "Lighten up. You need to take this to Grey. That wasn't my fault."

Her features softened a bit. Her hands dropped away from her hips. "Well, Grey wasn't at his house when I stopped by, but you were here. I guess you were handy."

Logan rubbed the nape of his neck. But that wasn't all. Libby never set foot on the Circle H if she could help it. He couldn't remember the last time he'd seen her in this barn. Wearing killer high heels and a suit. She was here for some other reason.

"We can't keep on like this, Libby. For one thing, it's not good for Nicky. It's not good for us either."

"There *is* no us."

"True," he had to agree. "I shouldn't have to tell you this, but the flood, the divorce and losing Nicky have been the low points of my life so far. I'd give anything for all of that not to have happened. You want to rub it in again?" He turned back to the colt. "Go ahead. But I'm not listening to any more of this."

She trailed a hand over the colt's sleek black neck as if she'd forgotten he might nip and had remembered her love of animals instead. They'd shared that at least, other than Nicky, though they weren't sharing him now.

"I don't want to see Nick hurt."

"Kids climb, Libby. That's what they do."

"You're calling me a helicopter parent."

At first Logan didn't respond. *If the term fits...*

"He needs the freedom to make mistakes, just like we did," he said. "That's how we learn."

"Oh. I see. So now you're saying our marriage was a mistake."

Among other things—like his absence when he was needed most. Logan snapped a lead line on the colt then unlatched him from the crossties.

"Maybe I am," he muttered. "All I know for sure is, you're wrong to shelter Nicky the way you do."

He started down the aisle to Cyclone's stall.

Libby caught his shoulder. "You weren't here during the flood. But you should have been, and the weather reports didn't lie. You grew up on this ranch. You knew how bad it could get."

"Yeah, and I guess we're going to rehash this forever."

He released the horse into his stall, rolled the door shut then hung the lead rope on a hook outside. Automatic motions he'd made a thousand times without having to think. Muscle memory.

Still, he didn't intend to stay here any longer than he had to. Or suffer through another tirade from Libby.

As he'd learned the hard way and from talking with Shadow last night after his lunch with Blossom, good feelings didn't last.

He leaned back against the closed stall door, listening to Cyclone root in the hay for stray bits of grain.

"Libby, we loved each other once. Didn't we?"

She didn't answer. For a long moment she looked at him, as if trying to decide whether or not he'd ever appealed to her. Whether they'd shared any common goal.

"All right," she said. "I admit, Grey bringing Nick over here wasn't your doing. But don't let it happen again."

"You'd better tell Grey that." Logan added, "Now, why don't you let me know why you're really here when a phone call would have done the job?"

She shifted, folding her arms over her chest and avoiding his gaze. "You know me too well. So here's the thing—and, God, I hate to ask this—but I do need a favor."

"From me?"

"I know. Astonishing, isn't it?" Libby focused on the open barn doors at the end of the aisle. "I have a doctor's appointment tomorrow morning. Nick's school is closed for parent-teacher conferences. He's too old for day care except the after-school program, and my usual babysitter called in sick today. My friends all work full-time. And Grey's going to Montana to buy cattle. Could you possibly…"

"Consider it done." He paused. "You came all the way out here to chew me up about the other day—when all along you needed me to help you?"

"I guess I did." She smiled a little. "I had to work up to it."

"Ah, Libby."

She tucked a strand of blond hair behind one ear, reminding Logan of all the times he'd done the same for her. "I hate to ask you for anything."

"Maybe you need to think about that." She was almost to the barn doors when he called out, "Hey. You feeling okay?"

"Perfect. It's just a…checkup." She couldn't resist adding, "I'd rather he didn't come here tomorrow. You can do something with him in town."

Then she turned her back, marched off without another word, her slim form moving farther and farther away. She was distancing herself from him physically just as she had emotionally before she left him—and took Nicky with her.

He hoped she wasn't just saying her appointment was only a checkup. He hoped nothing was wrong with her.

For Nicky's sake.

BLOSSOM SET ANOTHER can of peaches on a pantry shelf. She hadn't had time yesterday to unload everything. She ducked back into the kitchen for the last bag of nonperishables. Maybe tonight she'd ask Logan to grill steaks while she baked potatoes and cooked green beans, the meal he'd asked for. The traditional men's favorite should be simple enough that she wouldn't mess up.

At the window she glanced out to see a sleek sedan sail down the driveway toward the main road. Another visitor she didn't recognize. Whoever it was must have been here on business because no one had come to the house.

At least it wasn't Ken.

Humming to herself, she rummaged through the grocery bag.

A second later the back door flew open and Logan walked in.

She took one look at his face and thought, *Uh-oh*. His dark brows were drawn low, his mouth set. Pouring himself a mug of coffee, he said, "My ex was just here. She wasn't happy that Nicky showed up with Grey the other day."

Blossom had quickly learned to keep a full pot of coffee available at all times. He came and went and sometimes so did Willy or Tobias.

"Don't you have visitation rights?"

"Yeah, but she makes it hard to see him and it's upsetting to Nicky whenever I have to leave again. He was only three when Libby and I split up. Sometimes I doubt he remembers me that well."

"That wasn't my impression." Blossom saw the flash of pain cross his face again. He wasn't angry, as she'd first thought. "I think he misses you very much. I did when my father was away, and after losing your parents, you should understand… I'm sure he wants you to be part of his life."

"That won't happen," he said, taking a careful sip of the hot brew, "until I can go to court—and sue Libby for joint custody."

"How would that work? If she's here and you're in Wichita?"

"I haven't gotten that far," he admitted. "I may have to settle for summers and holidays. We'll see. I need my promotion first to afford lawyers. I'm still paying off the last suit."

"You lost," she said. "Based on what?—if you don't mind me asking."

"Libby convinced the court that Nicky might be in danger if he stayed with me. The ranch was no place, she said, for a little boy. There are too many things that could happen here—which I can't argue with. The same message, basically, that she delivered today."

"So you need to get back to Wichita."

"Yeah."

"I could take care of things while you're gone," she offered. "Sam doesn't mind my cooking and we get along well."

Logan blew on his coffee. "Can you also run a ranch? Give orders to Willy and Tobias? Deliver calves if need be? Treat an abscess or sew up a cat?"

Blossom bit her lip. She couldn't tell him about last night in the barn with Willy. Nothing had really happened except that she'd almost panicked. She'd left the kitten with some fresh bedding in an empty stall for the night.

"I guess not," she said, feeling as she always did when Ken criticized her.

"And the Circle H can't run itself. Could you really control Sam on your own? The better he feels, the sooner he'll be falling down the stairs trying to prove he's a hundred percent again." He added, "The doctor said he may have the balance problem, and some fuzzy thoughts, for a while."

"Oh." He'd reminded Blossom of her conversation with Sam. A safer topic, she hoped. "I forgot to tell you. The other day your grandfather confused me with your ex-wife." Her face warmed. "He thought you and she—or me, in that case—should have another couple of babies."

"God, no," Logan said. "I mean, nothing against you or even Libby. But you think he's that confused?"

"Only for a moment," she said. "I thought you should know, though."

Blossom dug into the grocery bag once more, in part to hide the heat in her face. She didn't welcome this constant awareness she had of Logan not as her temporary employer but as a man. She was in no position to start another relationship she couldn't handle. And one Logan probably didn't want.

Beside her, he dipped into the bag and then handed Blossom a can of green beans. "Put this stuff wherever you want it. My grandmother never liked any of us meddling in her pantry. I'll unpack the rest."

In the next second, she knew that was a mistake.

Logan held up the smaller bag from the Baby Things shop. She'd forgotten the tiny cap was in with the groceries. "This yours?"

"Yes. Thanks," she said, trying to take it from him.

But Logan held on to the bag. He peered inside with a pointed look.

"One of your errands in town?" he asked, as if he also knew she'd gone to the Mother Comfort agency.

"My...friend is having a baby." Blossom looked away.

To her relief he didn't pursue the matter.

Instead, he said, "I think there's still some of Nicky's baby stuff in the attic. Libby kept his clothes in real nice shape. You're welcome to them."

For your friend.

CHAPTER EIGHT

BLOSSOM DROVE INTO town by herself on Friday—finally, her first payday, and the day after Logan had seen the bag with the baby hat. Leaving her old sedan parked behind the red Mustang that belonged to Shadow Moran, she headed into the Mother Comfort Home Health Care Agency again.

To her disappointment, Shadow presented her with a check. Blossom stared at it for a moment, feeling the regular thud of her heart speed up.

Shadow looked apologetic. "I talked with my accountant. Dispensing cash messes up our system so I'm not willing to make an exception. I'm sorry, Blossom." Shadow didn't meet her eyes. "I hope this won't be a problem for you."

Well, it is. Blossom's pulse was beating like a trip hammer now. Her hand trembled on the paper check. "I don't have a bank account here."

"I'd be happy to recommend my bank. I can steer you to the person I deal with there. She's quite good. Friendly, too," Shadow added, as if that would make all the difference to Blossom.

"I'd rather not, but thank you. I know you tried."

Shadow leaned back in her chair to study Blossom. "I understand. You don't expect to be here long, so why put down roots? I get that." She thought for a moment. "So... I know. There's one of those payday loan sites on Sycamore Street around the corner off Main about four blocks down. The cowboys use it all the time. You can cash your check there."

Blossom frowned. She couldn't take that chance either. Logan had told her the ranch hands were often itinerant workers, and it appeared she was one of them now. But soon after she'd left Philadelphia, she'd let a friend who would worry about her know where she was staying. Ken had called Tammy, intimidated her—he was good at that—and Tammy had given up Blossom's location at the time. If Tammy hadn't warned her, he would have found her. Dragged her home.

Within hours of Tammy's call she'd sold the Lexus, which Ken would probably report as stolen. Twenty minutes after handing it over to a private buyer, no questions asked, Blossom had been on the road again in a different car. Like a cowboy moving on to another ranch, another job.

She turned away from the reception desk.

"I'll take care of it," she said. "Thanks again. Goodbye, Shadow."

She hadn't reached the door when Shadow stepped out from behind the desk.

"Wait." She hesitated before laying a hand on Blossom's forearm. "I've talked with Logan. We agree. You're running away from someone. Aren't you? I can understand why you wouldn't want to confide in Logan because he's your employer. But why don't you sit down and tell *me* all about it?"

Blossom shook her head. "Really, I'm fine. I like to stay loose, that's all." She looked pointedly at Shadow's hand. Her mouth had gone bone-dry. "I appreciate your interest but I need to go now. I promised I'd be back in time to make Sam's lunch. If I don't hurry, he'll be out of his bed and down the stairs. He's not steady enough yet."

With a frown, Shadow stepped back. "I won't keep you, then."

Blossom tucked the check into her bag.

She lowered her head and slipped through the door onto the sidewalk. Then she stopped and pointed toward the other end of Main Street. "The payday loan place is that way?"

"You can't miss it," Shadow said.

Blossom had no other choice. She would have to cash the check. Then she'd drive back to the Circle H to pack her things. She could be on her way again long before Logan came home from his outing today with Nick.

"Come back anytime," Shadow called after her.

But Blossom would be gone, and neither Logan nor Shadow could tell Ken where she was going. They wouldn't know.

Neither did she.

"I WON'T BE gone long," Libby told Logan. She'd met him at the local strip mall on the outskirts of Barren as if they were two spies about to exchange information.

"I have all day."

"Thanks. We'll see how this goes." She'd already transferred Nicky's booster seat to Logan's truck for the drive back to her house later and was turning toward her car. Nicky had walked away to inspect something on the sidewalk.

Logan hardly knew her these days. In the past three years Libby had reinvented herself. She'd been a rancher's wife when they were married, but since the divorce she'd built her own business. Logan didn't quite understand what she did, but it had something to do with people's estates. She'd recently opened an office in Barren. Now she was always in a hurry.

She turned around again. "You have my cell number so if anything—"

"Nothing's going to happen, Libby."

"I hope not. But just in case—"

"I already have Doc's office, home and cell numbers, too."

But Logan was clearly out of his element. He hadn't spent much time with Nicky in the past three years, which made him feel even more guilty than he already did about the flood.

Maybe this would work out, and Libby would learn that he was a capable parent after all, not the daredevil pilot in her mind who risked his life at every opportunity. Who'd risked Nicky's life, too.

He held out a hand to Nicky, who'd discovered a big bug on the sidewalk and hadn't heard much of their conversation. "Come on, buddy. Let's eat."

"Pancakes?"

"Whatever you want."

Nicky chose the nearby IHOP. They sat in a booth with a big selection of syrup bottles on the table, and Nicky ordered a blueberry stack.

Logan studied the picture in the menu. "You sure you can eat all that?"

Nicky raised dark blue eyes that matched Logan's. Only his son's eyes held some underlying emotion he couldn't quite read. Maybe Nicky was remembering his visit to the ranch with Grey. He didn't answer Logan's smile with one of his own.

"I love pancakes."

"So do I."

After that, while they waited for their meals, the conversation lagged. Logan didn't know how to talk to him. He fidgeted with his knife and fork, asked about school—any adult's usual question for a kid, especially one he didn't know well—and Nicky's plans for summer (which wouldn't include Logan) and, finally, about his friends.

"I have a bunch," Nicky said, his eyes lighting up as the waitress served their breakfast. He picked the strawberry syrup then poured it on thick. "But I also got a girl friend—not a *girlfriend*," he added. "She's more like the boys."

"A point in her favor," Logan said, fighting a smile.

The following silence made him twitch. He and Nicky had been best buds, practically inseparable, until Libby left and filed for divorce. Now he hardly knew what to say. He hadn't met any of Nicky's current friends. He didn't know what he liked other than pancakes—which he'd learned only moments ago.

Logan focused on his plate of waffles with bacon and home fries. But his stomach tightened at every bite, and he soon gave up trying to eat. The way Nicky was shoveling in his pancakes, he'd probably get sick. Then Libby would have more ammunition to use against him. He had to make this work or it wouldn't happen again.

"So." He laid aside his fork. "Now we've got all that out of the way, I miss you, buddy," he said. "You know that, don't you?"

"I guess."

"I mean, really miss you." He started to reach for Nicky's hand but drew back. The words almost stuck in Logan's throat. "You miss me?"

"A little." Nicky's face had shut down. He took another huge mouthful of pancake. Because he didn't want to talk? Or he remembered Logan's coldness at the ranch?

He was casting about for something brilliant to say when a man walked up to their booth. Nicky glanced up and grinned.

"Hi, Mr. Caldwell."

"Hey, Barney," Logan said. They shook hands. "Join us, if you'd like."

It was rare not to run into someone you knew—or had known, in Logan's case—whenever you came to town. He hadn't seen Barney in years.

"No, I'm on my way back to the bank." He eyed Nicky's almost-empty plate then Logan's full one. The syrup had pooled in the butter on his now-soggy waffles. He hadn't touched the potatoes or the bacon. "Surprised to see you here."

The rumor mill in Barren was apparently open for business. As vice president of loans at the Cattlemen's Bank, Barney usually got wind of things first. "I'm staying at the ranch while Sam's laid up."

Barney clicked his tongue, making Nicky giggle.

"Heard about his accident. He's getting pretty old to run that place."

"Maybe so." That was one of Logan's worst fears. What would happen to the Circle H if Sam couldn't manage it again? Sawyer wasn't here and Logan wouldn't stay. "Well. Thanks for stopping by."

"You get a chance, come on in. We'll talk."

Logan tensed. He didn't need a loan—unless Barney wanted to lend him money for a lawyer. "About what?"

"The ranch could use some renovations. Last time I drove by even your sign was hanging by a thread. I've got a home equity line of credit with the Circle H on it."

"I'll talk to Sam," he said. And he needed to fix that sign.

Barney lifted a hand. "I'll leave you, then, with your boy." He smiled at Nicky. "I know how precious that time can be."

No, he didn't. The banker was a lifetime bachelor—no wife, no kids.

Logan got the message. He was an absentee father.

The story would be all over Barren by nightfall. *Neglect pays a visit.* Barney's sighting would have tongues wagging for days. Logan watched him go.

"You finished, Nicky?"

"One more bite." He wolfed it down. "Mr. Caldwell was nosy."

Logan almost grinned. "You bet." He had to make the most of this outing. Make it a real success. The problem was, how? He glanced out the window at the strip mall. "What do you want to do next?"

Nicky shrugged. "I don't care."

Logan spied a store that might be of interest. "The toy shop's right over there. Let's do some shopping."

As soon as they cleared the main doors to the store, Nicky took off and so did Logan's pulse. Afraid he'd lose sight of him, he set off at a jog, already feeling the effects of trying to keep up with a six-year-old boy. Or was Nicky that eager to get away from Logan? Where did he get all that energy?

Logan wasn't complaining. After all, Libby had let him take Nicky for part of the day— to help her—as long as he didn't set foot on the Circle H.

Nicky had spied a large floor display of child-size vehicles that looked like a real car dealer's lot and was running from one to the next. A red convertible. A blue race car. A yellow Jeep. A shiny black monster pickup that closely resembled Logan's own truck. Nicky went right to it.

"Look at this one! Wow!"

His cheeks had flushed with obvious excitement. His small hands shook as he tried the horn, and even kicked the tires. "Can I get this?"

"I don't think so, buddy."

"Why not?"

Mommy wouldn't like it. Yet he couldn't say that. He might have lost custody of his only child—temporarily—but he'd never bad-mouth Nicky's mother. Or use his son as a pawn in his testy relationship with Libby.

"Why don't we find a soccer ball instead?"

Nicky's mouth set. "I don't want a ball. I want this truck."

Logan suddenly wished it wasn't spring. There was no snow or ice on the ground or a blizzard in the forecast. His best argument that a truck would have no use outdoors for months wouldn't hold water. "You're going to start soccer pretty soon. We could practice today."

"You're not a soccer man. You're a *pilot*."

Logan had brought him a set of gold wings on his last visit.

"I used to play soccer," he said. "Come on, let me show you my moves."

Nicky didn't budge. He climbed into the truck then sat there, fiddling with the dials on the dashboard. Logan had to admit, the battery-driven, motorized toy was impressive. If he was Nicky's age, he'd want it, too. In fact, he had the real thing.

"Please?"

Logan pushed aside his misgivings. He checked the price tag. Ouch. But the truck would be cheaper than a custody suit, and Nicky's birthday was coming up. He saw no harm in buying the pickup for him—except for Libby's probable reaction. He didn't have a better argument after all than "Your mother would say no."

Nicky rolled his eyes. "She always says no. She doesn't know how cool it is."

When Logan didn't respond, Nicky got out of the truck. And planted both hands on his skinny hips. Logan had seen that pose many times from Libby.

"Aren't you still my daddy?"

Logan's stomach sank. "Yeah."

Nicky's eyes lit up, as if he'd just had a brilliant idea. "Then you can say yes."

I wish I could, buddy.

"Give me a break." Logan turned back into the aisle. "Let's buy a ball. Next time we can talk about a truck." Assuming Libby allowed him to see his kid again. Frankly, the only reason he had Nicky today—"get him home by noon," she'd warned him—was because no one else was available. Nothing like being her last resort. She hadn't even let Logan come to her house to get Nicky.

His lower lip stuck out. "No. I want it *now*."

Clearly, he was being manipulated by a first grader, Logan thought. But if he showed up at Libby's house with that truck, this would likely be the last outing they took. Unless a judge decided otherwise, which wouldn't happen any time soon.

"Nicky, let's go." Logan started down the aisle toward the sporting goods department. Alone. He turned and saw Nicky still at the end of the other row, patting the monster pickup's hood as if to say *I'm sorry*. His eyes brimmed with tears.

"Can I keep the truck at your house?"

Logan opened his mouth to say, *Sure, but please don't tell your mother.* But the potential lie, like Grey's fib the other day, didn't sit well. He and Libby had always been honest with each other, at least. He couldn't destroy that now. The truck would go with them to her house when he took Nicky home. He'd deal with the fallout later. "No, but we can buy it."

Nicky flung himself at Logan. "Thanks, Daddy! I love you."

"I love you, too, buddy." *More than you'll ever know.*

Nicky drew back. "Can we get the soccer ball, too?"

SHORTLY AFTER NOON, Blossom heard a crash and came running into Sam's room. He'd managed to lift his lunch tray and then dump it on the floor. On purpose, she supposed from the look on his face.

"Oh," she said. "You didn't like my tuna salad?"

He couldn't meet her eyes. "Never had pecans in it before. But, sure I did."

"Then why…?" She eyed the mess on the wooden floor then shook a finger at him. "You didn't try to get out of bed, did you? I would have come if you needed anything. Why didn't you call?"

"I know what you're up to," he said, scowling, as if she planned to rob a bank. "Where d'you think you're going?"

"To the kitchen." Blossom knelt down to scoop up the splattered tuna salad, which was

mixed in with his buttered peas and apple-
sauce. The lunch was a complete loss. He'd
even dented his metal tray with that display of
anger. "I'll make you another sandwich, Sam."

"Don't want another sandwich."

Blossom hid a smile. He sounded like a
surly child.

"Then maybe some soup." She tried to keep
her tone brisk to take charge. "I think we have
tomato and cheddar-broccoli in the pantry. Let
me check. There might be bean with bacon,
too, if you'd prefer that."

His gaze lifted to hers. "No soup."

She set the damaged tray on his bedside
table. "Sam. What is it?"

"I heard you in your room, opening and
closing drawers, shutting the closet, too. Then
you zipped that suitcase of yours. You're leaving, that's what."

She sat down on the edge of his bed. She'd
changed his sheets that morning before she
left for town. The house was probably cleaner
than it had been in a long time, and after a
brief stop at the market the fridge was full
again. He and Logan would be all right—until
Logan found someone else to care for Sam.
So why was her heart breaking? She'd never
intended to stay.

"I have to leave. I need to…be somewhere."

"This have anything to do with Logan?" Sam focused on her with the intensity of a laser beam. "I know he can be cantankerous. Hasn't been right ever since you two split up."

Blossom bit her lip. "Sam, I'm not Olivia. I'm *Blossom*."

"You remind me anyway," he murmured, making her blink in surprise. Sam glanced around. "Of better times, I mean, of my own… wife. She picked this yellow daisy wallpaper print." His gaze moved on. "That six-drawer walnut dresser, too, these nightstands and the bed I'm in." He poked at a hole in the worn quilt. "We shared this room for over twenty years. Spring, summer, fall, winter… That garden out back is hers…filled with flowers then. She had hollyhocks by the back door. They're gone now, too. And roses," he said, worrying the hole in the quilt until his finger went through the fabric. "That was my Muriel. Growing peppers and tomatoes every summer. I can still taste them, the best I've ever had. And melons…their runaway vines covered the rear yard until my boys—Logan and Sawyer, that is—decided every melon needed to be carved into a Halloween jack-o'-lantern with a candle inside."

"You miss her," Blossom said, reaching for his hand.

He choked up. "I do. I always will. That woman was the brightest spot in my life—along with this ranch and my boys. While she was with me, I had everything."

"Oh, Sam." She couldn't blame him for throwing his lunch on the floor. He spent all day in this room with only his memories for company. *My boys*, he'd said. They weren't his, of course. Logan and his brother didn't share a drop of common blood with Sam. Yet he'd taken them, raised them…been the closest thing to a father they had after losing their parents.

"Now I'm stuck in this bed—by myself. And you're leaving." He frowned. "I like you, Blossom. You go, too, you'll take the last of my sun with you."

Sudden tears welled in her eyes. Sam had shown her more love and acceptance in the short time she'd been here than anyone else in her life.

He studied their linked hands, his fingers warm and dry and stronger than she would have imagined. "Give Logan another chance. That's all I ask. I'll straighten him out for you."

Had he confused her again with Olivia? "It's not about Logan."

"What do you take me for? I got eyes." He bent closer to her. "You need to *stay*. I'm begging you," he added.

Blossom let go of his hand. She looked deeply into his eyes.

"You don't have to beg."

"I will," he insisted, "if that keeps you here. Logan needs you. That baby you're carrying needs a home, too."

Her fingers turned icy cold. How could he know about her pregnancy? Or was that more wishful thinking? "Sam, I'm not going anywhere except to the barn."

BLOSSOM HAD BEEN looking out the window while she packed, as if Ken had seen her at the check-cashing place and then followed her as she drove out of town, her week's pay warm in her jeans pocket. She'd been minutes away from quitting the ranch.

Now, reluctant to leave Sam alone, she ran out to the barn then into the tack room and, finally, to the outside corrals. Logan's truck was here so he must have come back from his visit with Nick, but Logan didn't seem to be anywhere. Standing by the rail, she shaded her eyes against the sun and squinted into the far distance.

She could stay a bit longer. Just a bit. She'd panicked after her trip to town, that was all, but she had a little more time, at least until Sam was more himself again.

She scanned the area. Not a cloud of dust rose into the air, and from here she could see almost to the horizon. This part of the land was pancake flat without any obstruction, perfect terrain for twisters and just right for spotting anyone unwelcome who might approach. All she heard was the occasional bellow or bleat of a cow or calf—and even those sounds might be coming from Grey Wilson's property. She had no idea whether bison sounded like cattle, too.

"Logan!" she shouted but no one answered.

Blossom headed back to the house. She wouldn't call out again for fear of rousing Willy if he were nearby.

Because of Sam, she wasn't going anywhere for now.

Even Ken couldn't find her this fast.

She hoped.

CHAPTER NINE

LOGAN RODE BACK into the barnyard late that afternoon to find company waiting. His shoulders ached, his legs burned, his neck felt as if someone had lit a fire under his skin. After leaving Nicky and the toy truck at Libby's house, he'd come back to the Circle H to work, but he'd neglected to take sunscreen with him. Hours in the saddle were a lot different from time spent at the controls of a jet. All he wanted now was a hot shower and some food, which would have to wait.

Grey Wilson's truck was parked next to his by the barn doors.

As Logan got down from his horse, or rather Sam's horse, Grey emerged from his pickup. The door slammed and Logan tried to ease the kinks from his neck, his back, but every muscle had tensed. What had brought Grey here? "Thought you were in Montana buying cattle."

"Just got back. Got something for you."

"I don't need any cows." He glanced toward the pickup, but Grey wasn't hauling a trailer full of beef. "Sam keeps telling me how great his bison are."

Grey grinned. "To each his own."

Logan led the gelding into the barn. Sundance was a good mount, easygoing and steady with no apparent inclination to shy or bolt at the slightest sound.

Which met all of Logan's requirements. It had been a while since he'd spent so much time on the back of a horse. He preferred a reliable one. Half-dead was even better. It wouldn't do to get thrown in some gully or dry wash, to lie hurt or broken where no one would see him. Then what good would he be to Sam? And Nicky?

In the barn he unsaddled the horse while Grey stood nearby, hands shoved in his jeans pockets. He'd never been the talkative sort, although when he decided to, he could sure make his point.

"I'm worried about Libby," he said at last.

Logan remembered her doctor's appointment, the sole reason she'd actually let him see his son without a fight for once.

His stomach tightened. "She okay?"

"She went to see her OB/GYN. You don't think...she could be pregnant?"

"Not by me."

Grey frowned. "I didn't mean that. She has been seeing that other guy for a while now. The antiques dealer."

Logan gritted his teeth. "The smooth talker."

"Yeah, a real charmer."

"You don't like him."

"She's a rancher's daughter, Logan. She grew up on a horse—until Mom turned her against our dad. And she seemed happy enough with you at the Circle H to me—unless I missed something? Now she's all 'downtown,' dating this guy from Kansas City in a suit and tie."

Which wasn't that common in Barren, Logan had to agree. Maybe Libby had just wanted to get as far away from him as possible in every way.

"Guess you didn't see her change." He removed Sundance's bridle and hung it on a hook on the stall door after slipping on his halter. Pretty smooth for someone who hadn't ridden in years. As a kid, he'd thought about a career in rodeo—until the urge to fly had hit him, hard.

"I don't trust him," Grey went on. "What if Libby…?"

"She's a grown woman. Trust *me*. She can take care of herself. I can see Libby wanting some male companionship, but I can't see her letting an unplanned pregnancy happen. She's focused on Nicky."

"Then maybe she's really sick."

"Did you ask her?"

"I wasn't here. You were," Grey said. "Did she say anything?"

Logan shook his head. "Like she'd tell me if there was something wrong."

Grey shrugged. "When I saw her an hour ago, she seemed okay. Maybe a little thinner than she should be. She says she's been working too much, spending her time at the office instead of outdoors. She forgets to eat."

With a twinge of old guilt, Logan led the horse into his stall, gave him a pat, then stepped out and slid the door shut. Libby was trying to finish an MBA online now, but her business also kept her hopping. "You said you had something for me?" Grey wouldn't drive over if he only wanted to fret aloud about his sister.

"Oh. Yeah." He left the barn, went to his pickup then returned a minute later.

Logan stifled a groan. Grey wheeled the kid-size truck Logan had bought Nicky at the toy shop to the doors of the barn. Logan stared at the ground. "Why am I not surprised?" He'd meant to talk to her, but she hadn't given him the chance. When he dropped Nicky off, she'd led him inside then shut the door. Logan had left the truck in her garage. "Libby couldn't bring this back herself?"

"I'm her emissary, she said." Grey turned toward his truck. "I promised her I'd bring this over. And I did."

But that wasn't all either.

"What's the rest of her message?" Grey wouldn't want to deliver that, but there must be one. Libby wouldn't miss the chance to remind Logan that he wasn't a good father.

"Next time—if there is a next time, and that's a direct quote—she will personally choose where that outing with Nick—not in a toy store—will take place. Or else."

Logan's back teeth ground together. "What?"

"There won't be an outing."

"That's in violation of the court's order."

Grey looked at him. "I'd hoped you two would become sensible about this."

"I'm not the one who probably caused Nicky

to cry when she took his new toy away—just to get at me. That's on Libby."

"I'll try to talk to her." Grey retraced his steps to the truck.

"No, I will."

Libby wouldn't win this one.

He watched Grey back out, waiting until his brake lights blinked red at the end of the driveway. Taking another moment to tamp down his anger, Logan refilled Sundance's water bucket then started toward the house.

The way his luck was going, Blossom had likely made curry for dinner.

"Why is this animal in the house?" Standing in the hallway later outside Blossom's bedroom, Logan held up the kitten she had called No-Name. "I nearly fell down the stairs when she shot past me."

She looked away. "I thought she seemed cold. So I brought her inside. I'm sorry. She got out of my room."

"I told you. She's a barn cat, Blossom."

She met his eyes, trying to gauge the degree of his irritation.

"Maybe she has higher aspirations. Maybe she wants to be more than that."

Just as I want to be more than Ken's punch-

ing bag. Her first week on the road, putting miles between her and Ken every day, she'd experienced a real taste of freedom. The rush of wind through her hair, the sun on her face. Having no one to give her orders. Even the motel rooms she'd stayed in were preferable to Ken's spacious condo. She wouldn't let Logan intimidate her now. A first, but still…

He handed her the cat. "Before you know it, we'll all be scratching. We try to keep the flea population down, but we're not that successful."

She refused to look away. "I didn't know."

"Now you do. Take her back to the barn."

Her mouth flattened. "If I do, she'll only leave the fleas behind. They'll move on to a secondary host—that would be you. And me."

"Fleas aren't the only issue," he said. "Cats can carry parasites, among them toxoplasmosis—especially bad for pregnant women." Blossom froze even before he finished, "I mean, what if you were having a baby?"

That hadn't been a concern for her until now. She'd never been pregnant before.

Perhaps she should worry, but Blossom didn't have to respond. As she set the cat down, his grandfather bellowed his name from down the hall. "Perfect," Logan said.

Leaving the kitten to make her way downstairs for now, Blossom followed him to Sam's room, mentally crossing her fingers. She hadn't forgotten her conversation with his grandfather, especially the part about her being pregnant. But by now, maybe Sam had forgotten and wouldn't bring up the subject.

If he did, she was still packed and ready to go.

"What is it, Sam?" Logan strode into the room where his grandfather was working on the remains of his dinner. Blossom had made beef stew tonight, or tried to. The dented tray drew Logan's gaze. "Something happen here?"

"Sam dropped his tray at lunch," Blossom began.

"I threw my tray. It's my tray. I'll do whatever I please with it."

Logan glanced at the ceiling. "Deliver me," he said.

Sam glared. "You ever stop moving long enough to see around you?"

"Not while I'm running your ranch for you, no," Logan said.

"This girl's car will be halfway through town before you take notice."

Logan turned to her. "Is he making any sense?"

Blossom met his gaze. "Yes. I told him it was time for me to move on—"

She didn't get to finish. To tell him she'd changed her mind.

"Not yet," Logan said, looking grim. "I lost a newborn calf this afternoon. Another one became an orphan. Tobias is feeding it with a bottle at the barn, which takes up his valuable time. The whole herd needs to be moved tomorrow to better grass. So much," he said with a glance at Sam, "for bison being easier than cattle."

Sam scowled. "Just because you don't know what you're doing doesn't make them difficult, Flyboy."

Logan's gaze homed in on her. "You can't leave. There's no one to replace you."

"Not that you haven't tried," she said. "I know you still call the agency. So why does it matter if I leave in a month, a week or tonight?" Sam's health didn't seem to be an issue. Earlier, he'd simply gotten worked up.

"You're not leaving me with Sam."

"Hey," his grandfather said, "I'm right here."

"And you're more than a handful."

"See?" Sam eyed her. "I told you. He needs you."

"So do you," Logan said. "Are we done with this conversation? I have a ton of bills to deal with before I can get any sleep." Logan pushed past her and out into the hall.

Blossom's gaze followed his tall, broad-shouldered frame. He was probably much better with the bison than Sam claimed. He was certainly the very picture of a cowboy. Her pulse was still running riot, and Sam wasn't done yet. His eyes were shooting sparks. Yet she saw the underlying sorrow she'd detected before. He missed his wife. He also missed his grandsons.

"He loves you, Sam."

"Stubborn cuss. Why I ever had those hospital folks call him, I don't know. Should have asked Sawyer to come help me when I got tossed by that cow. Until he decided to turn tail and run from the Circle H, he was better with the stock anyway."

"You got that right," Logan called from down the hall.

"Go, then! Back to those fancy jets you fly. Keep trying to kill yourself." Sam fell back against his pillows. The dented tray slid to the floor, beef and gravy, carrots and potatoes oozing onto the wood. "See if I care."

Oh, dear. Apparently, Blossom's work here wasn't done. She needed to stay for Sam's well-being, yes—but now for Logan's, too. She picked up Sam's napkin then scooped up the spilled food—twice in one day.

Before Blossom left, Sam and Logan would admit how much they needed—and loved— each other.

At least Sam hadn't mentioned her pregnancy or thought she was Olivia.

SAM KEPT HIS eyes shut until those two had disappeared. When he no longer heard his grandson's voice saying *You got that right* in his head, he sat up straight, opened his eyes then looked around.

Nothing had changed. Why did he expect it to? Or fear it would?

He'd been sleeping in this room for many years, nestled into this old feather bed that fit his bones just right. But in what he now called the old days, he'd had Muriel beside him. Sam and Muriel. He'd always liked the sound of that.

Sometimes, as Blossom had seen, he ached

with missing her. All afternoon he'd drifted in and out of sleep, dreaming of her.

When they'd married, long after Sam had thought he was fated to be a permanent bachelor, she'd insisted on changing the name from the McCord Ranch—after her first husband's family—to the Circle H for Hunter. That was his Muriel, and a serious sign of her love and acceptance of Sam. Yet now that he'd become practically an invalid, he worried. Worried all the time.

If only illness hadn't taken her from him. And here he was, laid up with a bum leg—the cast was starting to itch—and his head messed up by a concussion. Powerless. He'd turned his back on the bison cow that day and paid the price. She'd only tried to protect her calf. Sam could relate to that.

He had an orphaned boy to fret about now, too.

Logan had always been a kid with other things on his mind, sometimes more than one at a time. When Sam had first come to the ranch, Muriel's new diamond ring sparkling on her hand, Logan had been a grieving boy. Both parents gone, and Logan and his brother not much older than Nick was now. Sawyer seemed to take things easier. If he'd been married to Olivia, Sawyer would never have let her go. He'd have found a way. Instead, Logan had traded her and his son for some fancy jet plane. He'd turned his back on the ranch—and Sam.

He sniffed. That needed to change—and he usually got his way. Maybe Blossom could help with that. She seemed to like it here.

But first, he had to get on his feet again. Prove to himself and Logan that he could still run the Circle H.

LOGAN SAT BACK in Sam's old desk chair. He remembered when his grandfather had bought it, not long after he'd moved in to take over the Circle H. The worn leather seat was now permanently shaped to the curve of Sam's rear, which didn't fit Logan's larger body. The chair seemed like a metaphor for their prickly relationship.

Still regretting his words earlier that night, he tossed a pen down on the scarred wooden desktop. He closed the ledger then the checkbook. He'd paid half the bills tonight, but there were plenty more, several of them overdue. Maybe he'd have to sell some stock before fall to cover the rest. The Circle H, even with the market price for bison higher than beef, was no longer as profitable as it had once been. Why didn't Sam sell and divide the profit with Logan and Sawyer? Move to Wichita? Logan's one-bedroom apartment wasn't that big, but he could sleep on the couch and give Sam his room. They could manage until Logan got his promotion and could afford the custody suit and then a larger place where Sam wouldn't be able to get himself in trouble again.

Logan's cell phone rang and he glanced at the display. It was his boss.

"Yeah, Joe," he said, both happy and not to hear from him.

"Got a sweet new baby for you." Joe sounded excited. "You gotta see this. Eighteen-karat gold trim everywhere. Bedroom. Fully stocked kitchen…" He named the latest model his company made. Sweet, all right.

Logan's hands twitched. "Avionics?"

"State of the art. You won't believe this thing. It's less than a year old—and we just redid it nose to tail for the new owner." He paused. "When can you be here?"

Logan glanced upward. He hadn't heard a peep from Sam's room in the past hour. His grandfather must be asleep by now. Logan's guilt was keeping him awake. And then there was Blossom… She'd almost left. For some reason, that still tied him in knots.

"Tell you what," Joe said. "Let me send Garvey for you."

Logan groaned. "He'd probably fly us into a building on the way just to get rid of me. You know that."

"He's here, you're not," Joe said. "Unless you can sprout wings, I'll have to use Garvey. Short trip and he's a good pilot."

"We're up for the same promotion, Joe. In case you haven't noticed, we barely speak to each other. And that's how I like it."

"You don't have to talk. You just have to get here."

Sure. No problem. All he had to do was leave Sam with Blossom—and hope the ranch didn't fall apart, hope she didn't take off in that rattletrap sedan. Logan had known she was planning to leave from the minute she'd arrived.

"Sorry, Joe. I'm not free right now."

"Your grandfather doing any better?"

"Some," he said, "but the concussion still has him a little loopy. I wouldn't feel good about leaving him alone just yet."

Joe's voice cooled. "Thought you were going to hire a male nurse."

"Caregiver," he said, which wasn't the same thing. Sam wasn't sick. "The woman who's here can't handle him plus everything else."

As if anyone could.

"Forget it, then. I'm going to have to go with Garvey instead for the test flight. He's already champing at the bit—notice the cowboy term you might understand—to get his hands on this corporate baby."

Logan was no cowboy, and didn't want to be one, but Joe's underlying message seemed as clear as Libby had been about the black toy Ford F-150. "You're saying I'm putting my promotion at risk."

"If the client likes Garvey's work, their influence will be critical."

"You're killing me." Logan knew he might be signing away his chance for a new job title with better pay, better assignments. Joe had just offered him one. "Keep me in mind for the next job, okay? I'll be back as soon as I can."

Joe didn't answer. At first, he'd seemed to understand Logan's dilemma, but apparently his patience had run out. "Good luck with your grandfather."

He hung up without saying goodbye.

Damn.

If he didn't win that promotion, he'd have to wait even longer to take Libby back to court. He wouldn't have a proverbial leg to stand on because nothing would have changed. He doubted the judge would go for letting Nicky sleep on his sofa in Wichita on a regular basis.

Interrupting his thoughts, Blossom appeared in the office doorway. She looked hesitant—which she hadn't earlier. "I don't want to disturb you…"

"Where's the kitten?"

Her chin went up. "I put her in the tack room."

"Sam asleep?"

"Fighting it, but on his way," she said.

They exchanged a look as if they were a couple with a mutual concern for a family member. Sam was crusty but lovable. Logan liked it that Blossom also cared about him—not that she'd be here much longer.

"Come on in." Logan spun the desk chair. "We need to talk."

CHAPTER TEN

BLOSSOM EDGED BACK into the hall. The overhead light shone on her red hair. She didn't wear a trace of makeup, but to his mind she didn't need any. "I only wanted to let you know that Sam is resting now."

Logan waved a hand. "Take a seat. It's time we got to the bottom of this."

"The bottom of what?"

"You." He rubbed a tension spot between his eyes. He kept hearing Joe's words on the phone moments ago, fearing he'd lost his chance for a promotion. "I'll find out sooner or later." He paused. "I prefer now."

Her shoulders rounded. Her gaze slipped to the floor between them. Her lips pressed tight. Logan recognized the posture.

"*Who* are you running from, Blossom?"

She smoothed a hand over her stomach. "Maybe I have a dozen creditors looking for me. Or I robbed a bank in Kansas City—"

"Is it that father of yours? Or some boy-friend?"

Blossom didn't sit. She drifted over to the window. She stared out at the black night sky, at the security arc lights in the barnyard, at nothing. Maybe she was seeing some even darker part of her own past. The one she wouldn't share.

He shouldn't care.

She was temporary help, as she'd pointed out herself, and in the morning—as she'd also said—he would call Shadow again on the off chance she'd found a male caregiver.

Was he that determined to replace Blossom? Or to save himself from getting involved any deeper in her life, her problems? From letting the unwanted attraction he felt for her become even more? With Sam and the ranch, his troubles with Nicky and Olivia, he didn't need another responsibility. And yet...

She turned from the window. "His name is Ken."

"Go on," he said when she didn't continue. He could hear her swallow.

"He's a big-deal developer in Philly. We met at a cocktail party. I'd finally moved out of my father's house only the week before. I was excited to be on my own, and that afternoon I'd gotten my first job." Her eyes were wide pools with what he could only call hurt in them. "I guess you could say I was an easy mark. That night I wanted to celebrate. I had a new life. A new job."

"Doing what?"

"I worked for the caterers." She sent him a rueful smile. "Yes, I was the hired help then, too. I didn't wear a fancy gown like the other women who were guests at the party. I wore a black-and-white uniform and a little white lace cap. Dark shoes with rubber soles." She shook her head. "Not a pretty picture."

He didn't know where the words came from. "You're a pretty woman, Blossom. Whatever you wear."

She eased onto a chair. "I've never thought so. My father didn't like me dressing up or wearing makeup—'making yourself look cheap,' he always said."

Logan's mouth tightened. "I can't imagine that."

"He had a point, of sorts. We did live on military bases. There were young guys everywhere. I didn't blame him then for wanting to protect me."

She still wore the baggy pants and loose shirt she'd had on the first day. Or similar ones.

She was probably the least available-looking woman he'd ever met, even when he suspected that underneath those shapeless clothes she had a more than decent figure. What she didn't have was a scrap of self-esteem.

"Your father was wrong," he said. "So then, you got involved with this developer. Ken." Already he didn't like where this was going. Maybe he shouldn't have asked. Or insisted she tell him. *None of my business.*

"He had his pick of women. I've never understood why he chose me except that I must have looked…naive."

"Blossom."

"I sure fell for his charms. He gave me a real rush, like some Don Juan, called me every day, woke me in the morning and tucked me in at night, so to speak, with his voice in my ear on the phone. He took me nice places. I'd never been…courted before—that's such an old-fashioned word, but that was how it felt— and it was a heady experience."

"Some guys do that. But once they've got you under their spell—"

"You mean, dependent on them." She nodded. "Before I knew what had happened, I was living in his high-rise condo. In a building he'd actually built, or rather his company had. It had the best of everything, from the furniture in the living room to the bathroom fixtures. It had *towel* heaters, a heated floor. There was a gourmet kitchen where I hardly knew how to turn on the eight-burner stove. For a girl who catered parties, Ken told me, I wasn't very good in the kitchen." She hesitated. "Or anywhere else, really, as it turned out."

Her gaze fell.

Logan could understand why, because of her dad, she'd been such a target for Ken. That kind of denigration, humiliation, was all she knew.

And her mom was his second in command, she'd told him. There hadn't been anyone to stand up for Blossom. She sure hadn't learned to defend herself. In effect, both of her parents had beaten her down. She had a real tendency to excuse everyone else.

In a different way, she reminded Logan of himself. He'd lost his mother and father then set himself up to fail with Libby, who'd been the wrong person for him from the start. Another pattern that had only led to more loss with Nicky. Because, except for Sam and his grandma, that was what *he'd* known.

"None of that was your fault," he said. "How old were you then?"

"Twenty."

"You were with him how long?"

She thought for a moment, as if she'd forgotten. "Eight years—no, almost nine."

"Kids?"

Her gaze fixed on a point above his head. "No kids."

"Well, that's something," he said. "I can't recommend having a family when I'm still fighting my ex for Nicky. Or I will be." In the meantime, he intended to speak to Libby. She wouldn't use Grey to deliver her message the next time. "Blossom, were you and...Ken ever married?" He didn't even like saying the guy's name and he'd never met him.

"I wanted to get married at first, wanted to start a family. But he always had some reason why we should wait. He wanted children but he was too caught up in his new project, or we'd already bought tickets to spend Christmas in Barbados and what if I got morning sickness and ruined the trip? Or we'd have to build a house first..." She shrugged. "Well, you know."

"He strung you along. Since you weren't legally bound, why did you stay with him?"

Her voice lowered until it was almost a whisper. "I couldn't leave. Ken controlled everything, gradually, until I had no choice but to stay. I'd quit that first job—not that it paid much—and he saw no reason for me to look for another. Or to enroll in college classes. Or to get job training of any kind. He needed me at home—and why be unhappy there? I was living in a palace. Other women would envy me, he said. Most would jump at the chance to trade places."

"All lies."

"He gave me a strict allowance. I had to explain any purchase—even though he bought me designer clothes. Beautiful things. I'd never dressed like that before. I didn't need anything else, he said. All the accounts were in his name. So was 'my' cell phone." She cradled a hand to her stomach. "After a while even my parents stopped calling, or I stopped calling them. We never went to visit, and he always had a reason for why they shouldn't visit us. My friends drifted away. They didn't like Ken and he didn't like them. He got angry when I saw them on my own—until I didn't see them anymore."

"You're a stronger person than you think, Blossom. You finally left."

"I'm trying," she said with a familiar glance out the window.

Logan's blood chilled. "You think he's looking for you." So that was why she checked the driveway, jumped when the ranch phone rang, why she'd asked Shadow for cash on payday. "That's why you packed your bags."

"Yes." She wrung her hands.

"What makes you think he can find you?"

Blossom shrugged.

"The first few days after I left, I let the only friend I had by then know where I was. Otherwise, she'd think something had happened. That Ken had really…hurt me."

"Did he?"

"Only…a few times. Nothing serious. He'd shove me or put his arm around my neck, pretend he was teasing then tighten his hold so I couldn't get away. He'd laugh but his words were always a warning."

"Verbal and physical abuse. Escalation."

"I knew one day he might really hurt me and my…" She trailed off. "Anyway, Ken called Tammy to see if I was with her. He's good at bullying people. He even boasts about it. In his business, no one dares to say no to him, that kind of thing…" Blossom breathed deeply. "I took the battery out of my cell phone, smashed it."

"No trail," he said.

"I hope not."

Logan got out of the desk chair. He crossed the room to her. He wanted to take Blossom in his arms and hold her close, his body feeling cold inside with anger for Ken but his hands warm as he cupped her face. In that moment he wanted to kiss her, to tell her everything would be all right. But he didn't. He couldn't. He only reached out to smooth her hair, then stepped back so as not to touch her.

He was in no position to pursue a relationship. He had to keep telling himself that or he might risk everything for this vulnerable woman on the run. He still had Libby to deal with.

Yet in that awkward, almost-moment, Blossom had a big part of his heart.

Ken had better not show up at the Circle H.

LOGAN HAD NEVER been inside his ex-wife's house on Liberty Street. Several blocks from the main drag in Barren, it stood square and squat, a one-story cottage that reminded him of a sentinel standing guard. The front door was painted a shiny black.

Maybe there was an explosion of bright color inside, but he doubted that.

There was no bell to ring. Logan rapped on the door.

A small sign beside it announced that solicitors were unwelcome.

But then, so was he.

Libby peeked around the filmy curtains covering the sidelights.

With a frown, she opened the door a crack.

"Yes?" she said in a cold tone, as if he were a peddler hoping to sell her something, not the man she'd married. "What is it?"

"You want to discuss this outside for the neighbors to hear—or let me in?"

"I have nothing to discuss."

Dead wrong. It had taken his outing with Nicky to show him how mistaken he'd been. In pulling back to keep the peace with Libby, he'd only confused Nicky. This was his first opportunity to give notice to her. From now on, after Blossom had told him about Ken last night, things were going to be different.

Logan took a breath then shouldered the door open into a small entryway, where the aroma of dinner, barbecued chicken—one of her specialties—still hung in the air. Libby stepped back. Surely, she didn't think he'd hurt her, but that look reminded him of the way Blossom's glance always slid away from any confrontation or criticism. Made him think of the things she'd told him.

"Keep your voice down," Libby said, although he hadn't raised it.

"Where's Nicky?"

"In bed. It's after nine, Logan. I wasn't counting on a visitor tonight. If you wanted to see him, you should have called."

So she could say no? The word *visitor* set his teeth on edge. In any normal relationship, he would be welcome here. He supposed their divorce had changed that, too. Of course it had. He'd heard Grey speak often enough of the wrangles he and Libby had endured as kids with their parents. Their acrimonious split-up had affected Grey even more than he liked to let on—and Libby, too. Which reminded Logan why he was here.

"It's not to visit Nicky. I'm here to see you."

He glanced around the small entryway. Beige walls. Cream woodwork. No pictures, not even a photo of Nicky on the little table that held a single basket, presumably for mail.

"Nice place," he said.

"It's too small. The bigger Nick gets, the smaller it will seem."

She didn't ask him into the living room, but he could see it from here, off to the right through a wide archway. More tan and white. Even the furniture—he recognized the sofa they'd bought together—was neutral. The only color he saw was the bright red of a small fire truck Nicky must have left on the floor before he went to bed. Did she have some plan to leave Barren? Was that why everything was so pared down, even minimalistic?

"Guess you're keeping your options open."

"I am." She folded her arms. "I can guess what this is about."

Logan abandoned any pretense of small talk. Any attempt to be tactful in getting his message across went out the window.

"You have anything to tell me, Libby, say it. Don't ever send Grey to do your dirty work again."

"I could hardly lift that huge truck into the trunk of my car."

"Then you should have called me. We might have 'discussed' the options."

"The only option is to return it. To the store." Her eyes flashed with the temper she usually kept under tight control. "How dare you. You used my little boy! Of course he wanted that truck. That's bribery, Logan."

He stepped back as if she'd pushed him. "Huh. Never thought of it that way."

"Of course you didn't."

"I was only trying to show him a good time."

"Which means spending money I can't afford to spend?"

"So that's it. You're not mad about the truck."

Her mouth tightened another notch. "I will not get into a competition with you for his love."

"Neither will I. I could never buy his love—even if I wanted to—for any amount of money."

"Then what is it?"

"Has it ever occurred to you that our divorce has confused Nicky? Saddened him? Made him wonder about my role in his life now? I didn't see that until Grey brought him over. And you should have seen us at breakfast after you dropped Nicky off. Trying to talk to him was like pulling teeth." Logan held her gaze. "I've lost touch with him, Libby. You have no call to keep me from seeing him."

"Don't be paranoid. Why would you think that? It's rarely convenient for me to drive Nick to Wichita." She frowned. "I have a shop to run, places to be. My work involves a lot of travel to nearby towns and counties. Assessing the contents of people's attics and basements and overstuffed garages takes time. I can't drop everything whenever you decide you want to see him."

"I've offered to come here. Pick him up. You always have some excuse."

She didn't deny that. "I'm a single mother now. In part, that's because of you. So tell me. How do I juggle my demanding job and Nick and running this house—tiny as it is—around your latest whim?"

In a flash, every hostile meeting he'd had with Libby in their lawyers' offices raced through his mind again. For a long moment he stared at the wooden floor and the rag rug at his feet.

"I'm not in Wichita now," he said at last. "While I'm here, don't even think of denying me my son again. If I want to see Nicky, I will."

"Really? And how long will you be here? The rest of this week? A month?"

"Until Sam's on his feet again."

"I spent Nick's first three years waiting around for you. Either you were somewhere on that big ranch all day or in the barn half the night or you were off to some interview hoping to work as a pilot instead."

"I can't argue with that but—"

"I'm not waiting anymore. I don't have to now."

Logan shook his head. "Then that's your decision. I told Grey I wouldn't have any luck changing your mind about me." He paused. "Tell you what. You do what you have to. I'll just point out—I've missed too many 'visits' with Nicky in the past three years. I want to be a better father to him, repair our relationship while I'm taking care of Sam. You say no the next time, I may have to call my lawyer. Could be there's even some provision in our agreement that says I have retroactive rights. Makeup time. Nicky could end up staying with me for months."

"You wouldn't."

"If I have to, yeah. I will."

Libby bumped his shoulder with the heel of her hand, nudging Logan off guard and out of the way. She flung open the door. It banged back against the wall, but she didn't seem to notice the noise it made that might waken Nicky. Her voice trembled. "Good night, Logan. Thanks for stopping by."

CHAPTER ELEVEN

BLOSSOM SHADED HER eyes against the morning sun. In the distance dust rose, billowing over the long driveway from the gate, and for a second her body tensed. Sharing her story with Logan the other night had been a relief, but at the same time it had brought back reminders of Ken.

The closer this car came, though, the more she began to relax.

Shadow Moran had called earlier looking for Logan, and Blossom had taken the opportunity to ask a favor.

Her classic red Mustang, which Blossom had seen parked in front of the agency in town, stopped at the front porch steps. Shadow climbed out of the car, all graceful limbs as she uncoiled from the driver's seat. With her sleek, almost thin build and her height, she could have been a top fashion model. She wore a pair of new-looking jeans that fit her like the proverbial glove and a Western-style top in a red-and-rust pattern.

"Hey," she said, extending a hand. "You surprised me when I called. You're still here. A few days ago I thought I'd seen the last of you." She glanced toward the near pasture before her eyes tracked a route, as if by instinct, that led to the crossroads. "I brought what you asked for on the phone." She held out a bag with the pet-store logo.

"Thanks." Blossom looked inside. "These will be perfect."

Shadow wasn't listening. When she didn't respond, Blossom saw that her gaze had fixed on the bare land between the Circle H and the Wilson Cattle Company.

"I don't often come this far from town." Her admission came with a rueful smile. "Not that Barren is especially urban, but I don't care for horses and cattle. I grew up dirt-poor on a scrap of farm one fraction of this ranch's size." She frowned. "Or the one next door. Every time I leave the town limits, I start to twitch. I can't wait to get back. Talk about lonely out here."

"I know what you mean." Blossom hadn't been raised on a farm, but there were all sorts of confinement, all kinds of poverty and isolation. Even in Ken's condo, or maybe especially there. After her talk with Logan, and the confession she'd made, every detail of those nine years seemed as clear as yesterday.

Shadow groaned. "Don't get me started on chickens. You're from back East, if I remember right from your application?"

"Yes. But I've lived everywhere, really."

Shadow's eyes brightened. "Tell me."

Blossom mentioned a few exotic places. "You've never left Kansas?"

"Only to spend some time in KC on the Missouri side. Then I came back for my father's funeral. I ended up staying to start the agency."

She was looking at the crossroads now. Or, no. Shadow was staring hard enough to make out the gates at Grey Wilson's ranch.

She shook her head as if to clear it of some troublesome memory. "Anyway." She half turned, surveying the barnyard. "I'll head back now, since Logan doesn't appear to be home yet. I'll catch him later."

"Do you have a few minutes? He rode out to inspect fences. Not far, though. He should be here soon. I just made a fresh pot of coffee. And there's apple pie from dinner last night. While you wait, I'd welcome your company."

Shadow glanced around then nodded. "All right, I'll take that coffee—and the pie. I do need to tell him something."

"If he doesn't get here before you have to leave, I can give him a message."

"It's personal," Shadow said.

Did she have an interest in Logan? Shadow didn't care for country life, but on the other hand Logan didn't intend to stay here. Wichita wasn't New York, but the smaller city might appeal more to Shadow than Barren. And Logan was an attractive man.

Blossom wouldn't let herself care about that. Even after he'd almost taken her in his arms—she'd been sure of that by the look in his eyes—Ken was still too much of a threat. She had the baby to worry about, and Logan had his own issues with Nick. He and Shadow would be a better match.

In the kitchen Shadow took her first bite of apple pie then moaned.

"Oh, this is good."

"I bought it frozen," Blossom admitted, "but don't tell Logan."

"You don't like to cook?"

"I don't know how to cook for him. And I don't dare serve curry again—even though everyone else liked it." Blossom toyed with her pie. She'd made an herbal tea for herself, but her stomach still felt queasy this morning, though she didn't normally feel nauseated. Lucky for her. With Sam and Logan in the house, it would be hard to hide morning sickness.

Shadow leaned back in her chair. "Let me see. You wanted cash for last week's pay. You don't cook what I might call cowboy style. Which tells me you weren't qualified as an in-home caregiver for the Circle H when you accepted the position."

Blossom had been tempted to use a fake name on her application but she hadn't. Lying about her experience was as far as she would go, and she'd only planned to stay a week. "I had an abusive relationship. I left. Logan knows that now—and in spite of my lack of credentials, he's been more than generous in letting me stay."

"No one's likely to find you here," Shadow pointed out.

"Maybe not, but feeling safe isn't something I'm familiar with." She hesitated. "I'm learning—a little—to trust my better instincts, but I'm not there yet. All I can do is try to become a better cook so Logan doesn't choke on his food while I'm here."

"Where will you go after this?"

"I don't know." She wouldn't tell Shadow, or Logan, even if she did.

Shadow finished her pie. She pushed her coffee mug aside.

"Well. I wish you luck. Logan has an edge sometimes, but he's mostly bark and no bite. And he's not alone. Men can be…men."

They shared a woman-to-woman smile but Shadow said no more.

She glanced in the direction of the Wilson Cattle Company again. Then she stood and walked to the back door to stare toward the barn. "I think I heard Logan and the guys ride in. I'll go talk to him now."

Someone—Grey Wilson was Blossom's guess—had broken Shadow's heart.

"SHE'S A MESS, LOGAN."

"Yeah. I know." Standing in the barn aisle, he told her about Ken in a few choice words then jerked a thumb toward the ranch house. "We had a talk. That guy sure won't hurt her while I'm around."

Shadow assessed him. "What do I see here? No more bitterness over Libby? A definite liking for Blossom? Good for you."

"She works for me. As long as she's here,

she's under my protection." He looked away. "That's it."

"Why don't I believe you?"

"Because, ever since you and Grey split up, every guy has been suspect in some way."

"With good reason." She shifted from one foot to the other.

Logan let that go. His friend and neighbor's feelings for Shadow, or hers for him, were none of his concern.

"Why did you want to see me?"

"It's something that might test your convictions. About Blossom."

Logan pitched another forkful of straw into an empty stall. He'd let Cyclone out into the corral to soak up some morning sun. Nothing but rain was predicted for the next week, and Logan wasn't looking forward to that, even though the ranch needed water right now. When the first drops fell, he'd be fixated on the lower-lying stretch of land that passed for a driveway.

"You're not curious?" Shadow asked.

"I figure you'll tell me when you're ready."

"I *may* have found her replacement." He heard the triumphant tone in her voice but didn't look at her. "I'd almost given up. Then, yesterday while I was combing through my file of applicants again, I got a call. About Bertrand O'Neill."

"He's still around? Bertie must be ninety-five if he's a day."

"And as you might have heard, he hasn't been well."

Logan pitched more fresh bedding into the stall. He needed to think about the colt's training. Or find someone to take that on because he'd be gone soon. "I doubt Bertie would make Sam a good companion."

"I agree. But that's not who I meant. One of Bertie's relatives has been staying with him for the past few months. Until recently he didn't need much help except for a daily reminder to take his medications, someone to do laundry once a week and drive him to his doctors' appointments." She paused. "Then a few days ago, he took a turn for the worse. He's in the hospital in Kansas City now."

"His cousin—or whoever—needs a new job."

"He's a bit quirky and, frankly, kind of a drifter, I've heard. He called himself a Renaissance man—a jack-of-all-trades—on the phone, and he never gave any thought to working as an in-home caregiver before, but now he's had some experience with Bertie."

"Might work. Sam mostly needs someone to keep him from getting too mobile before he's ready but—" Logan suppressed a twinge of regret that Blossom would be replaced "—from my own selfish standpoint, can this guy cook?"

Shadow smiled. "Yes, he does. He started as a line cook—chef, he said—at the old road-house outside Barren."

"That place—a real hole-in-the-wall—closed years ago."

"I'm only telling you what he said, and he claims he hasn't forgotten what he knows. In fact, he's since had some formal training—in France. He has plans, he said."

For some reason—Blossom, he had to admit—the thought of this new caregiver who was also a good cook didn't please Logan, but he said, "Great."

Shadow beamed. "I went to visit Bertie. He knows his release from the hospital will probably be contingent upon his going to a facility. Medicare rules," she said. "Sad, but I think he realizes he'll never be able to live at home again."

"Did you check out this caregiver guy?"

"He's coming in today to fill out the application."

Shadow was clearly waiting for Logan's agreement. He slid the stall door shut. He envisioned Blossom in the kitchen, humming to herself while she fixed lunch. He remembered wanting to hold her in his arms. To kiss her until she forgot about Ken, and he forgot about his need to leave the Circle H and get back to Wichita.

"I like Blossom," Shadow said, as if she were speaking for him. "I can empathize with her obviously unhappy past, though she didn't tell me much. But I don't feel as if I'm undercutting her with this. She won't stay much longer anyway, and you wanted a male caregiver. I think I've found you one—although it's certainly not a done deal yet."

Logan looked at the floor, knowing this was what he'd wanted. "We'll see how this goes, see if his references check out."

"I'm hoping they'll be stellar. But as I said, he's moved around, had a number of different jobs. He could be 'enhancing' his résumé or glossing over some failures."

"I'm sure you'll get to the truth. You're good at what you do." He paused. He'd meant to avoid the subject that was guaranteed to make Shadow prickly. "Not so good with Grey," he said anyway.

"Are you trying to probe a sore tooth?"

A sore heart, maybe. "No, I just—"

"You are. Don't bring him up again, Logan."

She stalked from the barn, her shoulders set, sunlight streaming over her dark hair.

Logan raised his eyebrows. He'd gotten what he'd asked for.

And he wasn't the only one with mixed emotions.

AT THE CIRCLE H, lunch really meant a full dinner to Blossom. Today she'd served fried chicken with mashed potatoes (lumpy) and gravy (too thick), corn (overcooked) and green beans (crunchy). As usual Sam devoured every bite, and even Logan had claimed it was okay except for the breading on his chicken, which was soggy, but when he'd finally pushed back from the table, he left his plate half-full.

Cowboys, she'd quickly discovered, even reluctant ones, needed plenty of fuel to get their ranch work done and leftovers were rare.

Something was wrong now other than her cooking.

Blossom had lots of experience at reading other people's signals. Often, though not as often as she wished, that had saved her. She suspected this had something to do with Shadow's visit.

But she would have to wait to find out, and even then Logan might not tell her.

In the barn she tried to corral No-Name, but the cat kept scooting into corners and crevices until Blossom's hair was dusted with cobwebs from trying to lure her out. She blew wisps of the sticky stuff off her face.

The other night, after she'd told him about Ken, she'd asked Logan if she could use the computer in the office. Alone, she'd explored the topic of toxoplasmosis. To her relief the danger didn't seem that great. It was unlikely, unless she cleaned a litter box—which she didn't—or dug in a garden bare-handed, that she'd risk contracting the parasite. Still, it wasn't a good idea to let the kitten in her room again.

"Gotcha!" She finally snared her just as Logan wandered in.

Shadow had talked to him earlier. She hadn't wanted to leave a message with Blossom. This couldn't be good.

She'd taken a liking to Shadow. Under other circumstances, they might have become friends. But had she merely been setting Blossom up that morning with what she'd thought was a simple girlie chat? Maybe Shadow had been probing Blossom's weak spots. And the

few things she'd said about Ken had only confirmed Shadow's suspicions that she'd lied to
the agency.

She reached into the bag Shadow had
brought from town. The collar she'd bought
at the pet store on her trip into Barren hadn't
lasted long—Blossom had found it abandoned
on the tack room floor. She hoped for better
luck this time, minus the kitty glamour.

"What's that?" Logan asked.

"It's a flea collar."

He looked at the ceiling. "You serious?"

"I tried a regular collar with a little bell on
it. But the other night you mentioned—"

"You'd have to put one on every barn cat
on this ranch."

"That's my plan." She showed him the rest.
"You didn't want fleas in the house, remember."

"I don't want cats in the house. In case you
haven't noticed, the dogs don't come in either."

"Haven't you seen the weather report? It's
going to pour rain for days."

"These cats are used to bad weather," he
insisted. "The litter this one came from was
born during a late-winter blizzard. She spent
her first weeks in the hayloft—snug as a bug
in a rug—until her mama decided to take off."

"See? Now she has no one."

"She has you, I guess." He couldn't hide a smile.

"And you," Blossom said, handing him the kitten. "Hold her, please."

It took both of them another twenty minutes to get the flea collar on No-Name. Blossom had to admire her spunk. The little cat wouldn't do anything she didn't want to do.

She wished she'd been able to handle Ken that way.

Her uneasiness returned. What if, after Shadow's visit, she had to leave the Circle H? Just when she'd decided to take the risk and stay longer.

Well, she was packed at least. Ready to go. But if she left, she'd be on her own again. Which was what she'd wanted. She needed to know.

"What did Shadow tell you?"

Logan tensed. "Not much. She never does."

"I don't mean to pry, but she came to the ranch for some reason."

"Apparently, to bring you a bunch of flea collars."

"That, too." Blossom realized she'd forgotten to pay Shadow. "You talked about me. Didn't you?"

"No need to worry." Logan moved past her to the first stall. He had that edgy look about him and couldn't seem to meet her eyes. "What are you doing this afternoon?"

"Distributing the other flea collars. Then I'm making a pot roast."

"Two big meals in one day. You're spoiling us." But he was smiling, his blue eyes warm, as he led a bay horse from the stall into the aisle.

Blossom stepped out of the way. Was he thinking instead about the other night in the ranch office? And that near-kiss? Or had she imagined that?

"You live on this ranch—you need to get on a horse."

Willy had said that, too. She didn't want to think about him. "Really? Kittens are more my style."

He groomed the horse with the brush in his hand, long, sweeping strokes over its powerful shoulders and flank. "I have more fence to ride. It's boring work. I'd welcome having you along—this'll be our last nice day for a while—and this bay is bombproof. Meet Ginger."

"Bombproof?"

"Gentle as a lamb. Quiet as a mouse." Setting aside the brush, he began to saddle the horse. "I'll ride Sundance—Sam's horse. Sam likes him to keep in shape. He's a happy boy. You'll be perfectly safe on this one, too." He knew how important that was to her.

"I've never ridden." Yet she felt tempted, and this might be her only opportunity. It was a beautiful day. "You really want me to go with you?"

"That's what I said."

But would she even be able to stay on? And what about her baby? Blossom eyed the horse he'd chosen for her. This wasn't a good idea, but she couldn't tell Logan why. And risk losing her job. Not yet.

He saw her hesitation. "We'll just walk. I can lead you, if you want. Like a pony ride at the county fair." He gestured at her clothes. "You got any jeans? A long-sleeved shirt? A light jacket to put on? Maybe you could bring us a couple of sodas."

If he'd meant to put her off balance, it had worked. This was the first time, except for their trip into town, that Logan had invited her to do anything. Maybe, after their talk the other night, he felt guilty about planning to fire her. Was that what he and Shadow had talked about?

She was torn between wanting to go with

him and protecting the child she carried, but she couldn't admit she was pregnant. If she was careful, and she trusted Logan to keep her safe, this one time might be okay.

"Could I take potato chips?"

Logan grinned. "You a chip lover?"

"I am."

"Me, too. Bring a big bag."

Before she left the house, Blossom put the roast in the slow cooker—her new best friend. This might be the final meal she cooked here.

Not that she hadn't planned to leave. Even Shadow had picked up on that.

Still. The air felt good, clean and fresh, as Logan had said. And she felt free for the first time in longer than she could remember. A couple of the border collies trailed along, and in the middle of the open range, on a clear early spring afternoon, any threat of Ken seemed far away. Nonexistent, even. His world was so different from this one.

The horse she rode was indeed gentle, and riding mostly involved just sitting there holding the reins loosely in her left hand, Western-style. Logan didn't have to lead her. She liked how warm the bay felt under her, and the land stretched out before them like a green blanket of new grass.

Blossom could see forever. There would be no surprises from this vantage point. She and Logan rode close together at a slow walk, checking for any breaks in the fence line as they went and talking about everything but Shadow.

Finally, she decided to circle around the question she wanted to ask.

"When Shadow was here, she kept glancing that way." Blossom pointed in the direction of the Wilson Cattle Company, where she glimpsed the rise of a barn roof in the distance. "I don't mean to pry, but were she and Grey—"

"An item, as people like to say? Years ago they seemed more than serious. Grey—who was barely nineteen—asked me to help him pick out a ring. But then, well, something happened. He and Shadow broke up—and since she's come back to Barren, she avoids him. You want to know more, ask her. You like her, huh?"

"Yes, but I know she told you something today. I think it must have been about me."

He nudged his horse closer to hers. Logan's leg brushed Blossom's, sending a rush of warmth through her. He reached for the bag she held then helped himself to another handful of potato chips. He washed that down with his soda. And looked beyond her. "We'd better turn back. I need to get home before sundown. These horses are getting antsy for dinner."

"But—"

She never said the words.

Did she find my replacement?

LOGAN STILL HADN'T figured out what to say. How to feel about Shadow's news that she'd found a potential new caregiver for Sam. A male. And a cook. Just as Logan had requested.

Instead, he'd asked Blossom to go riding with him, and having her company had temporarily eased his mind. But as soon as he and Blossom rode back into the barnyard, he heard snuffling from inside the stables. The horses were stirred up—and he doubted it was anything good.

There went his troubled thoughts again. Should he keep Blossom close to protect her from Ken, if necessary? That was his inclination. Or hire the male caregiver, the one he'd hounded Shadow for? His life would become simpler again if Blossom wasn't in the picture. No matter her growing bond with Sam, she tested Logan's resolve not to get close to a woman when his focus should be on Nicky and the coming custody suit.

One of the dogs barked.

Ears laid flat, Sundance picked up his pace and Logan sniffed the air. Fire—his first concern—didn't seem to be the problem. No smoke issued from the open barn doors. Maybe as he'd thought, the stock were just anxious for dinner. Sundance, too.

Then he heard a low groan.

"Sam!" Blossom said at the same instant he thought of his grandfather.

"Stay here." Logan slid from the saddle, tossed his reins to Blossom then ran inside. He found Sam dangling from the side of a horse in the aisle, his left foot awkwardly wedged in the nearby stirrup, his casted foot in midair. The horse Sam had managed to saddle was prancing in place, nostrils distended, snorting.

Logan caught the bridle. Carefully, he turned Sam's foot enough to ease it from the stirrup. If the mare had bolted, Sam might have been dragged halfway to the Wilson ranch. Seriously injured, or worse.

Sam rubbed his head. "What happened?"

"That's my question."

Blossom hurried into the barn and dropped down beside Sam, who now lay flat on his back.

"I tied the horses outside to that old hitching rail," she said.

Logan left her with Sam while he settled the mare in her stall. He gave her a pat on the rump. She'd remained steady enough not to let Sam get in more trouble than he already was. He returned to Blossom. "How is he?"

Sam said for her, "Stop fussing."

Blossom continued to gently hold his hand. "The cast seems intact but his other leg doesn't look good. Not that I'm an expert."

"Neither am I. I need to drive him into Barren. The walk-in clinic there should be open till eight or so."

"There's no hospital nearby?"

"This isn't Philly, city girl. Other than the clinic and one doc in private practice who should have retired years ago, medical care is hard to come by." Which meant going into KC for anything serious.

And, if Sam was really hurt, possibly more time for Logan to spend on the Circle H.

He suppressed the thought. Except for Nicky, Sam's well-being was his main priority. What if he'd broken his other leg? Or his neck? If he had to stay bedridden longer than expected, even here at home, he'd be in danger at some point of getting pneumonia, which at his age could be deadly.

Sam blinked up at him.

"Who am I?" Logan asked.

"The stubborn cuss who makes my life miserable."

Logan frowned. He hadn't inherited Sam's orneriness through his genes, but it was part of him anyway, and it would sure be the last thing to go for Sam.

He grunted. "Stand back so I can get up."

Logan held him down. "What did you think you were doing?"

"I've ridden horses all my life."

He glanced toward the nearby stall. "Good thing you picked Gumdrop."

"See? I know what I'm doing."

"The jury's still out on that. Where were you headed anyway?" Not far, he thought. Gumdrop's cinch had been so loose the saddle would soon have spun around to her belly and Sam would have tumbled off. At least he hadn't made it out of the barn. Logan hunkered in front of him. "Wait here. I'll move the pickup."

Blossom laid a hand on his arm. "Let's take

my car. Then Sam won't have to climb up into your truck."

Logan looked at her. He could lift Sam if need be, yet she hadn't hesitated to include herself. Or to make plans. She had a selfless side. He would definitely miss her when she left. Logan's mind flashed back to that kiss he'd almost given her in the ranch office.

But Sam was still his problem. "You can stay here, Blossom. I can take Sam."

"No," she said. "I'm going, too. And we're wasting time."

Logan stood. He wouldn't argue with her. Later, he would think about that hard decision he needed to make. But for now he had to see to Sam.

CHAPTER TWELVE

SAM HAD STRAINED a major ligament in his foot. The doctor at the local clinic had done what he could, but his main recommendation was for Sam to rest. This new injury would take weeks to heal, and he should spend as much time as possible off his feet. But Logan didn't seem satisfied with the diagnosis or treatment plan.

"I ought to take Sam into KC after all." He drove Blossom's car on the way home as he had on the way into town. "Get a second opinion. We could check with Doc—our family physician—too. He's good but not as spry as he used to be or up on the latest methods."

Sam had fallen asleep on the backseat. Blossom turned to check on him again. The painkiller he'd gotten had done its work. His face appeared serene, and she didn't see a flicker of an eyelid or the twitch of a lip. He didn't quite fit lying down on the rear seat, so his position looked uncomfortable, but she figured he was too exhausted to care.

"The clinic doctor said there was nothing more to be done. It's not as if they can set the ligament like a bone."

"Thank God he didn't rebreak the other leg."

Blossom tried a smile. "At least he didn't fall down the stairs."

Logan shot a look at Sam in the rearview mirror. "How did he get from upstairs out to the barn? Without killing himself?"

"I'd pay money to have seen that."

He smiled weakly. "Me, too."

Sam was still out cold when they reached the ranch. Logan managed to nudge him awake long enough to get him into the house, hobbling with Logan's support, and half carry him up to bed. Blossom tucked him in. By the time they came downstairs again, Sam was snoring.

And she was still expecting Logan to lower the boom. She'd waited all day.

"I don't know what to do." He leaned against the kitchen counter, arms crossed. "Now more than before, Sam needs supervision. The way things are going, I'll never leave here."

"I have to admire his ingenuity—his determination—in saddling that horse," Blossom said. "But how did he manage? And as you said, where was he headed?"

"In the exam cubicle at the clinic, he admitted he was looking for us," Logan told her. "He woke up from his nap but nobody was here. Of course, he felt certain he could get to the barn and ride out on Gumdrop without help."

Blossom winced. "I shouldn't have left the house. I wasn't hired to go horseback riding with you." *And risk my own safety.*

"Maybe he panicked with us gone, I don't know. Or maybe he thought he was okay—hadn't broken his leg—and was off to ride fence with me."

Which only reminded Blossom that her stay here might be coming to an end. She stirred the now-cold tea in her cup. She added another spoonful of sugar. "When are you going to tell me?"

"What?"

"About Shadow. She didn't come to the ranch today just to bring me half a dozen flea collars. Please be honest with me, Logan."

He rubbed his jaw where a five o'clock shadow had sprouted. "She found a man to take care of Sam."

That was no surprise—she'd expected it—
yet hearing him say the words made her shrink
inside. She didn't need to worry, he'd said. But
unlike Sam, Blossom wasn't his responsibility.
She cradled her stomach where the tiny bulge
was growing. When she'd changed clothes to
go riding, she hadn't been able to snap her
jeans. She hadn't told Logan about her pregnancy for fear of being fired. She wouldn't
have to tell him *now*.

"Sam's not easy for any of us to deal with."
Logan's gaze avoided hers. "He wasn't before
but after this—"

"I know. You're right. I should probably…"
She gestured toward the ceiling. "Oh, wait.
I'm already packed."

"Blossom."

"No, I'm glad Shadow found someone. This
male caregiver is probably bigger and stronger
than I am, and he'll keep Sam from getting
hurt." Someone Logan might feel more com-
fortable with. "We both benefited from my
being here…at least I did, for a while, but…"

Blossom set her cup in the sink. She ran
water, rinsed it out then slid the cup into the
dishwasher.

"I don't know if this man will even work
out," Logan said to her back.

"He must have more experience than I did."

He took a step closer. Blossom could feel his heat only inches away. "Where will you go?"

"I can't tell you," she said with a thin smile.

"Because of Ken."

"I've already stayed too long. If he did track me here, he might convince you to give me up. Like he did with my friend Tammy."

"I don't knuckle under to bullies. I'd throw him off this ranch, off your trail so fast—"

Blossom turned. Her eyes suddenly moist and her throat tight, she wanted to believe. But if she stayed, she'd be relying on Logan, leaning on him when she needed to rely on herself. And only herself.

Logan didn't seem to agree. "Blossom," he said in a thick tone. He turned her toward him, and she didn't stop to think. His voice had been enough. Without considering why this was a bad idea, she glided into his arms. "This doesn't help anything. We shouldn't…"

"Right now it helps me." He began to lower his head toward her, his mouth angling ever closer to her lips, his breath a whisper as he said, "Maybe we should."

But at the last second Blossom drew back.

"Logan. I have Ken to worry about and…" *My baby.* "You have Nicky, Sam—"

"And you haven't completed your on-the-job training here." His eyes looked somber. "Stay," he said softly. "At least until Shadow vets this guy to see if he's all right."

And to her surprise, Blossom agreed. She was used to not having choices, but this time she did. She hoped she'd made the right one.

As THE WEATHER forecast had threatened, the rains had come. The constant downpour dampened Logan's mood and shortened his temper. It reminded him of the flood three years ago and of Nicky, of his own guilt. His impatience grew until Willy and Tobias began to avoid him again whenever they could.

Yet, to his growing irritation, Blossom bothered him most. By the end of the following week, Logan had seen her only a few times— once at dinner when she served a birthday meal for Tobias and those mornings when she'd passed Logan in the hall on her way to the bathroom. He'd tried not to notice her sleepy eyes or tangled curls. He tried even harder not to remember the night he'd all but begged her to stay until her replacement came. There had been no word from Shadow except to say that Bertie was still in the hospital and she was checking Jack Hancock's references.

"He's an odd duck," she'd added. "I'll make sure to check them all out thoroughly."

Then, as the rains continued to drench the pastures and make deep puddles on the drive and the horses grew as cranky in their stalls as Logan was, the kitten disappeared.

Blossom paced from the kitchen to the front door to peer outside.

"Where can she be?"

Logan tracked dirt through the house to follow her. The yard was a sea of mud. Where once his mother and grandmother had planted petunias in the flower beds every spring and mums in the fall, Logan saw only a few straggly shoots poking up through the rain-sodden earth.

"I've told you. The cats come and go."

"No-Name is different. She likes to stay near—and she's still a baby." The word seemed to catch in her throat. "How will she defend herself? Her leg has barely healed. There must be predators around."

"Blossom, she'll either come back on her own. Or she won't."

"Cougars," she said. "Mountain lions."

"Same thing. Different names."

"Coyotes, then."

She was on the verge of tears, which was nothing new. Ever since she'd agreed to stay a while longer, she'd been on edge. Logan suspected the only thing keeping her here now was the kitten. She hadn't come near Logan since that night she'd decided to stay on. He wanted to believe that was a good thing for both of them.

He sighed. "By dinnertime she'll probably be in the barn waiting for food like the horses."

That didn't reassure her. "What if she gets stepped on?"

Logan stood behind her at the front screen door. "On a ranch you can't be a bleeding heart, but you've fed that kitten, watered her, carried her around as if she was a baby…a human one." He frowned at her suddenly stiff back. She'd become too attached to that barn cat. Or maybe the weather was getting to her, too. She could be worried about the distance from the house to the road, the chance that on this low-lying ground, typical of most of the state, the driveway would flood and trap her here. The way it had with Nicky. At least Blossom wasn't sick, he told himself. She was determined.

"I need to look for her."

"Not in this rain, you don't." He turned her toward him. "I'll saddle Sundance and look around the property. The cat could have wandered off and then taken cover in the rain."

Her chin hitched. "I'll go with you."

"No, you won't." The last thing he needed was Blossom riding next to him again, her leg brushing his thigh now and then. Just his luck, they'd find the kitten lying in a watery ditch somewhere—or electrocuted by one of the corral fences, some of which were wired. Blossom would fall apart. "I'll call you on my sat phone as soon as I find anything."

Blossom glanced back at the yard. "You won't forget?"

"I promise. I'll find her." Her tone had sounded vaguely hopeful, and he appreciated that she'd held her ground with him. "In this rain I've got nothing better to do," he said.

Logan eyed the dark sky. Thunder rumbled overhead.

The days were ticking by and Joe had already given Garvey that sweet assignment. Logan was losing ground—but at least not today.

The weather was too bad to fly.

Which, right now, worked for him.

WITH A DEEPENING SCOWL, Sam eyed Blossom from his bed. She bustled around the room, straightening a dresser scarf here, a cushion there. Sam was in a rotten mood, and he couldn't help notice that Logan was, too. As the rains went on and the stream that paralleled the driveway rose almost to its banks, he knew his grandson's mind must be on that flood three years ago. Sam remembered it, too, but he couldn't completely blame his bad mood on concerns about the weather. Being flat on his back again had turned him into a grumpy old man. In trying to prove he was on the mend, able to take over the ranch again, he'd only made things worse.

"I've never seen rain like this," Blossom said.

"Every spring."

"How can you grow anything? Corn, hay or whatever?"

"With my fingers crossed behind my back." He watched her fluff the same pillow she had minutes before. Everyone seemed to be on edge. "That's the risk of ranching. Farming, too. We must all be crazy—except for those big agribusiness boys. They can afford the losses."

She raised an eyebrow. "There are no agri-business 'girls'?"

"I'm sure there are."

"I thought the Circle H was doing well." Her smile didn't quite cover the sad look in her eyes. Sam guessed she was worried about the missing kitten. Logan had been searching for her without any luck. "Except for the sorry sign that was hanging at the gate, aren't things good?" She smiled. "I'm glad Logan finally fixed it for you."

"I'd have fixed it myself if I hadn't busted my leg."

"Well, you did." As if she'd been waiting for the opportunity to scold him, she said, "Then you just had to hurt the other one falling off that horse."

"I didn't fall. I got hung up. If you two hadn't come in at the wrong time, I'd have worked my foot out of the stirrup, and been on my way."

Blossom studied him. "You remember where you were going?"

"Sure. Why not?"

She hesitated. "Sometimes…you don't get things exactly right."

"Now, that's a darn lie."

She stepped closer to his bed. "I'm not

lying, Sam. Several times you've mistaken me for Olivia—Logan's ex-wife."

"I know who Libby is." He looked past her. "Why would you say that?"

"Because you and I are friends. You deserve the truth." Blossom sat down on the chair beside his bed. "You don't remember calling me by her name? Thinking—" she hesitated "—that she and Logan are still married."

His jaw tightened. "They're divorced."

"You're definite about that?"

"Sure as it's raining again right now." The sky was dumping another inch on the already-saturated ground. There'd be no riding fence today, no checking on pregnant cows, no feel of a horse under him.

Blossom looked relieved. So was Sam. For a minute, he'd thought they were going to get into some wrangle about things he'd never said. Or done.

He tangled enough with Logan. Yes, Sam's mind had given him some trouble after that bison cow tossed him against a tree, but he hadn't suffered a headache now in days. He didn't feel as dizzy. But did Blossom and Logan discuss him at dinner every night? Did his grandson think Sam could never take over the ranch again? And if he didn't…

This wasn't really his property and he wasn't true family. Yet Sam had to stay here. Somehow. He couldn't leave Muriel behind.

Blossom took his hand. "Why did they break up?"

"Logan and Libby? That was between them," he said.

"But you do know."

"I raised Logan from a boy. There's not much I don't know about him." Sam didn't go on. Not many ways in which they connected these days.

"I didn't mean to pry, but I'm curious. He and Olivia don't seem to get along well—and Logan doesn't spend much time with his son."

"Nick's a good boy. Libby smothers him, though."

"There must be a reason."

"All I can say is, she was never the right woman for him—or this ranch. So why would I confuse her with you?"

"I shouldn't have asked." Blossom rose from the chair but Sam caught her hand again. He'd noticed she had a habit of backing off, of apologizing when there was no need.

"Don't go. I'm bored and I don't know how much longer I can stay in this bed like a hogtied calf."

"If you behave, the doctor thinks you can get up for a bit in a few days."

Blossom didn't sit down, but she let him keep holding her hand.

"That'll be a relief."

"So be a good boy." She let go of his hand. "I need to start lunch." She was almost to the door when Sam spoke again.

"Tell the truth. You have an interest in my grandson?"

"I guess I do," she admitted. "Which won't do either of us any good."

Sam eased back onto his pillows, hurt again and all but helpless, which scared him. Logan and Sawyer had no interest in the Circle H except for their two-thirds share of the ranch. Together they held the majority vote on any decisions. If Sam could no longer work, would they sell? And throw him off the ranch? Right now Sawyer was missing like Blossom's cat, which bought him time. But his and Logan's only real connection to Sam was through Muriel.

Everywhere he looked she was still here. He could feel her love, and Sam tripped through a few good memories. He wanted Logan to be happy in that way.

He straightened in his bed. *Blossom*, he

thought. He was no matchmaker, but if she stayed at the Circle H maybe Logan would, too. Sam wouldn't have to quit the ranch when this was still his home, if not really his property.

He stared out the bedroom window at the rain.

Maybe the idea was too far-fetched.

Face it. He was an aging man with nowhere else to go. And at the moment, it seemed, he couldn't get out of bed anyway.

A FEW DAYS later the rain finally moved on, soaking the plains to the east and heading for New England. For Philadelphia. The sun came out and bathed the Circle H in light again. The ground began to dry out in the front yard—and, with the small rake and shovel she'd found in the laundry room cabinet, Blossom basked in the beautiful morning. She would plant flowers. Another first for her.

On a day like this, she could almost believe she was safe here. As if nothing bad could happen to her in such a sunny spring. As if she could stay. There had been no more word on Jack Hancock, her replacement, and as a bonus Nick had come to visit today. "With a laundry list from Libby," Logan had told her.

"Don't do this, don't let him do that… It was like listening to fingers scraping on a blackboard."

"At least she let him come."

"I guess my talk with her had some effect. I still can't believe she allowed him to visit the ranch, though. Will wonders never cease."

He was keeping an eagle eye now on Nick, who was kneeling in the grass by the neglected flower bed in front of the house. He was Blossom's helper.

"There'll be more rain." Logan stood above them on the front porch. "You two are wasting your time."

"This dirt's nice and soft now." Wearing sturdy gardening gloves, so as not to make direct contact with the soil that could contain toxoplasmosis, she held up a handful of rich, dark earth. "It's the perfect time to plant these flower seeds." *I think.* "Right, Nick?"

"We're making a garden. It's going to be pretty."

Logan smiled. "But I'm warning you. Those will wash away next time it rains."

She raised her face to the sun. "No, with any luck they'll get wet and germinate, Mr. Hunter. I'm giving them a head start today. Isn't the weather gorgeous?"

His gaze stayed on Nick. "I see I can't change your mind."

"You'll eat those words when the first flowers bloom."

"Blossom," he said, shaking his head. "I bet your mother was a gardener."

"No, they just loved the name. My father didn't like plants. They made his nose itch, he said. And we moved so often Mom never had a garden." She looked up at him. "She did risk a house plant or two in her kitchen, but they always got left behind."

She didn't point out that these would, too, when she left.

Jack Hancock was never far from her mind. Maybe Shadow had checked all of his references by now and Bertie had left the hospital for a nursing home. This might be her last day here. Maybe Logan was right—she was wasting her time. Several days ago when she'd tried to talk with Sam, she'd stepped over another boundary. *You have an interest in my grandson?*

Digging in the dirt was supposed to distract her.

"Thank you for finding No-Name," she said, making a small hole in the ground. Logan was right. It was too wet, but she dug anyway, as if she might really become a part of this place, of a life here with Sam and Logan and Nick. The kitten had bounded across the grass to plop down in Nick's lap. He giggled as she purred and rubbed against his face.

Logan's gaze softened at the sight. "She's pretty smart. The hayloft was a natural hiding place for her, the same spot where she was born. It stayed warm as well as dry."

"But thanks again."

"I gave up," he said. "Between you and Nicky, I'm outnumbered with that cat."

"Yes, you are." Blossom sprinkled seeds into the first hole.

She should enjoy their light teasing and let it go at that. Instead, she watched Nick abandon their project to chase after the kitten. "May I ask you something?"

Logan was looking at Nick. "Don't go as far as the barn," he called out, waiting until Nick veered off toward the nearby field, then turned back to her. "He hasn't seen that toy truck. It's hidden in the barn."

"My question is personal," she said. "You might not like it."

She sprinkled seeds into the second hole. She could feel Logan's gaze on her from the porch. "Shoot," he said. "If I don't want to answer, I won't."

"It's about you and Olivia…"

"Libby goes her way. I go mine." His voice had hardened.

"That doesn't help Nick," she murmured. "I meant, what happened before?"

"Why did we split up?"

She nodded but kept digging more holes, planting more seeds.

Logan came down the steps. He sat on the bottom one, which was likely still damp, then laced his hands together between his knees. "Rain" was all he said.

Blossom decided to wait him out. She patted dirt over the seed holes, hoping she was doing this right.

"That flood I mentioned once." Logan's serious tone made her sit back on her heels. She looked up at him, but his gaze avoided hers. "Nicky was only three then. He was pretty sick the day I had a final interview for my job, so I wasn't here. We were still living at the ranch but had plans to move to Wichita. We hadn't found a good house yet we could afford and were waiting to make certain I got the new job."

"While you were gone, the storm came," she said, urging him to go on.

"By nightfall the driveway was under water. Deep. It's been that way for generations, and there's no real way to change the lay of the land out here without spending a ton of money for the few days now and then when it floods. The truck bogged down halfway to the road when Sam tried to get out with Olivia and Nicky, who'd had the flu but seemed to be getting over it when I left. While I was gone he got worse. At first Libby thought he'd developed croup—which sounds awful but isn't usually that serious. She bathed him to keep his fever down that night, even put him in the shower once or twice for humidity." He shook his head. "Nicky kept coughing. He couldn't breathe very well. Because it wasn't croup—he had developed pneumonia."

"She must have been frantic."

Logan didn't deny that. "And in Wichita, my interview had been canceled so I had no reason to be there. No flights were going in or out and the helicopters couldn't fly either. By the time I managed by car to get to Barren…"

"Nick was trapped."

He nodded. "Grey's ranch sits on slightly higher ground. He and I rode cross-country that night on horseback. We cut fence to get here, which risked letting his herd run free, and in the dark we prayed our horses didn't step in a hole. Break a leg. Even then, once we got here, there was nothing else to be done until morning."

"You were with Olivia, though."

"I doubt she noticed by then. She was hysterical and still blames me." He hesitated. "I blame myself, too."

"You did what you could, Logan—just as you do what you can now. With Sam," she said, "and Nick, too."

"I wish I could do more—"

"Maybe we can think of something."

Logan's gaze turned soft. "*You're* something," he said. "You have no reason to help yet you always try."

She set the shovel and rake aside. "I know one way. We can get Sam on his feet tomorrow. See if that helps his bad mood."

"I know he's frustrated, alone in his room. I'm grateful for you spending so much time with him. That's over and above your job requirements."

"You really care about him," Blossom said.

"I do. Sam's been like a father to me."

She repacked the garden tools in a bag. She

started to rise from her knees but couldn't get up. In the past week or so her center of gravity had begun to shift. With the new weight she was gaining, she felt awkward, even clumsy. And as she'd expected, none of her shapeless clothes really disguised her condition now. For an instant she regretted trying to stand.

Logan got off the step to help her. He put a hand under her elbow, and his fingers brushed the side of her stomach. Blossom felt him recoil. Then she finally stood, her loose top pulling tight against her as she straightened.

His gaze shot to the swell of her abdomen before it rose to meet hers.

"Yes," she admitted. "I'm pregnant."

"Why didn't you tell me?"

Before she could answer, Nick came running across the lawn with the kitten at his heels. Without waiting for him, turning his back on Blossom, Logan climbed the steps then stalked into the house. The screen door banged shut behind him.

Her secret was out.

CHAPTER THIRTEEN

LOGAN LOCKED THE TRUCK. He strode along Main Street the next day with Blossom beside him—or rather, walking a step behind. She stayed close by his shoulder but not touching. He hadn't said an unnecessary word to her since she'd stood up by the flower bed and he'd seen the plain evidence of her pregnancy. Quite a shock until he recalled the bag from the baby shop tucked in with the groceries. It sure wasn't for her *friend*.

The tension between them on the drive into town had felt like another coming storm. He shouldn't shut her out but couldn't seem to help himself. In a way, he felt betrayed. Logan had opened up to her about Nicky and the night of the flood, but the whole time, and for all the time she'd been at the Circle H, Blossom had been lying to him.

"How long will you be at the ag store?" she asked in a small voice that only set his teeth on edge. He didn't like that submissive attitude any more than he liked the way she turned aside from any confrontation.

"Not long."

"I need to pick up my paycheck."

"Meet me at the truck when you're done."

Logan noticed she didn't mention the grocery store this time. Either the pantry and freezer were still full or Blossom had leaving on her mind again.

He'd been expecting that.

Earlier, she'd caught up to him as he was about to drive into Barren. Blossom had asked to come along—the only thing she'd said to him since yesterday.

Logan stopped in the middle of the sidewalk.

"Blossom. You should have been up-front with me. First thing."

She took a breath. "Would you have hired me if you knew I was pregnant?"

"No way." His mouth set. "I've got enough on my mind with Sam. You expect me to overlook the fact that you're not who I thought you were?"

"I'm the same person," she said, a hand on her stomach. "Just bigger."

"Yeah, well you'll get a whole lot bigger before it's over." An image rolled through him. At first, it was Libby when she was carrying Nicky. He remembered how exciting it was to watch their baby grow. But then Libby turned into Blossom, huge with child. Ken's child. Nothing to do with Logan. Which, for some reason, only made him angrier with her.

"I could still have done my job."

"Until when?"

"Until I decided it was time to leave."

"Maybe that would have been too late. Maybe by then, we'd have more rain or snow or a tornado warning. If I know one thing, it's that Mother Nature always wins. Especially out here with nothing to stop her."

"You think I'd have the baby during a storm?"

"That's a good chance, yeah."

"And like Nicky, I'd be stuck at the ranch."

"Makes perfect sense to me."

"Babies come when they're ready, Logan. And you can't always predict bad weather any more than you can a medical emergency. It wasn't your fault Nick was there on the Circle H—"

"He had pneumonia!"

"And the doctors—antibiotics—cured him."

She shook her head. "Not every story has a bad ending."

He glanced along the street. "How's this for an ending? I lost my wife, my marriage, my kid… Is it any wonder I hate that ranch? If it weren't for Sam, I wouldn't be here right now."

"I know you're worried about your job—"

He scowled. "Don't do that. We're not talking about my career. Or Sam. We were talking about you—your…" He gestured at her stomach.

"Stubborn." She took a step away then turned back. "But just your luck, I happen to agree with you. I'll see Shadow. Then as soon as we get back to the Circle H, I'll say goodbye to Sam and be on my way," she said, confirming his suspicions.

"I won't be here, Logan, but someday you're going to realize—have to realize—that you couldn't keep Nick from getting sick or being trapped. Just as you can't keep this baby from coming when, or where, it wants to."

"Maybe not but—"

What? For a moment he couldn't think. He didn't want a relationship with her, or with any woman. All he wanted was to get back to Wichita, win his promotion and challenge

Libby's sole custody. Seeing his son more often was a good thing, but right now it still depended on Libby's whims. He'd likely have to pressure her down the road again until he went back to the courts. But those weren't the only things weighing him down. Logan realized something else: he liked Blossom, maybe too much, and he was about to lose her.

The fact that he was getting what he'd wanted—a male caregiver—didn't improve his mood. Blossom would be heading off now before Jack Hancock was on the job, leaving Logan with Sam. Logan was still waiting for Shadow's go-ahead but apparently, to everyone's surprise, Bertie was doing better, so things were still up in the air. He watched Blossom set off down the street. She didn't look at any of the shops she passed. Why would she? She wasn't staying.

His fault, partly. He shouldn't have groused at her.

Logan sidestepped a man who'd cut in front of him to enter the local clinic, a storefront operation that was half of the medical care available in Barren—the place they'd taken Sam the day they found him hanging from the horse's saddle in the barn.

Blossom had no sooner walked away when the back of Logan's neck prickled. He was being watched. He turned and saw Libby standing in front of her shop a block down on Main Street, arms folded across the jacket of her navy blue suit.

Round two, he thought, sooner than he'd expected, then walked toward her.

The building space she'd rented recently suited her. Neat as a pin, the windows sparkling, stylish letters that read Olivia Wilson, Proprietor in flowing gold script. Estates, Sales, Auctions. He hadn't seen it before. And using her maiden name.

"Congratulations," he said. "I like the new store."

"I needed room." She didn't smile.

"First, the house was too small, now you have a new shop... You want to spread out everywhere, huh?"

"I do. Business has been good."

Maybe if they stuck to such simple subjects, they wouldn't end up in yet another go-round about Nicky.

Libby's gaze shifted to some point over his shoulder. "Well, maybe *good* isn't the word. Lately, I've been handling a number of ranch properties that are being sold, foreclosed on or even abandoned. I have a sale coming up next week—lots of equipment at prices meant to unload it. I feel bad for all those people, but you might be interested."

"Ask Grey instead. Sam has the barns stuffed full." He added, hoping he didn't sound exaggeratedly polite, "But thanks for thinking of me."

"Nick has a playdate this afternoon," she said, as if out of the blue.

I wasn't asking to see Nicky.

"I have to meet the vet at the Circle H soon—if that bison cow doesn't break out of the pen before then and run off. It took Willy, Tobias and me to corral her. She's not going to give birth as easy as the others. Looks like a Cesarean in the making." He added, "My day's full, too."

Libby glanced down the street behind him again. "Who's that?"

Logan looked back. Blossom was halfway down the street in the opposite direction on her way to Shadow's agency.

"You seemed to be having an intense conversation," Libby said. "I couldn't see too well, but she looked…pretty."

His jaw tightened. "She's Sam's caregiver." Or she was, he thought. If Blossom followed through, she'd be gone by evening. He wasn't sure that wasn't the right decision. Last thing he needed on the ranch was a pregnant woman. Guess he'd made himself clear about that.

"A caregiver," she said in a tone he didn't like.

Logan shifted his weight. "She helps him dress, brings his meals, straightens his room, changes his sheets, does his laundry… She gives me a progress report every now and then. She cooks for us."

Libby arched a brow. "That's all?"

"I don't happen to have a detailed invoice with me for her services."

And why explain himself? She continued to stare at Blossom's retreating back, raising a hand to smooth her hair, which already looked tight as a drum. He'd never liked that bun coiled up at the nape of her neck, but at one time it had also lured him to loosen the pins and watch the silky blond strands slide through his fingers. He'd known her every habit then, every expression and mood, but Logan wished he couldn't read her face now.

"You're sure? She's just a nurse?"

"Not a nurse—"

"I suppose she's living in the house."

"Yeah."

"In the spare room across from yours."

He tensed. "I don't like what you're saying, Libby. Look. I'm sure you haven't forgotten, but we're divorced. You're apparently a Wilson again. So what I do, where I go and who I'm seeing—which I'm not—are no longer your business."

"Nick is my business. The only one where you're concerned."

"What does that mean?"

Blossom had headed into Shadow's office. Libby hadn't glanced away once.

"It means I won't hesitate to 'make excuses' when you want to see Nick. If I get the least whiff of any goings-on in that house—"

"Come on, Olivia."

"—or a hint of inappropriate behavior—"

"You're way out of line."

"—I'll be talking to *my* lawyer."

Her gaze stayed on the agency office. Blossom was inside now to collect her last pay. Logan was darned if he'd let Libby know she was leaving.

She hesitated before she turned to open the door to her shop. "You know, a six-year-old boy can be a font of information. Every time you see him he gives me a full 'report.'"

BLOSSOM MARCHED INTO the Mother Comfort Home Health Care Agency and Shadow looked up from her computer. Her eyes darkened.

"It's not Friday."

"Not yet. But I need whatever pay is coming to me."

Shadow rose from her desk chair. "Are you all right?"

"I'm fine."

"You don't look fine. Why don't I make coffee—or tea—and we can talk?"

"I've already talked. To Logan." Not that their conversation had been friendly, she had to admit, but she'd actually hoped he might take her pregnancy more kindly once he knew. That he would ask her to stay, safe as she could be from Ken. Unlike Logan, the Circle H had become a haven to her, not a trap.

"I know you were planning to leave once Jack settles into the job—"

"I can't wait." Blossom would be gone before that could take place. "There's no reason for me to stay any longer."

Shadow perched on the edge of her desk. "No reason?"

"Logan doesn't want me here," she said. "He never did. But now, because..." She sighed. "He knows I'm pregnant."

Shadow's eyes widened. "You and Logan…?"

"No. There's nothing between us, and I certainly haven't been here long enough. But he didn't welcome the news about this baby—which, I'm sorry to say, I let him find out for himself."

"Ah. I see."

"And, really, it's time." Blossom leaned against the closed door. "My ex-fiancé is probably looking for me right now." Her shoulders drooped. "I've already stayed longer than I should have."

"What did Logan do when he found out?"

She sent Shadow a sad smile. "He pulled back into his shell like a turtle."

Shadow nodded. "When are you due?"

"Four months from today."

"Boy or girl?"

"I don't know." But Blossom could hazard a guess.

"You haven't seen a doctor?"

"In Philly. I'll find another one somewhere."

Shadow tilted her head. "You passed the clinic right down the street."

"That would be a one-time visit. I won't be in town again."

"Blossom, I wish you'd reconsider. There are people here who care about you—even

Logan, I'm sure, if not *especially* Logan—and I know you've become close to Sam. At the ranch you have some protection. Away from here, you won't."

"I'm aware of that. But I can't endanger anyone else. Sam," she said, "and Nick, too. I won't jeopardize an injured man and Logan's child."

"So you'd endanger your baby instead?"

"Oh, of course not…"

"You would be if you leave." She paused. "I'm one of those people who care about you. I'm in a very good position here to intercept any inquiries that ex of yours might make. If not in this office then anywhere else in town. I can keep my ear to the ground. At least then you'd have some warning."

"That's very kind of you—"

"I'm not trying to be kind. I'm trying to help you." Shadow went behind her desk, punched a few computer keys. "I've pulled up your application. Give me more information for your profile—and I'll know who to look for." She frowned at the screen. "First, tell me his full name. With a description. A photo if you have one."

When Shadow glanced up, expectantly

waiting, Blossom was already on her way out the door.

"Thank you, but no."

She hurried away from the agency.

She'd spent her life with people who said they cared about her but didn't—her own parents, then Ken—and she wouldn't make that mistake again. Logan had been clear. Shadow was wrong.

Her baby was hers to protect. And hers alone.

She had neared the local clinic when she saw a man coming out the door—and stopped. Was she seeing things? Still far enough away, she couldn't make out his features, but he appeared tall enough and was built much the same way as Ken, enough to send a shiver down her spine. He wore a well-tailored, familiar-looking suit. His hair looked the exact color of Ken's ash brown. And the confident walk that was almost a strut…had he found her? Asked about her at the clinic? Did he already know about the baby? How could he? Unless he'd gotten to Tammy again. Blossom turned to run.

And slammed into Logan's hard chest.

He steadied her. "Whoa. The truck's over this way."

She couldn't speak. The whole morning had been awful, even Shadow's unexpected sympathy and her offer to help when Blossom knew she couldn't trust anyone. Now she was all but gasping.

She wrenched away. *There.* Across the street, as Logan had said, she saw his truck. A few more steps with him behind her, already jangling his keys, and they could scramble in then lock the doors…

Blossom didn't check for traffic. She rushed into the street and another pickup suddenly flashed by, so close she could feel the heat from its metal side and the brush of air as it whizzed past. At the last second Logan yanked her out of harm's way.

"Easy," he said. "What's wrong?"

"Ken." It was the only word she could get out. Her heart thundered. All the weeks, the miles, the different towns… "I never should have stopped here. The longer I've stayed, the closer he's come. Maybe he pressured Tammy again, though how could she know where I am now?" How could Ken?

Logan looked up then down the street. "Your *ex*? Where?"

Still short of breath, Blossom pointed.

"That guy?" Logan drew her to him. "It's okay, Blossom. I know him—that's not Ken."

"Then who—"

"I almost ran into him earlier. He's a drug rep, works for one of the big pharmaceutical companies. He makes his rounds in Barren about once a month. He visits the clinic to drop off samples then heads for Doc's place on Cottonwood Street. See?" He gestured, his arm around her, his body warm against her back. "He's turning the corner now."

Blossom pressed against him. "I didn't see his face…but he looked so familiar."

"It's not him," Logan said again.

He held her close until she stopped shaking. Which didn't change her mind.

She had to leave. It didn't matter whether other people cared for her or not. She couldn't think about Logan's aversion to her pregnancy.

She needed to disappear again. Somewhere Ken would never find her.

AT THE CIRCLE H, Logan carried Blossom's bag down to her car. In the upstairs window he could see Sam peering out, frowning. A few more minutes, and she'd be gone. If only he had reacted better to her pregnancy…

There was nothing else to say. Those few

minutes on the street in Barren when Blossom had thought she'd seen Ken were engraved on his mind. His reassurance hadn't changed her decision. He shouldn't want it to.

Logan cleared his throat. "You'll be okay?" *Can't I change your mind?*

Maybe Blossom leaving was for the best. Libby was being unreasonable, but he had to consider his relationship with his son.

"I'll be okay." She rearranged her gear on the front seat of the old sedan.

"This thing doesn't look like it'll take you ten miles from here."

"Darla is more reliable than she appears."

"Darla?" She'd even named her car. He wanted to smile but couldn't.

Blossom risked a glance at him. "Thank you for holding me up in town, but I'm not that much of a wimp, normally. I really can take care of myself."

"Shadow doesn't think so. While you were upstairs, she called me."

She searched through a bag. "Where did I put my wallet?"

He steeled himself not to beg her to stay. Sam's face had disappeared from the window in his room and Logan could hear him now, coming down the steps. Sure enough, he barged out the front door, his eyes wild.

Blossom straightened. "Sam, you shouldn't be out of bed."

"I'm darned if I'll lie flat on my back and listen to your car going down that driveway." He pointed toward the road and took another shaky step.

"Don't you dare come down here," she said.

Sam only grunted.

"Jack will probably be here soon. He'll take good care of you."

"Not as good as you."

Blossom pressed her lips together. "Sam, please don't make this any harder than it is."

He jerked a thumb toward Logan. "This his doing?"

"No," she said. "The decision is mine."

Sam swayed a little. He knew the bare facts about Ken. "You need a man to protect you. I've got rifles in my office gun safe, another in the front closet."

"It won't come to that." Blossom rummaged in her bag again. "Oh, here it is." She opened her wallet, counted out bills then frowned. "I needed to pick up my pay in town. But then I panicked."

"You can get it tomorrow," Sam said.

Logan stepped in. "He's right, Blossom. What's the rush?"

"You know," she said, not meeting his eyes.

"But that wasn't Ken today. He isn't here."

"You are." She turned away. "We've both made ourselves understood. I need to do this—and I'm doing it now."

Not looking happy about that, she shut the car door. Blossom marched across the yard to the steps then climbed up to the porch. She hugged Sam tight.

Her voice sounded choked. "Do what the doctors tell you—I mean that—and Logan. I hope Jack works out."

Sam didn't respond. He stood there, swaying, watching her walk back down to her car, looking as lost as Logan already felt. He watched her slide into the driver's seat then adjust her mirrors. Sam glared at him. "Do something, Flyboy."

"I can't stop her."

"You won't," Sam muttered. "Both of you, durned fools."

Logan couldn't disagree. This was it. He wanted to call her back, but he didn't make promises he couldn't keep. He couldn't pursue a relationship with her after the disaster he'd made of his marriage, and he couldn't give Libby any reason to restrict his access to Nicky. They might both be fools, as Sam said, but he and Blossom had to deal with their problems on their own.

Blossom started the engine.

Panic clawed at his throat, and Logan put a hand on the open window frame.

"Wait," he said. "I forgot. I have something for you."

He ran past Sam into the house and upstairs, then up another flight to the attic. He came back down with two boxes piled one on top of the other.

"Unlock your back door and I'll slide these in. For your baby. They're Nicky's clothes I mentioned."

"You thought they were for—"

"Your *friend*. Now they're yours."

Things were changing, he thought. Even Sam was on his feet now for longer periods. Maybe within the next week or two, Logan could be in Wichita again, salvaging his job. And then he could concentrate on spending even more time with Nicky.

He stood watching with Sam for another moment as her car sped down the driveway, which was as dry as an old cow's skull now, before he turned his back on the sight, the cloud of dust, and went up the steps to help Sam inside the house.

She was gone.

His fault.

CHAPTER FOURTEEN

DONE DRIVING FOR the day, Blossom rented a motel room. She pulled one of the boxes from the backseat of her car. Surely, she imagined the scent rising from it, along with the attic dust, of Logan's woodsy aftershave. Barely able to see over the top of the carton, she carried it from her parking space toward her room. The motel wasn't much to look at, but it was cheap. And all she could afford without her pay.

One night here, then she'd be on her way, still headed west. Today she'd covered a lot of miles. She was almost at the Kansas border, approaching the front range of the Rockies. Not for the first time she wished she'd made the effort to get her paycheck from Shadow then cash it before leaving town and the Circle H behind. But she hadn't wanted to face Shadow again. To feel tempted to stay.

And she'd felt the need to hurry. To get on the road before she changed her mind.

Near the door to her room, she came to a dead stop. The blood rushed from her head to her feet. A tall, rangy-looking man stood there, blocking her way, with a broad smile Blossom didn't trust. She'd seen Ken grin like that right before he pushed her, throttled her or slapped her for some unknown offense.

"Let me take that for you." This man had pale hair, and a stray lock flopped on his forehead. He wore a battered cowboy hat, a pearl-buttoned shirt with jeans and scuffed boots. Blossom tried to memorize every detail of his appearance in case she needed to make a police report. "Any more of these in the car?"

"Just one. I can get it." Wanting to run, she tried to move past him. This was what she'd decided, wasn't it? To leave the Circle H and take care of herself? Prevent any danger from coming to the ranch? Run from Logan's disapproval of her baby?

The man tipped his hat back. "You one of those feminists?"

"Not officially," she said. "Why?"

He frowned. "'Cause I notice you're not letting me help you."

"Thank you, but I don't need any help."

"Little thing like you, of course you do." A

second later he took the box from her hands, and Blossom's heart began to pound.

"Please. Leave me alone."

Instead, he turned to her room, deposited the box beside the door then faced her again. She could see no threat in his dark eyes, unlike Ken's, which always seemed to hold an underlying danger. Blossom stayed several feet away. She was truly on her own now—and she hadn't seen anyone else nearby. The motel office was around the corner in a better-lit section of the parking lot.

"Come on," the man said. "Looks like we're the only two guests here tonight. I'll get that last box—they'll be okay by your door—then we can get a bite to eat in the restaurant across the way." He tilted his head toward a café that wasn't part of the motel. "Tell me you're not hungry."

"I'm not—" Her stomach growled.

He grinned. "I hear you are. My treat," he said.

Blossom decided he wasn't going away. And in public, she'd be marginally safer, if it came to real trouble, than having him force his way into her room in this shadowed corner of the property.

A few minutes later she was sitting across

from him in a red upholstered booth under the bright overhead lights of the café. Staring out into the night, she caught a glimpse of her reflection in the window. She looked so vulnerable and forced herself to sit up straighter, look more confident. "Where you headed?" he asked.

"Nowhere in particular," which wasn't the wisest thing to say. Better to let him think someone was waiting for her. Somewhere. The Circle H popped into her head, the peacefulness she'd felt there, at least for a while. "I mean, my family…expects me tomorrow."

"Parents?"

"My…husband, too."

He looked at her hand. "No ring."

"It's being…resized. I've gained a little weight."

He moved a saltshaker on the table between them. "You're having a baby. That's one reason I tried to help you. Damsel in distress, and all that. I couldn't watch you wrestle with those heavy boxes in your condition."

When the waitress came to take their orders, Blossom tried to catch her eye, but the woman's attention was on the man across from her. Blossom chose a hamburger—she had a craving lately for beef—with a side of coleslaw. He ordered chicken-fried steak with gravy and grits.

"What's your destination?" she finally asked, the tension easing from her shoulders and the back of her neck. He hadn't made any threatening moves so far, and she did feel lonely tonight. In the brightly lit restaurant, his company seemed almost welcome as long as he didn't try anything.

"Tulsa. Blew a tire on my truck an hour ago. Decided to stay the night here."

What would she do after they ate? Blossom polished off her meal then, stalling, let him talk her into dessert.

He leaned back to study her, his arms crossed. With his shirtsleeves rolled back, she could see that, despite his leanness, he had a powerful build. "What are you running from, darlin'?"

She tensed again. Could everyone see that in her?

"Nobody."

"You had that panicky look about you."

Blossom pushed the last of her banana cream pie aside.

She didn't know what to say. She wouldn't tell him about Ken, let him any deeper into her life.

"Whatever it is," he said, "traveling by yourself doesn't seem the best idea."

"No," she had to agree.

He motioned for the check. "I'll walk you back."

"Oh, you don't have to—"

He held out a hand to help her up from the booth.

Outside the restaurant, Blossom breathed deeply of the spring night air. For a few brief moments it felt like the freedom she craved. But could she ever really find that as long as she knew Ken might be in pursuit?

By the time they reached the motel, she'd stopped keeping so much distance between them. He hadn't made a wrong move or pushed her to talk about her past. Maybe they really were just two strangers passing through and she had overreacted at first. Big-time.

At her door he waited for Blossom to unlock it.

"Thanks for dinner," she said.

"My pleasure. Put the dead bolt on when you get inside. Not because of me," he said. "Because of you. So you won't feel afraid." He hesitated. "You want some free advice?"

Blossom wasn't sure. She didn't answer.

"Go home, I'd say, but if not, good luck to you."

She didn't have a home. There was no one waiting for her now. Her parents were in Alabama…or maybe not. She'd broken those ties a long time ago—or they had—after she moved in with Ken. But this man, as kind as he'd turned out to be, didn't have to know that. She'd never see him again.

"Night, Blossom. You take care."

"You, too." For a few more moments after she went inside, she imagined him still standing outside her door.

Then, like Logan, he was gone.

IN HER ROOM with the dead bolt on, Blossom sat alone with all the lights blazing, the draperies closed. *Home*, she thought. She'd never had one with Ken, just as she hadn't with her father. The only connection to her former life was her one true friend. Tammy.

Tomorrow she would repack her car. She'd check out of this cheap motel, drive on…to somewhere. Farther away from the Circle H. From Philadelphia. But tonight, there'd be no harm, no risk, in making just one call. Blossom picked up the phone by the bed. It wouldn't matter if Ken could somehow trace it. She'd paid cash for her room, and by then she'd be gone.

A minute later she had Tammy on the line. It was so good to hear her, even when she said, "Blossom, I'm sorry. I can't talk—"

"Tammy, I just want to make sure you're all right."

Her voice rose. "I'm not all right! Ken calls me at least once a week to put on the pressure. Have I heard from you again? Have I seen you? Do I know where you are?"

"I'm sorry. I didn't mean to put you at risk."

"Well, you did. I don't blame you for running from that guy. He's crazy." Tammy's voice quavered. "I didn't think you'd call again, but I'm almost glad you did. He hired a private detective, Blossom, who tracked you as far as the place where you sold your Lexus. If he could do that, maybe he can find you wherever you are. Make this the last time you call. For both our sakes." Unable to say a word herself, Blossom was about to hang up when Tammy added, "Are you okay? The baby? Don't tell me where you are but—"

Blossom managed, "Still on the move," then disconnected the call.

Her hand shaking, she put the phone down.

Now she knew for sure. She'd lost her best friend, her last link to Philly.

What was left? Blinking back tears, she opened one of the boxes Logan had given her. It was filled to the brim with beautiful baby clothes. The labels were all well-known, high-end brands. Nicholas Hunter had started life with a killer wardrobe. Now her child could, too. It was like getting an entire layette for free.

Still trembling after her call to Tammy, Blossom laid out the one-piece suits and sleepers and little pants and tops with elephants, giraffes, puppies—and airplanes—on them. Of those, she liked the sunny yellow ones most, especially a tiny bathrobe with ducks on it.

At the bottom of the second carton, which contained slightly larger clothes, she found another, smaller box bound with white satin ribbon. Inside were what appeared to be mementos, and she almost closed it again, not wanting to intrude on another person's cherished memories. But something stopped her. The need to share a part of Logan's life?

They were birthday cards, saved by Logan or Olivia from Nick's first-, second- and third-year celebrations. She would have to send them back. Unlike the baby clothes, they weren't hers to keep.

One card had a playful pony on the front.

It was an invitation to a party for Nick's fourth birthday at the Circle H. There were more of the same, none of them sent. She guessed it was the time that Nick was so sick and the ranch road flooded, isolating them. After that, Olivia had left Logan, taking their son with her.

The date on the invitations was only a few days from now. It would be Nick's seventh birthday this year. Had Logan remembered? She hadn't heard him say a word about any upcoming plans. *I don't care much for birthday parties*, he'd said, because of his parents.

She wondered how he and Olivia handled their son's birthday now that they were divorced. They were still Nick's parents. One day of the year, at least, should belong to him. Special.

He was an innocent child, like the one she carried now.

Blossom gently closed the box. And set it aside.

She'd cut her last ties tonight to Philadelphia—or Tammy had. But instead of thinking of her or Ken, she thought now of Logan,

Sam and Nick. She'd made another mistake by leaving the Circle H. And what she was about to do was risky but...

Blossom went to bed early. Before dawn she rose and dressed, lugged her bag and the boxes out to her car, set the cartons on the backseat again, then approached the sleepy front desk clerk to check out of the motel. She bought a milk shake at the restaurant where she'd eaten dinner with the stranger last night.

Then, not seeing his truck this morning, Blossom, too, hit the road again.

She drove back the way she'd come, back to the Circle H.

CHAPTER FIFTEEN

LOGAN STOPPED AT the open barn doors. A car was speeding up the driveway. *Blossom's car.*

"Well, what do you know?" he said to Sundance.

He'd been about to saddle up. Now, with a grin, he went to greet her.

Blossom got out of the car, an expectant smile on her face. "I came back." Then, as if uncertain of her welcome, she just stood there.

Logan had never been so glad to see anyone in his life—unless he included the helicopter pilot who'd come during the flood to fly Nicky to the hospital in Kansas City. Logan had thought he'd never see Blossom again.

"You forget something?"

"No, I brought something back."

He shifted from one foot to the other. She'd gone to her car and was pulling out a box Logan recognized. "I gave you those baby clothes, Blossom. I don't want anything ba—"

"Is Jack Hancock here?"

"Not yet. Bertie's still in the hospital but has been doing a lot better. Shadow has gone through Jack's references. I don't know what to hope for—that Jack can come here or, even better, that Bertie can go home." He held his breath. "In the meantime we can use a good caregiver at the Circle H. You want your job back?"

Her face broke into a smile. "If you'll have me."

That was a loaded question. "You're looking at a desperate man."

Blossom took a step toward him, and he took the box from her arms. Her whole body appeared to relax, and she beamed a wider grin at Logan. "Thanks. I'm just in time to start lunch. How does curry sound?"

"Almost good." He could have stayed here all day just looking at her, which wasn't where his attention should be. "After lunch I've got a cow to tend to. That bison with the Cesarean before you left? She had twin calves. I need to make sure they're okay—and she is, too."

For a long moment they shared another smile, or was it the same one?

"I think you like this ranch more than you let on," she said.

He set the box down. "It's got a lot of memories, that's for sure."

"You should try to focus on the good ones."

Maybe she was right. Bringing Libby to the ranch after their wedding. Nicky's birth. Those first few years before the flood… He had some even better ones, though, since he'd met Blossom. When he framed her face in his hands, she didn't pull away.

"I kind of missed your curry." He'd missed more than that but wouldn't say so. "All I could think of was you driving west, getting farther and farther away from here."

"I didn't get that far."

Logan said, "Maybe the Circle H isn't a bad place to make a stand, if it comes to that."

Blossom eased out from under his touch. She turned toward her car again to get the second carton.

"I have something to show you."

In the house, Logan didn't expect to see, of all things, a bunch of old birthday cards. At first he didn't recognize them. Then he saw the invitation and remembered that Libby had picked it out for Nicky's fourth party, which had never happened. "We had a great time planning the event, but then the rains came and after that she and Nicky were gone. Now

I have a monster toy truck in the barn I don't know what to do with, and Libby and my son are living in Barren."

"When I found this invitation with the clothing you gave me, I wondered." She added, "Thank you, by the way. The clothes are beautiful."

"Won't be needing them again," he said with a pang of regret.

"What are you planning to do for him this year?"

"There'll be something in town, I suppose. Libby's call."

"You don't celebrate Nick's birthday together? For his sake?"

He glanced at the blue sky. "I guess he had a big do last time with his friends from kindergarten at one of those bounce-castle places. Pizza, prizes, the works."

"You should have gone."

"And been a gate crasher?"

"You weren't invited? Logan, he's your child, too. How could she leave you out?" Blossom's mouth had tightened. "I don't like her for that. She hurt you."

"Nah, I understood. Better for me to stay home than for Nicky to see us fight in front of everyone." He thought of their run-in in town before Blossom had left.

Her eyes took on a gleam he hadn't seen before.

"Well, this year is going to be different."

"How so?"

"*We're* going to throw the party. Right here at the Circle H."

"Blossom, I just told you. That's not a good idea." Neither was his urge to take her in his arms and kiss her senseless. He was leaving for Wichita as soon as he could—as soon as Sam could take over management of the ranch, if not before. Maybe Willy and Tobias—and Jack Hancock—could handle things after all. Blossom was still carrying Ken's baby, and that wouldn't change. She might feel the need to head off again. But for now...he was glad she was here.

Blossom cut off his thoughts. "The first person we'll invite is Olivia."

He almost rolled his eyes.

"I'm serious. It's time you both stopped snarling at each other."

"I don't snarl." But Libby sure had yesterday outside her new office.

"You have to make some kind of peace between you."

"I've tried to tell her that. We don't sound like good parents, do we?" Logan gazed at her. "You're going to make that baby of yours a real fine mother, Blossom."

"I am," she agreed without any hesitation. "But for now, let's work on this party. We have a lot of planning to do."

BLOSSOM CALLED OLIVIA right after lunch. Sam had given her the phone number for Logan's ex-wife, but she hadn't been prepared for the way their conversation was going.

"Excuse me? A party at the Circle H?" Olivia said again.

"We'd love for you to be here."

Another silence, longer this time.

"Olivia, please." Blossom tried to maintain a friendly tone even when her patience was dwindling. "This is important—for Nick."

"If you've become part of the household out there, then you must know I don't like Nick coming anywhere near that place."

"But he was here not long ago. We planted flowers. How dangerous was that? I understand what happened before, but that was three years ago."

Olivia's tone hardened. "It will take the rest of my life to forget being stuck at the end of the world. With Logan gone, of course. If it wasn't for Sam, I'd have been completely alone with a very sick child."

"Nick will turn seven next week. He looks healthy to me."

"Who do you think you are? I'm his *mother*. This phone call is over—"

"Olivia, wait. Nick isn't a toddler anymore. He's a little boy who needs his father, too. I'd hoped things were getting better between you and Logan."

"Logan—and you—may be planning a *party*, but he'll leave the Circle H for Wichita again any day now. I assure you, that's all he thinks about. *Flying*." Blossom knew that wasn't true. Olivia drew an audible breath. "I don't know what *your* relationship with him may be—"

"I *work* for him," Blossom said. "Nothing else."

"That's not what I hear in town—and I told him so. My ex-husband has a pretty, young woman living in that house. A woman who apparently knows very little about giving care, at least to Sam."

Blossom blinked. The only person she knew in Barren was Shadow Moran, who didn't seem like the type to gossip. If she'd been the one to spread that kind of speculation, Blossom wouldn't see her as a potential friend any longer. Or had the woman who owned the children's clothing shop been talking? She'd seemed overly curious. Or even the clerk at the pet store? The market. Blossom had encountered more people here than she'd thought.

Was Olivia really jealous?

"The gossip mill often gets everything wrong." That gave her the idea for another tack. "Maybe you should come see for yourself. I don't have time for intrigue—or romance." She paused. "I hope you'll reconsider, Olivia."

Blossom hung up and found Sam standing in the kitchen doorway.

"No good?"

"I left her to think about it. We'll see."

Sam shuffled over to a chair and sat down. "I'm awful glad to have you back." He laughed. "That party could be full of fireworks, all right. But if you can pull it off, it'll be the first time Logan's spent a birthday with Nick since the divorce."

"We'll pull it off." Blossom had even more ideas. "Since this is a working ranch with plenty of livestock, what if we give pony rides?"

"No ponies," he said. "Logan was going to buy one for Nick's fourth birthday, but by then he was living in town. Got a few gentle old horse souls here that would work just as well, if not better—ponies can be ornery— but, believe me, they'll seem too dangerous to Libby. She's kept Nick off a horse so far."

Sam had gained back a bit of strength and confidence in his abilities, and spent more of the day on his feet again. His mind also seemed better. Which, of course, would mean she'd be out of this temporary job soon, even without Jack. But she wouldn't think of that now.

"Dangerous?" She poured Sam some coffee. "Then maybe not."

"You should have been here in the flood, then you'd understand why she's so overprotective when it comes to Nick and the ranch. The water reached the house and up the porch to the front door. Seeped in underneath. All the rugs were done for. Some of the furniture, too, including the dining room chairs Libby had just bought. We had to lay all new wood on the first floor." Sam gazed out the kitchen window. "Those horses were swimming in their stalls. We lost our power for a week."

"Yet Nick survived. That's the important thing, isn't it?"

"Sure is. Thanks for trying to change Libby's mind, but I wouldn't count on that. Still…" He rose from the chair. "Think I'll go make a list. Pick out those 'ponies' for you."

He left the room, and Blossom went back to her work. She wasn't done yet with Olivia. Nick would have a perfect birthday this year—with both of his parents.

LOGAN EASED THE truck into a parking spot in front of the ag store. Today was go-to-town day again. The weekly shopping junket with Blossom was becoming a habit, one Logan wasn't sure how he felt about. Not that he spent much time examining his feelings.

He'd learned three years ago to keep a tight lid on them. If not, his sorrow and guilt over Nicky would have killed him by now. He didn't trust there'd be a repeat of Nicky's visit to the ranch to plant flowers, especially after he and Libby had argued again the last time in town.

Blossom sat close to him now, her light scent teasing his senses, as it had all the way from the Circle H into Barren. That shouldn't seem right but—

"Oh!" Blossom covered the now-visible swell of her abdomen.

Logan sent her a sharp look.

The memory of his urge to kiss her when she'd shown up at the ranch a few days ago tightened his gut again.

"The baby. Aaron kicked—a real kick," she said with the kind of smile that belonged on a Madonna.

Logan got out of the truck. "You so sure it's a boy?"

"Pretty sure."

He almost smiled. She'd already given her baby a name as she had the barn kitten. And even her car. "Has it moved before?"

"Flutters, that's all. This is amazing."

He rounded the pickup to her side. "You haven't seen a doctor."

"I've been meaning to, but then I left the Circle H and didn't think I was coming back." She lifted one eyebrow. "I guess I need to do something about that. I just haven't gotten around to it."

But there was more to it than that, and Logan could guess what it was. He opened the passenger door then handed her out. "Libby went running to Doc the minute she suspected she might be pregnant." He didn't mean to accuse Blossom of neglect, but that's how it came out. "For you, better late than never."

"You know why," she said.

"You didn't want a medical history that Ken might be able to access."

"I've tried to be careful—no caffeine, no alcohol—and except for that one horseback ride you and I took, I watch where I go and how I step."

"That was more of a slow walk than a ride," he said. "Libby rode until a few months before she had Nicky."

Blossom met his gaze head-on. "She grew up on a ranch. I'm not Olivia."

Wow. "Sorry, I didn't mean to compare."

They made their way along Main Street until Blossom suddenly stopped.

"I thought you had to go to the feed store." She looked across the street toward the market and Shadow's agency. "Where are we going now?"

Logan kept walking. "To Doc's office. He's trying to sell his practice then retire, but he still sees patients. I bet he'll have a morning slot for you today. His client list has gotten pretty small. If he doesn't, I'll convince him to find one."

Blossom hung back. "I promise, I'll see

someone—maybe in Kansas City but not here in Barren." *Too close to the Circle H if Ken came searching.*

Logan didn't listen. He steered her around the corner onto Cottonwood Street. He needed to know that she and her baby were all right. Period. He wouldn't risk having her go into premature labor at the ranch during another flood or with the drive blocked by fallen trees after a tornado. If she was staying for now, she needed a clean bill of health.

Doc's office was the third building on the street. "You've waited long enough. Isn't this…baby—Aaron—your first priority?"

"You know he is. He's why I ran from Ken in the first place."

"Ran for yourself, too, I'd hope." He opened the door to the small office, where Doc's wife, Ida, reigned at the reception desk. "I'll check you in."

As he closed the door behind them, Blossom insisted, "Since we're already here, I can check myself in." Leaving him standing in the middle of the waiting area, she marched over to the reception desk and spoke to Ida, the most opinionated woman Logan had ever met. Ida, who loved to talk, kept glancing at him with that measuring way of hers that made

Logan feel like a kid called into the principal's office. Blossom had told him about her conversation with Libby—that the town gossip mill was having a field day about him and Blossom. Surely, Ida didn't think he was the baby's father?

"You can go in now." Ida eyed him again. "You too, Logan."

"I'll stay here. I'm not—"

"Doc is ready for you."

Blossom reached for his hand. "Please. I didn't mean to snap at you. I don't want to be alone."

He took a deep breath. "Bison calves are more my style these days—not human babies." *Especially one that's not mine.* But she looked white-faced, and he had bulldozed her into coming here.

In the exam room with Logan, Doc took her history, chatting away, then told Blossom to lie flat on the table. He shot a look at Logan. "Turn your back."

Logan was all too happy to obey. He sat on a stool and studied Doc's framed diplomas on the wall while he examined Blossom. Finally, Doc stood back with a nod.

"Young and healthy. That's how I like 'em."

Yet for some reason Logan's stomach

churned. Not seeing what was going on with the physical exam had made this worse somehow. He wanted to support Blossom—this one time—the way she was trying to support him about the birthday party, and she didn't have anyone else, but getting up close and personal here made him sweat. He sensed Doc's gaze on him again.

He'd never liked these visits with Libby, who'd had a rough pregnancy with morning sickness the whole nine months, pains here and there, and then a tough delivery.

He'd started to rise from the stool in the corner when Doc said, "Everything looks fine, Blossom. And isn't that a lovely name you have?" Logan turned to see Doc pat her arm. "Stay right there. Why don't we do a sonogram today?"

"I've had one before. It was blurry. Do you think I can actually *see* him?"

He winked. "The miracle of modern medicine. Just got a new machine."

"Logan." Blossom's eyes again begged him to stay.

He felt bad for her. Ken sure wasn't here. Another thing to be thankful for, but this wasn't his place...his responsibility... Logan reminded himself he didn't want one.

He wheeled his stool over to the exam table. "Go for it," he said.

As the images showed on the screen, at first he couldn't make anything out. Blossom said the same thing. It had been that way with Nicky, too, he remembered. Then the pictures seemed to sharpen and jell into two pairs of limbs, a head, a curved spine. Blossom clutched his hand so hard it hurt.

"Oh. Look. There he is," she murmured.

There were tears in her eyes, a look of sheer wonder on her face.

Libby had looked that same way.

Logan was pretty sure he would, too, if he'd looked into a mirror.

"All the basics are where they should be." Doc moved the tool over Blossom's abdomen a few more times, as if fascinated himself by the images.

"It's a boy, right?" she asked.

"Can't tell that. There's no cooperation at the moment. The baby has the vital parts covered. Maybe next time." Doc sat back on the opposite stool. "Well. What do you think?"

"I think I'm *pregnant*!"

Doc laughed. "Right you are, young lady." He turned to a nearby cabinet. "I'm going to recommend some prenatal vitamins. It's especially important to make sure you're getting enough folic acid. I wish you'd come in sooner..." He rattled off some other directions for Blossom's care. Then, while Logan's head was still swimming, they were out on the sidewalk again. Blossom was still smiling.

"What a nice man. He didn't even charge me."

"Doc gave you the new-baby package. His fee will cover everything from today until you deliver." Which implied she'd be here that long. "But don't worry about that now."

"One-stop shopping." She raised her face to his. "I need to get my last week's pay from Shadow—I meant to before I left. I'll get that while you order the feed, or whatever you need."

When she turned, he caught her shoulder.

"Congratulations, Blossom. You're on your way."

"Yes, I am. Thank you for staying with me." She paused. "Thanks for insisting I see Doc. You were right. I didn't like him taking that history, asking about the doctor I saw in Philly. I've been worried about that."

He leaned down, and in the bright morning, in the middle of Main Street, he kissed her lightly on the mouth. "Don't," he said, as if cautioning himself instead of Blossom. "We've got this covered."

She let him hold her for a minute before she drew back. "I feel like celebrating."

"I'll buy you lunch here in town this time."

"First, we have some birthday presents to buy—for Nick." She kissed him once more then started off toward the agency. "Meet me at the truck."

CHAPTER SIXTEEN

SHE'D ACTUALLY *MET* her baby! The pregnancy hadn't seemed quite real to Blossom before, even after she'd felt those first flutters or when she sang lullabies each night, or back in Philly, where she'd had one doctor's visit before any visible signs were there, but now…

At dinner she broke the news to Willy and Tobias. If they hadn't guessed before, Sam, who had come to the table tonight, already had. And Blossom held her breath. She should have warned Logan that Sam knew before she said anything. Sam was grinning.

"High time you had another one to carry on this ranch someday. When he's grown Nick will need help." He glanced at Blossom. "A boy, you say?"

Blossom rearranged her food, peas on one side of the dish, meat on the other. "I can't be sure. Yet. I think so."

"If it's a girl instead, we'll have us a cowgirl. Been a long time since we had one here at the Circle H."

"You mean, never." Logan glanced at Blossom as if to say, *What's he talking about now?* Linking them together. "The only kids on the ranch were me and Sawyer. Boys, and we weren't babies when you came here. When you adopted us."

But Sam looked as if he had all the inside information. His gaze homed in on Blossom. "I knew the minute I saw you. Now what you need to do is—"

Blossom forced a bright tone. "Everyone ready for dessert?" She began to stack plates. "I made bread pudding tonight."

Willy tried to make eye contact with her. "My favorite."

Logan pushed back his chair.

"Sit down," Sam said. "I know what I'm talking about." He actually cackled. "You two might as well get married, that's what I say. We can have a big wedding right here on the ranch."

Their eyes wide, Willy and Tobias dropped their forks. Logan's napkin fell into the remnants of food on his plate. He rose then strode from the dining room into the kitchen.

Her heart in her throat, Blossom followed him.

Logan spun to face her. "He's gone off his rocker. Why would he think that we...and here I hoped he was getting better."

"He is, Logan." Sam hadn't confused her with Olivia since her return.

"Now those two cowhands think we've been closer than we should be."

"No, I think Sam was just matchmaking." She could hear Willy and Tobias in the dining room, laughing and making jokes with Sam. All of her good feelings from her doctor's visit vanished. So did the euphoria she'd felt when Logan kissed her on the street, as if he didn't care what other people saw or thought. "You make that sound like a crime."

"Well, it would be." He studied her, his gaze uncertain. "Wouldn't it? I mean, sure, I'm attracted to you. I guess that's obvious by now after—"

"Thank you so much." Her stomach sank. She turned on the sink faucets. "And here *I* thought this morning in town you were happy for me—"

"I am." He turned her around. "I'm happy for *you*. Blossom, if I've misled you, I apologize. I owe you another one for bossing you around about seeing Doc. But I have all I can handle with Sam—and if I don't get back to Wichita soon I can kiss my promotion good-bye. If that happens, I'll never be able to get joint custody of Nicky—at least not very soon." He hesitated before adding, "Libby will likely get an earful about…us anyway."

A fresh wave of misery ran through Blossom. "I shouldn't have come back. Olivia thinks you plan to leave right after Nick's party."

When she saw Logan flinch, she knew Olivia had been right. After all, she knew Logan better than Blossom did.

"I want my son back, Blossom. I want to be part of his life. I'm grateful to you for his birthday party but, yeah, I can't stay long after that." He rubbed his neck. "In the meantime, I need to think what to do about Sam—"

"He did guess I was pregnant. I'd just hoped before today he wouldn't say so before you knew." When he turned to leave the kitchen, Blossom said, "You know I care about him. I care about—" She almost said *you*. But clearly, Logan didn't feel the same way about her. At least he was being honest. "—this place. I'll stay until after the party, too. Then, like you, I'll be leaving. For good."

LOGAN WAS IN no mood for a party. He'd been an idiot with Blossom a few nights ago. He'd spent the past two days in the barn or on horseback riding fence—an eternal job because there were always broken wires to be fixed and, frankly, Sam could use new posts here and there—until he wondered if Barney was right. The ranch could use some renovation and, for sure, upgraded technology. For instance, the office computer was ancient and the Wi-Fi here was inadequate, adding to their isolation from the rest of the world.

Now he'd have to face Libby if she showed up today.

At least it wasn't raining.

Logan watched No-Name scamper up and down the barn aisle, chasing shafts of sun and motes of dust while Logan shined up the black truck he'd bought, and kept, for Nicky. At the house he'd left Blossom—without a word—piling presents on the dining room table. In the oven the birthday cake had been baking, filling the air with the scents of sugar and vanilla.

He had to admire her spirit; he'd hurt her by suggesting she had more feelings for him than he did for her.

He was almost done waxing the truck when

Grey arrived. Logan fought a swift urge to hide the toy. Then he saw Grey was alone.

"I thought you were bringing Nicky over."

"Change of plan."

His stomach dropped. And he'd thought Libby had finally caved after Blossom's call. "Libby won't let him come?" What kind of party would it be without the birthday boy? "Not that I'm surprised."

"Quit letting yourself down easy. He'll be here." Grey said no more, and Logan wasn't in a mood to probe any further.

"Help me roll this truck back into the tack room, will you?"

"You bet. Wait till he sees it."

"It's supposed to be his last present—the crowning touch—not the first."

"Who said?"

"Blossom. She's in charge today." Quite a difference from the uncertain woman with the haunted look in her eyes who had first come to the Circle H.

With the truck secured, he dropped down onto a hay bale in the empty aisle and Grey joined him. The horses had been turned out for the day for exercise until they were needed for the "pony" rides later.

For now, he and Grey were alone, so Logan

told him about his quarrel with Blossom. "I really messed up," he said. "She's not even speaking to me."

Grey scratched his head. "You have a real way with women. What happened?"

Logan filled him in on his grandfather, too. "She's been overprotective of Sam ever since—as if I'll snatch him from the ranch any minute. It's like I'd throw him into a cell somewhere and chuck the key just for saying the wrong thing."

Grey let out a low whistle. "And—I can't believe this—Blossom's *pregnant*?"

"I should never have hired her."

"Do you hear yourself?" Grey eyed him again. "Yep. You look to me exactly like a lovesick calf. Man, you've got it bad."

"Grey, I learned my lesson with Libby. And no matter what Sam might think, I'm not going back there. With anyone."

"Sam must see you've got a real soft spot for Blossom. He sees what's between you. Maybe you should focus on that."

Logan stared at him. "Are you kidding? I can't fall for her. Yes, she's *pregnant*—with another man's baby. That's all I need."

"Sometimes we don't get to plan—or control—things."

Logan disagreed. The attraction he felt for Blossom was one thing; a new commitment, when he'd failed so miserably with Libby, was something else. Neither he nor Blossom should be thinking about love—and why call it *that*?

He stood up. Another car was coming up the drive. He didn't recognize it, which meant the first guest must be here. He tucked in his favorite denim shirt, which Blossom had ironed nice and crisp for the party. His best jeans, too. Maybe she hadn't been that mad at him. A little boy tumbled out of the car as soon as it stopped. His mother trailed after with a wrapped present. Logan looked at Grey.

"Well, right now there is a plan. Let's get this party moving." He just hoped Nicky, the guest of honor, showed up.

OLIVIA WAS NOT what Blossom had expected.

The yard was already full of six-year-olds when Olivia finally pulled up near the back door with Nick, and Blossom breathed a sigh of relief. She and Logan might be at odds, but if his son didn't come to the party, she imagined his heart would break. He wasn't as tough as he looked.

Slim and taller than Blossom, Olivia wore a

white suit with a pastel blue-and-green scarf. Her sleek blond hair was wound into a knot at the nape of her neck. Looking as far from Blossom's image of a ranch wife as possible, probably on purpose, she walked into the kitchen. "We're here." Her tone didn't sound happy.

She'd barely said the words before Nick exploded past her then straight into Blossom's arms. "Where's my kitty?"

Blossom hugged him tight. "I think she's at the barn." She leaned back to see his face. "Happy birthday, Nick."

He glanced at his mother with a solemn expression. "Thank you."

Blossom wondered if Olivia had lectured him all the way from Barren about how to behave. Blossom kissed the top of his head.

"Why don't you go say hello to No-Name? And all your friends are waiting."

Olivia was juggling a big box wrapped in *Star Wars* paper, and she dropped it on the table into a smear of icing Blossom had been about to wipe up.

She grabbed a sponge. "Let me get that. I think I can clean this package until it's as good as new."

Olivia's smile looked rueful. "Knock yourself out, but Nick won't notice. He'll tear the paper off without even seeing it's from his favorite movies. He has his father's impatience." She gave Blossom a once-over. "You must be the caregiver."

Blossom held her gaze. "That's me."

Then Olivia surprised her again. "I apologize for that day on the phone. I'm sensitive about Logan—not that I'd take him back. Or he'd have me. As you must know, he's still bitter about our divorce." She looked around the room. "So am I. I made enough memories here to last a lifetime. I don't need any more."

"Welcome to the Circle H anyway." Blossom rinsed the sponge then took the slightly damp present into the dining room, where the table was stacked with other gifts. Gleeful childish laughter floated from the barn and yard into the house. The aroma of meat grilling permeated the kitchen.

"I'm glad they're having fun." Olivia set her purse on a chair. "Now. As long as I'm here, what can I do to help?"

LOGAN PUT DOWN the saddle he'd been about to lift onto Gumdrop's back. The little buckskin mare was the gentlest horse in the barn other than Sundance.

He couldn't believe Olivia had come.

The quick rush of pleasure didn't last before Logan mentally crossed his fingers. They'd be lucky to get through the party without a quarrel, but he was more than glad she'd brought Nicky. Glad for Blossom, too. She'd really pulled out the stops for this birthday party to make sure it was one his son wouldn't forget.

"Daddy!" Nicky ran into the barn.

Logan held out an arm to stop him. "Hey, buddy. What's our first rule here?"

Nicky's mouth turned down. "No running. It scares the horses."

Logan ruffled his light hair, which was slicked into some kind of spike in front. Olivia had dressed him up for the party in tan khakis—a color too light for horseback riding—and a white button-down shirt. The mare didn't twitch an ear.

"Gumdrop's your ride today."

All he needed was for Nicky to have another bad experience, the perfect excuse for Libby to forbid his coming to the ranch again, even with her. Logan planned to watch him like a hawk, which was too bad, really. Kids needed to let off steam, especially boys, as the horde of six-year-olds buzzing all over the yard seemed to prove. The three girls Nicky had invited were part of the pack, too. They all wore sturdy jeans, and more than a few had boots. Ranchers' kids. Nicky wore a spiffy-looking pair of what appeared to be new boat shoes or loafers.

"Can I ride now?"

"Not yet."

Nicky looked around. "Where's my kitten? Blossom said she's here."

Logan pointed at a nearby hay bale where the little cat was snoring in the sun. "Let her nap for now. You can play with her later."

"She got a lot bigger!"

"Yes, she did. She's growing—like you. But your friends are waiting, Nicky."

"Oh. I forgot."

"Excitement will do that," he said.

Nicky ran out the barn doors to join his pals. A rowdy game of hide-and-seek was under way.

Logan was saddling another "pony" when Nicky ran back inside again.

"Can we ride now?"

Apparently, the game in the yard was over. "As soon as I finish getting Ginger and Trig ready." He pulled Nicky away from Ginger's hooves then pointed him in the other direction. His son had been about to get stepped on. "Would you fetch his bridle for me from the tack room?" He'd no sooner said the words than Nicky raced off and Logan realized what he'd just done.

"Daddy! My truck!"

Logan straightened Trig's forelock. "Whoa," he said.

In the tack room doorway Nicky was trying without success to tug his pickup into the barn aisle. Logan tucked the horse back into his stall.

"Leave it. You guys can ride now then we'll try out the truck. It was supposed to be a surprise for later."

But Nicky dropped the bridle in front of him and raced out again.

"Guys! Wait till you see this!"

More than a dozen kids were suddenly in the barn swarming around the tack room with exclamations of delight. They tested the truck's horn, the lights. The horn again. Country music blared through the barn.

"It's got a real radio and everything," Nicky told them with the obvious pride of new ownership.

Dirty hands explored every inch of the truck, leaving marks on Logan's fresh wax job. He didn't care. Nicky's joy was all that mattered. But wrangling a bunch of little kids sure wasn't easy, orders of magnitude harder than Nicky alone.

Someone bumped his shoulder, and he turned around. Libby, in a white suit that would probably look brown by the end of the party, glared at him. "You didn't return that truck."

He'd meant to tell her. "Libby, he loves it. What harm can there be—"

She kept her voice low. "You, of all people, should know. I agreed to attend this party— Grey convinced me and your Blossom made me feel guilty—"

"She's not 'my' Blossom."

"—but how could you?"

"I'm his father, that's how." Or at least he was trying to learn to be a father to his son again. "I have as much right as you do to buy something for Nicky." *Here we go.*

"I'm taking him home."

"No, Libby. You're not." Logan stepped between her and the tack room. "Let him be. He's having the time of his life. It's probably the first time he's been allowed to run and raise…Cain…since I last saw him."

The children buzzed past them, around them, running off to the yard again. After their thorough inspection, the truck had lost their interest for now.

Her eyes flashed. "No wonder the judge granted me sole custody."

"Yeah, well, that's about to change."

She blinked. "You're planning to take me to court again?"

"As soon as possible." He hadn't intended to reveal that just yet, but Libby had made him see red. He'd never thought that actually happened.

"And then what? If you win, you'll take him to Wichita? How would that work, Logan? Three days here, four days there—the way we lived when you were ranching and off looking for that job? It didn't work then. It won't now. You can't be serious."

"Libby, come on."

She glanced at her watch, a dressy thing he'd never seen before with lots of gold and silver and probably a price tag to go with it. She'd done well for herself and her business in the past three years. He wanted to feel proud of her. Olivia Wilson Hunter, now Wilson again.

Libby marched toward the barn doors. "Nicholas has exactly two hours. Then, whether this party is over or not, we're going home. Before any damage is done."

"You want to talk about damage…" he began.

But she was already marching toward the house in her fancy white suit.

CHAPTER SEVENTEEN

SAM LEANED AGAINST the corral's top rail and grinned. Those kids, six at a time on horseback, were whooping and hollering until every horse in the ring had its ears laid flat. Well-trained—he'd trained most of them himself, Sawyer the rest, maybe Logan one or two—they didn't react otherwise. Logan and Willy were directing the action now, and Sam felt a twinge of envy.

Grey Wilson ambled toward him. "How's it going, Sam?"

"Couldn't have put on a better party myself." There was nothing he liked more than to see life on the Circle H again, including Blossom's coming baby.

Grey stood beside him. "Look at Nick. He's a natural."

"If he was still living here, I'd have him in junior rodeo soon."

"Yeah, well…" Grey wouldn't say any more, but he had to be relieved that his sister had gotten here, at least. "I think all the women are having a good time." Grey frowned. "I left Libby, Blossom and…Shadow in the kitchen. Ten minutes, and it was time to make my exit. It smells way too good in there. My stomach's still growling."

Sam slid him a look. "Almost time for cake and ice cream."

"Not before Libby sees to it that Nick eats the lunch Blossom prepared. Kid favorites," he said. "Hamburgers, hot dogs, fries, mac and cheese, and milk."

"No soda." Sam shook his head. "Libby doesn't allow sweets."

"Well, she's going to allow that cake today. If I have to, I'll see to that."

"Thanks, Grey. I know you had to talk her into coming—giving us the list of his friends to invite."

"Blossom helped." He put a hand on Sam's shoulder. "I know it pains you to see her and Logan at each other's throats."

"I hope to live long enough to see them acting like reasonable adults."

Grey half smiled. "My view, as well."

The group of boys and girls streaked past on horseback, big grins on their little faces. Sam gave Logan a thumbs-up, but Logan didn't respond. His mouth looked taut and he didn't seem himself.

Sam remembered the night at dinner when Logan had bolted from the table with Blossom after him. Something Sam had said troubled him, but it seemed Logan and Blossom had argued, too, because clearly they weren't talking now. Sam never knew what would come out of his mouth, but maybe he shouldn't have mentioned marriage.

What if Logan thought his mind was gone? And decided to send him away after all?

"You okay, Sam?"

"Sure. Glad to have the wind and sun on my face. After all those days in bed upstairs, and dinner on a tray every night, being outdoors is like being born again."

"I'm glad you're feeling better."

"Next step," he said, "is getting on a horse again myself."

BLOSSOM STEPPED ONTO the back porch to ring the bell. Lunch was ready. In the outdoor arena the last group of children walked their horses toward the gate. The riding part of the day was over.

The door behind her opened again, and Shadow Moran joined her, wearing a slight frown. "Those horses must be dizzy by now. Going around in circles."

"They've had fun, though. The kids."

Shadow leaned her forearms on the railing. "Remind me to hire you the next time I give a party. You thought of everything, Blossom. I love the favors and the gift bags for each child. The dining room looks so colorful."

She flushed. "I enjoyed doing it. A birthday party's not as hard for me as cooking something Logan will actually eat."

"He should eat what's put in front of him, as my father always said." Shadow shaded her eyes with one hand, watching the kids lead their mounts back into the barn under close supervision. "He's gone now, but I'll never go back to that house."

"You won't have to. Your agency is doing well, right?"

"Well enough. Oh. That reminds me." She dug into her jeans pocket. "I brought your check with me. The last one and this week's pay, too."

"Thanks." On her most recent day in town, Blossom had never reached the Mother Comfort office.

Shadow sighed. "I really shouldn't have

come today. I should have known Grey would be here, too. After all, he's Nick's uncle."

Which told Blossom that Shadow had come knowing he'd be here, all right. She remembered Shadow's last visit and those looks toward Wilson Cattle. Grey was still on her mind, and Blossom couldn't help thinking their issue wasn't just heartbreak.

"You had to come. You're a friend of the family."

Shadow held her gaze. "Your friend, too, I hope. And I'm hoping you'll stay here rather than run again—not that I blame you."

Blossom told her about her one-night escape. "I'd like to stay, but Ken wants me back—what's *his*, he'd probably say—though he wouldn't miss a day of work to find me himself. He hired a private detective. He's far too 'important' to waste his time on a mere woman who, in his opinion, is worthless."

"I hate him already." Shadow let the silence build between them for a few long moments. Then she said, "The reason I came out here to talk to you alone… Blossom, I've heard from Bertie. I hate to bring this up today with the party going on…"

"Just say it."

"Bertie's being released from the hospital

then going into rehab for a month—which no one expected. After that, he may go home. Jack Hancock is ready to fill in here, at least while Bertie's away."

The sunny day, the laughter of children, the enticing aromas of food wafting from the kitchen, all seemed to disappear. The world went white, and sounds echoed in her ears. "What did Logan say?"

"I'm telling you first this time." The kids were spilling from the barn now and tumbling as if in a giant ball toward the house.

Why feel this stunned? She'd known this would come sooner or later, the announcement she'd waited for and then dreaded, and in the end it wasn't just Ken who would send her running. It was Logan, too. They'd both said they would leave after this party. Blossom squared her shoulders then linked arms with Shadow, forcing a smile. There was no reason to make her feel bad. "Let's serve lunch. I'm glad you came. Thanks for letting me know."

They were handing out hot dogs at the table when Grey wandered in. He propped a shoulder against the door frame to the kitchen, and Shadow stiffened then hurried from the room, sweeping past him without touching. Grey looked at Blossom. "Logan will be late. He's still putting up horses."

Or was he stalling, so he wouldn't have to be around Blossom as much? Shadow wasn't the only one with an obvious conflict.

Shadow returned from another trip to the kitchen, pushing by Grey, as if she wouldn't let him chase her away, to set a platter of hamburgers on the table. The kids, chattering among themselves, had dug in to their fries and mac and cheese, and their glasses of milk were empty. "He wouldn't be late if you'd help him," she told Grey.

His mouth turned grim. "Not here, okay, Shadow?"

"I'll say whatever I please, wherever I please," she muttered.

He put a hand on her back to guide her from the dining room, where all the presents were piled on the sideboard, then shut the swinging kitchen door. But Blossom had gone ahead of them, hoping to avoid what promised to be a scene. She'd had enough of that with Logan.

"Would you two like to be alone?"

Grey leaned against the counter, his long legs crossed at the ankles. His gaze fixed on Shadow. "No, I may need a witness." His mouth thinned. "What's your problem, beautiful? You left that old postage-stamp farm years ago, but you know what? You're still there. I've told you before—I'm not the guilty one."

Blossom stuck a last candle on the cake. "I need someone to carry this." Trimmed in blue icing, with a design of a pickup truck on top, the cake stood three layers high and was Blossom's pride and joy. Ken had been wrong about her. As Shadow had pointed out, there were things she could do, and do well. She rested a hand on her stomach.

"Sorry," Grey murmured.

Shadow echoed his apology. "I wouldn't have said a word, but then I don't expect to see Grey again. I thought I should make myself clear."

Grey only said, "I'll give you a call."

Shadow didn't answer. Tight-lipped, she grabbed the carton of ice cream from the freezer then disappeared into the dining room. Blossom heard cheers.

"She's not my biggest fan," Grey said, studying his boots.

"Oh, Grey." Blossom touched his clean-shaven cheek. "You love her."

"Yep. Since I was seventeen. We used to double-date with Libby and Logan when I was in high school. You know how that turned out."

"I wish you better luck."

"I'll need it," he said, but instead of joining the festivities in the dining room, he headed for the back door, leaving Blossom to carry the cake. "I'll fetch Logan for you. He won't want to miss the candles and the birthday song."

FROM WHAT LOGAN could see, Nicky had gotten more presents than any kid he'd known. But then, most of Logan's own birthday party invites had dwindled off after his folks died. Sam hadn't given him and his brother any parties that he recalled after his grandmother passed away, but Logan hadn't cared. He stood back now from the dining room table, watching the last frenzy of gift opening.

Blossom stood next to him but a foot away.

"Olivia knew what she was talking about." Blossom seemed to address no one in particular, but then she looked at Logan. "She knew Nick would tear open his presents. You need to cut each other some slack."

"That's still your opinion, is it?"

"I'd tell her the same thing."

He looked at her. And in spite of his vow not

to get involved, his heart rolled over. Her pregnancy had given Blossom a new glow. Or was it living on the Circle H? Far away from Ken. Despite the past days of righteous silence between them, she'd looked almost happy earlier—as if Logan had anything to do with that. So what had changed that look in her eyes? Their quarrel, but something else, too. Something new that had ruined her enjoyment of the party.

Nicky held up a foam weapon he'd pulled from a blue-and-green package with dragons on it. He crowed, "Look! I got it! Just what I wanted!" He grinned at his friend. "Now we can play war."

On the other side of the table Libby blanched. She'd made it through "Happy Birthday" sung slightly off key, then ice cream and the cake Blossom had baked—complete with sparklers among the lit candles—but the adventure toy was too much. He expected her to bolt for her car at any second, as she'd promised, taking Nicky with her. Logan had no idea when he'd see his boy again.

"Relax," he said, but of course Libby didn't. Any minute now she'd put an end to this party. By the time she and Nicky got to Barren, she'd probably have scolded his son into a state of misery. And the judge thought *she* was the more fit parent? She moved to take the toy from him, but Logan tilted his head toward the front entryway. "Leave it. I need to talk to you."

With Blossom and Shadow to manage the rest of the party, he went out onto the porch. Libby stalked after him. As soon as the screen door banged shut, she crossed her arms. "Well. What?"

"Thanks for bringing Nicky today. I appreciate that."

Her eyes snapped. "But, really, Logan…all those presents in there do nothing except teach him that violence is exciting, even desirable."

"I didn't buy him that toy gun."

"What about the *truck*? How macho. I'm trying to raise a gentle, caring human being— not Rambo."

"No, you're teaching him to become a sissy. He's a boy. Little boys like stuff that goes 'pow' and 'bam.' I don't know why either, but when I was a kid—Sawyer, too—we loved the same stuff. We grew out of it."

"Did you? Do you know how many nights and days I sat out here on this ranch, *praying* you'd come home safe without getting gored by some bull? As for *flying*—planes that may or may not have mechanical faults—"

"You worried?" From his standpoint he'd never viewed his job as any riskier than a lot of other types of work. He had confidence in his skills as a pilot.

"Yes, I did. And now I pray to keep my son safe."

"Libby, he's *our* son. We don't do him any good letting him see us throttle each other every time we meet." He sounded like Blossom. He tried to take Libby's hand but she resisted. "I'd never let anything terrible happen to Nicky. I love him, too."

"I know you do…"

"Today those kids in there have had a great time. He and his friends drove around in that truck, all over the yard…they loved *that*. I don't expect you to understand—"

Libby arched a brow. "My being a girl and all."

"Yeah," he said, unable to stop a smile. "And still quite a girl at that."

Libby stiffened.

Logan shook his head. "It's your choice if you want to stay all buttoned-up, though. A white suit to come to the ranch? And Nicky in khakis. With his hair like a tepee perched on his head."

"It's the newest fashion."

"Not around Barren, Kansas. Didn't you notice? He's the only one."

She gazed past him at the front door. "The spike is better than some mullet."

"The point is, his friends don't model for some high-fashion kids' clothing line. Most of them probably see *Modern Cowboy* or *The Horseman* magazine on the coffee table at home. They're Westerners—not from New York or Chicago."

"Rough and tumble," she said.

"You grew up here. You should know." He knew she'd become unhappy at the Circle H, but now he wondered if she really liked living in Barren. "It may be okay for Shadow and Grey to argue like they do, because there's no one else involved, but it's not right for you and me."

From inside the house, he heard a roar of delight. Another goal scored with a perfect gift to Nicky. A few giggles followed then a shouted group demand for more cake.

Even Libby had to smile. "They are having fun, aren't they?"

"Yeah."

To his surprise, she reached for his hand. "I hear what you're saying."

Logan did a double take. "You what?"

"Maybe I am a bit…protective with Nick."

He lightly squeezed her hand. "He's been fine today, Libby—more than. You don't need to worry when he's here."

"I'd still rather he didn't spend that much time at the Circle H, but perhaps that's something I do need to deal with. For now, I'm grateful that today turned out well. No one got hurt. But I'll hold you to your promise. If anything else does happen—" She didn't finish.

He didn't need the warning.

Libby withdrew her hand from his. And, to his amazement, said, "When would you like to see him again?"

STANDING ON THE front porch with Logan and Sam, but with her thoughts elsewhere, Blossom watched the party guests leave. One by one, mothers and fathers had come to collect their offspring. By then every kid's impressive energy appeared to be flagging. In the backseats of cars, SUVS and pickup trucks, little heads nodded even as car horns tooted another goodbye.

She sagged against a porch post. "I think that was successful."

Sam snorted. He'd loved the party and had named himself the official gift presenter for

Nick in the dining room. "They'll be talking about this for years, Blossom."

"I'd give today an A-plus," Logan agreed. "Thanks."

"You did your part."

Blossom glanced at Sam. His eyes looked as drowsy as Nick's had been when he and Olivia said goodbye. Sam wasn't as hale and hearty as he liked to think. Which gave her the excuse she needed to go inside.

"Let me help you upstairs," she said. "Take a quick nap before dinner."

He grinned weakly. "We have to eat again?"

"I made fried chicken this morning. Crispier this time. All I have to do is reheat it and you can eat as much or as little as you like."

But before she'd turned toward the door, Sam stepped around her.

"I'll settle myself."

That left her alone with Logan. At a loss for words, Blossom stayed against the post and stared out at the now-empty driveway, at the dust that was slowly settling back onto the lane. She hadn't thought about Ken at all today—until Shadow had told her about Bertie and Jack Hancock—but she'd thought about Logan. Blossom had never liked feeling cross with anyone. She'd always rushed to apologize to her father and to Ken. Now she couldn't seem to say the words. Or maybe she didn't want to this time.

"I should start cleaning up," she said yet didn't move.

Logan propped one shoulder against the opposite post. "I'm having a hard time believing you couldn't please Ken. You say you never did anything right, but Nicky's party was perfect, Blossom. I said thanks but I really can't thank you enough."

Her next words were knee-jerk. "I live to serve."

He unfolded his long frame from the post. "Don't talk about yourself like that. Since you've been at the Circle H, you've, well, 'blossomed.' You've become friends with Shadow and Grey—when they're sure not friends with each other—and you've managed to put up with me."

"It's not that hard." With the ice between them cracked, she went on. "Giving Nick the party was easy. Do you know what he said to me? I was taking the sparklers off the last of his cake when he came into the kitchen. He thanked me, too—I imagine, in part because Libby told him to—but then he thanked me for the kitten."

"No-Name."

Blossom smiled. "Nick said that isn't any kind of name for his kitten."

"What would he choose?"

"You won't believe this." She waited a beat before saying, "Blossom."

Logan grinned. "What did you say?"

"That there was already one flower on this ranch." Her eyes blurred. "Two would be confusing."

"And then he said?"

"He can tell a cat from a girl."

They both laughed. Blossom watched his eyes warm, the glow turning into heat. "He really likes you."

"I like him, too." She forced herself to straighten. "I'm going in. I have at least three loads of dishes to do."

"I'll help." He held the door open for her, then, before she could step through, let it close again. "No, I need to do more than help. I need to say I'm sorry. I shouldn't have gone after you like that…in town, then here." He gestured at her stomach. "I feel better since you've seen Doc and started those vitamins. I didn't mean to sound harsh about you…and me, but—"

"All you can do, Logan, is try to minimize the risks. Every risk."

He frowned. "I wish that worked for a natural disaster."

"A flood?"

"Or tornado. Or…" He didn't go on.

Blossom waved at the still-clear blue overhead. "Look at that sky. Do you see rain coming? A funnel cloud? I don't."

"Not today," he said, but they weren't talking about the weather. "In any event, I can't be here much longer. Joe's pretty hopped up about me staying this long. And Sam seemed…okay today. I *have* to get to Wichita. Seems like one of us is always planning to leave."

"About that," she said. "Did you talk to Shadow?"

"No." He lifted a stray curl from her cheek, tucked it back behind her ear.

Shadow had left the announcement to her. "Jack Hancock will be taking over here. I know you think that's better for Sam." She explained about Bertie's rehab. "So I'll be on my way, as we decided."

She couldn't read the expression in Logan's eyes. Relieved? No. Not happy either, but he didn't say a word. For a long moment, his hand stayed on the too-warm skin just beneath her ear. "Blossom. There's no hurry. Remember when you came back before—and I said I'd missed your curry?"

She smiled, a soft smile as if they'd spend the rest of their lives making such memories together. "Hard to believe."

Logan leaned closer. His lips brushed her ear then moved lower along her cheek to the line of her jaw, where his hand still lingered. As their mouths met at last, and she sank into him, she could feel the mound of her baby between them. "What I should have said, what I meant to say is—" With the words his lips moved against hers. A wave of tenderness, of need, washed through her, and maybe him, too, deep inside, like the sea coming to the shore. "I really missed you."

CHAPTER EIGHTEEN

JACK HANCOCK MOVED in two days later, not quite to Logan's relief. By the second night, Jack had taken full command of the Circle H kitchen. At dinner Willy stared down at his plate.

"It's *boeuf bourguignon*." Standing behind him at the table, Jack—or rather, as he preferred to be called, *Jacques*—looked down his nose and sniffed. "The French are master chefs."

"I can't even pronounce what I'm eating," Willy grumbled.

"I trained at the Cordon Bleu. With the very best," Jacques said.

"I don't know *parlez-vous Francais* from bull—"

"Willy." Logan fought a grin. Blossom's gaze had fixed on the Remington-style painting on the far wall. Tobias didn't seem to care about what had already become their nightly ritual. He'd filled his plate then began to eat

what she would have called plain beef stew.
No more. Logan covered his mouth with his
napkin. *Be careful what you wish for.*

As soon as Jacques had come to the ranch—
borne on a wave of praise from Shadow and
half a dozen references headed by Bertie
O'Neill's—he'd declared that the hired hands
would no longer eat any of their meals in the
bunkhouse. Devouring franks and beans or
canned spaghetti as they had before, Willy
and Tobias couldn't possibly have enough
energy to do their hard work on the ranch,
according to Jacques. So now they were "dining" in the main house every night—and none
too happy about it.

Willy pushed carrots and potatoes around.
"What's this white stuff?"

"Leeks. Some fennel. Pearl onions. A garni
of—"

Willy pushed back his chair. "Look here,
Jack. I eat regular food. I'm going right now
to open me a can."

"You are ruining your stomach, William."

"Yeah, well, it's my belly."

Blossom shot Logan a look. "Willy," she
said, half rising from her chair. "Sam loved
this casserole—and Jacques has been cooking all day."

Relieved that she was still here, Logan stepped in. "You're out of luck at the bunkhouse. Jacques already tossed all the cans."

Willy gaped at him. "My bags of Cheetos, too?"

"Everything," Jacques said. "Their nutritional content is *rien*."

Willy didn't blink. He'd quickly learned, like everyone else, the few words of French that seemed essential to communicate with Jacques. With a groan, he sank back into his chair then tugged at the collar of his Sunday go-to-church shirt with the pearl buttons. "Nothing? If I wasn't so hungry..."

Jacques sniffed again. He'd made it plain he considered the cowhands to be more than common.

Logan picked up his fork. The first bite sang along his taste buds. "Really good, Jacques. Another great meal." If he kept eating at this rate, he was going to weigh more than Cyclone.

Jacques disappeared into the kitchen as if he were part of some royal procession, the guy with the crown on his head.

"Weirdo," Willy muttered.

Logan sighed. "Shadow warned me the guy was different—though she barely mentioned the French thing." Jacques might have gone to some fancy French cooking school, but the Circle H didn't need that or the snooty attitude.

Tall and reed-thin, Jacques never appeared without his "uniform," a pair of black pants, a white tunic and the kind of shiny patent leather shoes normally worn with a tuxedo—which Logan had sported exactly once in his life, when he married Libby. He'd been meaning to call Bertie. It didn't seem likely Jacques had been so formal there. Maybe he viewed the ranch as some kind of vast estate and this job as an upgrade position and wanted to look the part.

"He's funny." Blossom smiled.

"I notice he keeps you moving."

He squirmed in his seat. The sooner Jacques got used to the ranch routine, the quicker Blossom was going to take her packed suitcase and leave. In fact, she'd probably never unpacked and was still ready to go at a moment's notice. Which had been her plan all along, just like his return to Wichita. Why feel so unhappy about that now?

He didn't quite appreciate it when Blossom tried to put a good spin on things. "At least with him here I'll have time to plant more flowers before I go."

Willy glanced up. "Bet old Jacques is a genu-ine horti—hortic—"

Logan said, "Horticulturist."

"Yeah, that."

But all Blossom said was "He does seem to be very good at everything."

AN HOUR BEFORE lunch the next day, the whole house sparkled. Blossom trotted along behind Jacques Hancock. Maybe the better decision would have been to leave the Circle H before her replacement moved in—as she'd tried to do once.

Already, three days after he'd turned up at the front door with his Louis Vuitton bag in hand, Blossom had become his assistant in the kitchen, just as her mother had been her father's second in command. But then, the faster Jacques adapted here, the sooner Blossom would be unneeded and could leave.

Jacques might be an odd person—as Willy and Tobias kept saying in more colorful terms—but he'd quickly picked up on the household routine.

In the upstairs hallway Jacques paused, holding the latest pile of Sam's sheets, which he insisted on changing each day. "I am grateful to you. I did not know about making these hospital corners. So neat and tight and much harder for Monsieur Sam to pull out from the mattress each night."

"My father taught me," Blossom admitted.

"The laundry—sorting, pretreating stains was his doing *aussi*? Separating the whites from the colored clothes?"

"No, my mother's."

"You are too modest. These details make all the difference."

"I'm being truthful. They trained *me*—not in the happiest way but—" She wouldn't mention Ken, who'd taken her parents' strict regimen to the extreme.

"Blossom, be proud of yourself. These are your accomplishments now. You must own them, and not take them lightly." He paused. "You are more skillful than you know. There is not a dirty piece of clothing in this house," Jacques said with satisfaction. "The furniture has been polished until it gleams. The windows shine."

"That took two of us."

He frowned. "I believe a chimney sweep will be needed for the living room fireplace— such a buildup of creosote is a fire hazard—but for now, we are done. You must believe me."

"Thank you, Jacques. I appreciate your vote of confidence."

"Confidence is exactly what you need."

Flushing, she swiped at her chinos. They had a hole over one knee. Work clothes, she thought. She didn't need anything more stylish. And her loose pants and flowing poet's shirt were practical, if too tight these days.

As if he sensed her discomfort at being praised, he brushed at the front of his spotless white tunic, which he seemed to wear day and night until Blossom wondered if he slept in it or had a dozen such outfits.

The Circle H had certainly gotten fancied up the minute he arrived.

"Now. It is time for today's cooking lesson. This is where I will contribute most." Blossom didn't think she'd need new recipes. She wasn't likely to be a caregiver again, or a cook. But she trailed Jacques down to the laundry room to deposit the sheets then up into the kitchen. "We will have *croque monsieur* for lunch."

"Isn't that like a ham and grilled cheese sandwich? A panini?" she asked.

He kissed the tips of his fingers. "A taste of paradise. You will learn."

Blossom could hardly keep up with Jacques. He whizzed from pantry cupboard to stove then back again for another ingredient.

"You may slice this *fromage*," he told her, handing Blossom a knife and a block of Swiss cheese. "Very thin, if you please. No, much thinner," he said after she'd made a first attempt. Then suddenly, he stopped swirling butter around in what he called a sauté pan. "You are a good student—but I have been meaning to ask about those cowboys. How do you tolerate such ruffians? I regret my inclination to feed them. I do not like William."

"I don't trust him," Blossom admitted. Her dinner with the truck driver at the motel had made her less fearful of opening up to someone she didn't know well, and a moment later, while carefully slicing cheese, she found herself telling Jacques about the night in the barn when Willy had cornered her.

Jacques scowled. "He is a Neanderthal. Have you told Monsieur Hunter?"

"No, and don't you tell him either, Jacques. It was nothing. Really."

Soon, it wouldn't matter. Blossom had made her decision. She was leaving tomorrow, this time for good.

"THEY'RE AT IT AGAIN."

Sam's voice snapped Logan's attention from

the ledgers on the desk to his grandfather in the office doorway.

"Who's at it?" He'd been drowning in a fresh stack of bills. Wichita seemed as far away right now as Paris. He'd be lucky to ever leave this place. And once Blossom was gone...

"Willy. Tobias. Jacques," Sam said, leaning heavily against the door frame.

"How would you know?"

Sam's chin jutted out. "I took my evening walk. Only a deaf man wouldn't hear the ruckus coming from that bunkhouse."

Logan blew out a breath. "Just what I need." A fight.

"Sounded to me like someone was trying to kill somebody."

He threw his pen down on the desktop. "Your evening stroll?"

"Walk, I said."

"Sam, you're supposed to stay in the house."

Ever since Jacques had come, and it looked as if Blossom would leave any minute, his grandfather had been out of bed more than he was in it, as if to make sure he was up when she left.

"I feel good," he said.

"Maybe, but you shouldn't stress that

strained ligament. You'll undo any progress you've made—again. Walking around inside the house is okay. That's been a gradual way to regain your strength. But the path to the barn isn't level in places. What if you fell?"

"I didn't. I did fine during the birthday party. But those three out there—"

Logan pushed back his chair. "All right. Let me see what I can do."

"I can help," Sam said, already turning back into the hall.

"No, you can't. For just once, will you do what I tell you?"

Blossom had managed Sam with far less effort. Now he was halfway to the back door.

"Treat a man like an invalid—with no worth left at all, no dignity—that's what he'll become. Useless. I won't be a shell of myself, Flyboy. You wouldn't like being in my position either."

"No, I wouldn't." He'd come close the night of the flood. "But let me handle this, okay?"

"Another bout of helplessness on the way," Sam muttered.

Still, he did what Logan had asked. In the kitchen doorway he grumbled to himself until Logan wished Blossom was in the room to restrain him. Logan went out and made a bee-line for the bunkhouse.

The fresh air cleared his head. It wasn't a bad night. No rain today, and in the blue-black sky a few stars had begun to pop out. Later, there'd be millions of them like a carpet for the heavens. And wasn't he the poet laureate of the Circle H tonight?

Halfway to the bunkhouse he heard the shouts.

"Frenchy, my…patoot!" Willy's familiar voice must have carried all the way to the house. Logan said a quick prayer that Sam wouldn't decide to join him after all. "I've had enough of your highfalutin ways. I won't eat another bite of some fancy concoction like that lamb stuff—"

Jacques cut him off. "*Mon dieu.* You seemed to eat your dinner tonight."

"Guess I'm just a polite cuss."

"You had three helpings, William."

"Well, I'm done." Logan heard boots stomping across the bunkhouse floor. "Don't you ever use that high-toned language with me again."

"*Incroyable.*" Jacques banged a pot down, probably on the old iron cookstove. "After all

I have done for you…no more stew in a can…
you should be grateful—"

"Oh, yeah. I just love having my denim
shirts starched, too." Jacques had taken over
the cowhands' laundry. "My everyday boots
polished until they look like mirrors—before
the manure gets on 'em again, did you ever
think of that? This isn't a Saturday night dance
here, *Jacques*. It's a working ranch. I'm a working cowboy."

"Uncouth," Logan heard Jacques murmur.

"Yeah? Well, my mother didn't raise no
fancy pants. I'm proud of it."

"That is obvious. You practically frightened
Miss Blossom off with such crude manners—
in the barn, too."

"What?"

A different voice piped up. "Darn straight."

"Tobias, this is between me and…" Logan
could almost hear the familiar sniff from
Jacques. "…William," he finished.

Another object of some kind hit the bunkhouse floor with a thud.

"There. That's what *I* think of your prissy
ways. Take that."

"Mademoiselle Blossom did not welcome
your 'attentions'!"

Logan's gut tightened.

"How did you know—?" Willy's voice rose with every word.

"He wasn't even here then," Tobias put in.

"I heard it from Miss Blossom herself. While we were cooking. She told me how you cornered her in the tack room one night."

"Why would she bring that up?"

"So you admit it."

"She's a good-looking woman. I'm something of a ladies' man—"

"You are a worthless cur!"

Logan's eyebrows flew upward. He had his hand on the bunkhouse door latch when the door suddenly crashed open. In a ball of rage, Willy, Tobias and Jacques tumbled out into the darkness, past Logan.

They knocked him off the short stoop, but none of them paid any attention to him. In the yard they became a knot of angry bodies, fists flying, their grunts and the sounds of flesh against bone filling the air. He couldn't tell who was punching whom.

Logan waded into the fray. "Cut it out! Now!" He hauled Willy then Tobias off Jacques. Logan waved toward the nearest tree. "Over there, both of you! Stay put." He leaned down to help Jacques to his feet.

"*Merci*, Monsieur Hunter."

"Don't *merci* me. Who started this?"

"As if he doesn't know," Willy muttered.

"*You* attacked me!" Jacques drew himself up to his full height. Blood trickled from his nose, which Logan could see even in the dark, then down his chin to drip onto his chef's tunic. "You are an evil dog, William. Don't touch me again. Do you hear? *Jamais!*"

Willy sank down by the tree trunk. He rubbed his jaw. He had a rapidly blackening eye. "What does that mean?"

"Never." Logan had picked up quite a bit of fractured French in the short time Jacques had been here. It got more frequent whenever he was upset, which seemed to be half the time. Logan shot a look at Tobias, who was cradling his arm against his side. "You in one piece?"

"I think my wing's broken."

Logan shook his head. "I ought to fire the three of you. Willy, what was that Jacques said about you and Blossom?"

"I didn't touch her," Willy said.

"Well, that's one for you." He took a breath. "But if I hear a whisper about you shoving yourself at her, I'll—"

"She gave me that come-on look, boss. The same one you give her—"

Logan stomped over to him. He balled his fist. "Shut your mouth, Willy."

"Yeah? Or you'll shut it for me?"

He pulled him to his feet. "Go inside. Put some ice on that eye—and don't let me see you again tonight."

"How 'bout I just take off, then?"

Logan ignored him. He knelt to examine Tobias's arm. "I don't think it's broken, but we'd better get you to the doctor in the morning. Too bad the clinic's not open now. At the least, you'll probably be in a sling." He rose with a look of disgust. "A fine lot you are. Fighting like a bunch of schoolyard bullies. Willy, I expect you to check the herd first thing tomorrow—no matter how that eye feels. I don't want to hear Blossom's name from you again, understand? Keep away from her. I'll take care of Tobias."

Tobias grunted. "I'm tougher than this arm, boss."

"That's what you think." His face glowed oyster white in the dark. Logan turned toward Jacques, who had dropped down onto the bunkhouse stoop and was examining himself by the light from inside. "What's your damage?"

"I believe I will be...*bien. Demain.*"

"That so?" He had a big bruise on one cheek and a split lip.

"Oui. Vraiment."

At that moment, Sam called out from the kitchen door. Blossom stood right behind him, apparently drawn by the commotion. "Logan?" they both said.

"Don't come out here. Everything's under control."

Or was that, as Blossom had said, only an illusion? Willy skirted past Jacques, then limped into the bunkhouse with Tobias beside him, holding his injured arm. The door slammed shut behind them.

Logan looked at Jacques. "If I were you, *Jack*, I'd sleep in the house tonight. I wouldn't stay out here with them." If they started up again, he would fire them all.

Jacques lumbered to his feet. "I will not stay in the house or anywhere else. I cannot work with those…animals. I quit."

CHAPTER NINETEEN

LATER THAT NIGHT Blossom sat with Logan on the front porch glider, the stars overhead in full display. The glider creaked a little, and she burrowed deeper into the too-big sweatshirt she'd borrowed from Logan. The spring temperatures were still cool, especially at night.

"Do you know what Jacques said to me before he left? He told me, basically, that I'm a more competent person than I give myself credit for."

"Jacques was right."

"Being here *has* helped. So have you."

What if she didn't have to leave? As she should have done much sooner, she finally told Logan about her call to Tammy the night she'd met the stranger. Had she only put herself in greater danger then?

"I've been thinking ever since about that—and Ken."

"Don't," he said but Blossom went on.

"At first, he seemed like the perfect guy, so

different from my father." She gazed up at the stars. "But then he turned from Prince Charming into a—I don't know how to say this—a worse man than the one I grew up with."

"I *didn't* help matters that first day or so," Logan insisted.

Blossom shook her head. "You just tried to keep me from getting hurt by the bison calf, tossed against a tree like Sam."

"Yeah, and what about the time I all but forced you to go to Doc's office?" he pointed out.

But Blossom had stopped listening. She'd felt a stronger kick against her palm. Logan must have noticed and covered the back of her hand with his.

"Wow," he murmured, pushing the glider a little with one foot.

"He's getting stronger."

He smiled in the darkness. "She's going to be a barrel racer for sure. With legs like that, she has to be. I'm thinking Ginger for her first horse—"

"That's a nice idea." Blossom pressed her lips tight. She had no business spinning fantasies, or dreams, about the baby, girl or boy. About Logan.

For a few more moments, she sat there anyway, feeling the warmth of his solid shoulder against her more delicate one—the shoulder Ken had slammed into a wall one night not that long ago—before she put distance between them.

All at once the remembered feel of Logan's mouth on hers and the way he'd said *I really missed you* was replaced by another thought of Ken.

"Tammy told me Ken hired a private detective who found that man who bought my Lexus—the first car I sold after I left."

"Could he find the others?" Farther west, closer to the Circle H.

"I traded with people who didn't care about transferring a title—if they even had one in the first place. I always paid cash, but—"

Logan stroked her cheek. "Then I can't imagine how he—how anyone—could track you here. Barren's a small town, Blossom. There's no reason to even drive through—"

"Ken has his ways. I guess I should have changed my name. Gotten contacts—green instead of brown eyes. Dyed my hair. But at first, I thought if I could get far enough away, he'd never find me."

Logan drew one of her curls through his fingers. "I like your hair the way it is."

A rush of heat streaked through her, but Blossom moved away from his touch. "You have enough to worry about with Nick. Libby's already suspicious about…us, and I wouldn't do anything to jeopardize your custody suit. That's what matters."

"I never know what she'll come up with next."

"Then you have to be extra careful. So do I."

"Blossom, what are you going to do after your baby comes? You can leave now, if you've decided you have to, but later on?"

"That's what Shadow asked me."

"A child changes everything. From the second I first saw Nicky, I became a father above everything else. It will be the same for you."

Logan leaned closer. In the distance a horse whinnied. A spring frog chirped near the pond. "Once the baby is born, you won't have the freedom to run—if that's even the word for it. You'll have to stay where you are, wherever that is, and in doing so, alone, you'll be risking your child's well-being and safety."

"Shadow said that, too."

He sat back. For a while longer, they studied the stars. "Doesn't really change anything right now, does it? For you and me."

"Change what?" Blossom asked, although she already knew.

She thought he whispered *this*, then he moved closer again and his mouth was on hers. His kiss was sweet, and all too brief, before he eased back to set the glider moving. "I think you should stay, Blossom. If Ken or that private eye does find you here, we'll take care of it."

"You bet we will." Neither of them had heard Sam at the screen door. His voice startled Blossom and Logan, shattering their brief romantic interlude.

"How long have you been standing there?" Logan asked.

"Long enough to see the way of things." With a satisfied smile, he turned back into the lighted house, and Logan shook his head.

Blossom had another dream in her mind. What if she and Logan could make a new, far better life together—one in which Ken would have no part? Then she and her baby would be safe. But could she take that risk? Stop running?

BLOSSOM COULDN'T GET to sleep. Well after midnight, hours after she and Logan had sat on the porch glider, quietly talking, then sharing more kisses after Sam had suddenly appeared then left, she lay staring at the white globe of the ceiling light in her room.

Tammy had given her a warning she couldn't ignore. Blossom had initially put her in danger, which was cowardly. The problem was hers, not her friend's. And Jacques had made her see how much she'd changed, how capable she had become. Maybe she wasn't the best cook in the world, and never would be, but she knew how to do other things and do them well. With Ken's impossible standards, she'd never been able to measure up. Maybe her own were enough.

Logan's earlier words echoed inside her head. *The Circle H isn't a bad place to make a stand, if it comes to that.* And now tonight, *We'll take care of it.*

Yet the first step was up to her.

In the darkness Blossom flung aside the covers, got out of bed and fumbled her way to the door. Being careful not to make a sound as she crept out of her room across from Logan's, she tiptoed down the hall to the steps. Breathing a little easier because she hadn't wakened anyone, she went through the living room, along the downstairs hall and into

Sam's office, which was where Logan managed the books now.

She sat in the worn leather desk chair and considered using the aged computer, but Logan had logged in for her before and she didn't know the password, and she wanted this connection to be more direct, more human. From her, and her alone.

Logan had left his cell lying on the desk. For another second she hesitated, her hand hovering just above the phone. It must also have a passcode, and if she guessed at too many combinations of numbers, the security measures would lock out Logan, too. If, instead, she was successful, she'd only be leading Ken to Logan.

Blossom reached for the landline phone on the other side of the computer. And, with a quick prayer for courage, she made two calls.

The first was to Ken. At one time she'd wanted to forget his number. Now, within seconds, she'd reached him—or rather, his answering machine. For an instant Blossom froze. She could hang up, try his cell, but this would do. Her hand shook, and so did her voice when she tested it before the beep sounded to record her message.

Blossom took a deep breath to steady it.

"Kenneth, it's me." Deliberately, she'd used his full name. "Don't ever bother Tammy again. No matter what you do, I'm staying right where I am. I'm outside of Barren, Kansas. Have a nice…life."

Blossom waited another second then hung up. She put the old phone—probably a first-generation cordless—back in its charging cradle then lifted it again.

Tammy didn't answer, but it was the middle of the night, so she left that message, too.

"Don't be afraid," Blossom said. "This is just to let you know I'm okay and so are you. Ken won't contact you again. I've told him where I am. I need to deal with him myself, Tammy. I understand why you don't want to hear from me again, but…thank you for being such a good friend."

With one hand on the silent phone as if to touch the woman who had been her only connection to her former life, she sat there until a slow smile began to form.

She'd done it. Taken that first step.

Until she faced Ken, she would never be free.

CHAPTER TWENTY

LOGAN HELD HIS breath while Libby lectured him. To his amazement, after their talk at the birthday party, she'd actually brought Nicky to the Circle H again, though now she was clearly having second thoughts.

The quiet time he'd spent with Blossom on the porch still made Logan smile. The past three years had been hard ones, and that night he'd felt like a new man again. Didn't he deserve some happiness?

"Nothing will happen, Libby. You were a reasonable person last time." And she'd almost seemed to enjoy the birthday party. "I promised him a picnic and I don't want to disappoint him, certainly not for some lame excuse that he might hurt himself."

"It's this *ranch*—it's just full of potential for tragedy."

You don't see any rain, do you? Any funnel clouds?

"Nicky can ride with me. He did fine in the arena with the other kids—"

"That's different from being outdoors on some trail."

"It's not far." He paused. "You and I used to go down by the pond, beside the willows there."

Her tone hardened. "Sounds harmless, doesn't it?"

Logan held her gaze. "Remember, I asked you to marry me there."

She arched an eyebrow. "You even got down on one knee. But *harmless*? I said yes because I was young. Foolish." She didn't mention love. Despite her words he could hear the slight give in her tone as if she'd run out of energy to quarrel with him.

"Libby, you did a good thing in letting Nicky come for the party."

"Because I was here, too. Keeping an eye on him."

"Now he wants to be with me for the day."

"And Blossom," she added.

He stared at her. "You're really jealous."

"Maybe. A little, but not for the reason you think. And Nick does seem to adore her."

"Then why are you so reluctant to leave

Nicky with us on his own?" Logan had never been able to figure her out.

She looked down at the ground between them. "Because, if you must know, whenever he's away from me, I remember that I almost lost him once." Her voice thickened. "I feel like I've lost him all over again."

He rubbed the nape of his neck. "Aw, Libby."

"True. So now you know."

To his relief, she finally gestured toward her car and Nicky clambered out. She kissed him goodbye with a big hug then said a few words in his ear, of warning, Logan supposed, before she drove off.

Logan turned to Nicky, but with only a quick "Hi, Daddy," as he passed by, he ran toward the barn.

Logan stopped him. "That kitten isn't coming with us," he said. "She'd only get lost in the grass or run into trouble with the bison. She has to stay here, buddy."

Nicky's jaw set. "She wants to come."

"Sorry, those are my terms."

As if he hadn't heard, Nicky headed for the barn again. And Blossom appeared on the back porch with a wooden picnic basket. Logan recognized it as the one his mother and grandmother had used when he was still a boy—before he'd lost them. Today he'd show Nicky and Blossom the kind of relaxed, peaceful afternoon that had been missing from all their lives.

She came down the steps then glanced at Libby's retreating car.

"Where's the fire?"

"Anywhere Libby goes." He was about to say something more when Nicky raced back from the barn with the kitten galloping behind. In his boots, he clumped to a stop in front of her.

"Blossom! Hi!"

She handed Logan the basket then hugged Nicky. "Hi, little cowboy."

"Uncle Grey calls me that, too. Daddy says we can have a picnic. We can ride there." Wearing jeans, a checked shirt and a straw cowboy hat, he planted both hands on his hips, glanced at the kitten then tried again. "Can we take Blossom? The two Blossoms?"

"Not today," Logan said. "We need to travel light, and if we don't get started, your mom will be back to get you before we do."

Nicky scowled. "She never lets me stay long. Can I come again?"

"I hope so."

"All you have to do is make her." Nicky's world was still a simple one.

Logan looked at Blossom. "Try that."

She took Nicky's hand. "While your dad gets the horses ready, let's go see if there are any of those oatmeal cookies left that I baked this morning."

"Yay! I love them!"

Off they went, the kitten scampering to keep up with them.

Logan was on his way back from the stables, almost to the house, when Sam came out. He had a cowboy hat clamped on his head and a worn roping-heeled boot on the leg without the cast.

"Seriously?" Logan said.

"I'm going with you."

This picnic wasn't starting out well. "There's no way I'm letting you get on a horse." Blossom either, he decided. "You know what happened the last time."

"I can drive the Gator."

Logan groaned aloud. The Circle H had recently invested in a pair of the vehicles that many ranchers now used with their herds, saving horses and manpower and covering vast amounts of uneven terrain in far less time than on horseback, but if Sam had ever actually driven one, Logan didn't know about it.

"Who says?"

"I've been driving since I was fourteen years old. You think I can't handle a simple machine like that? It's as easy as Nick's toy truck—and he's like a professional race-car driver in that thing."

"Not if his mother has anything to say about it." The truck permanently resided at the Circle H, so Nicky's opportunities to make use of it were limited.

Sam blithely ignored that. "Well, she's not here. Willy and Tobias could tell you, I'll be safe as a baby in church." Sam clumped across the yard. "Are we going to get moving before lunchtime turns into supper?"

FEELING MORE ALIVE than he had in weeks, Sam settled into the Gator's passenger seat. He laid his hat beside him, baring his face to the warm spring sun. And smiled to himself. At the last minute Nick had been torn between riding with Logan or with Sam, but Logan had settled that, too.

"Blossom isn't riding today. She'd taken one chance with her pregnancy the last time,"

Logan had said. "You get Gumdrop again, Nicky. She can go with Sam."

Blossom had glanced at Sam's leg cast. "I'll drive."

He finally had to admit that was easier than him trying with his bum leg.

Now she and Sam were bringing up the rear with a couple of the border collies behind them. As they set off, he watched the backsides of the two horses sway in time with their easy gait. He liked the way Nick looked, leg to leg with Logan, who rode next to him.

The divorce had torn his adopted family apart, but seeing this sight gladdened Sam's heart.

Nick already sat atop Gumdrop like a real horseman. And he shouldn't fret. Blossom and Logan seemed to be getting on together better than they had at first. Much better, which he'd seen for himself that night on the porch.

The ride to the pond took just long enough for the clean air to double Sam's appetite. By the time Blossom braked near the water, he was grinning.

The cast on his leg would come off soon. He could bear more weight now on his other foot, and he no longer needed crutches part of the time. Soon, he'd be on a horse. Running the

Circle H. Still living in the house he'd come to with Muriel years ago—the ranch where he'd finally found his place in this world. And if Blossom stayed, maybe Logan would, too, and this would still be Sam's home.

Mission accomplished? He could only hope.

LYING ON HIS BACK, Logan settled his hat over his eyes, arms laced across his full stomach. Blossom had outdone herself today, and he had to admit that she'd learned how to cook pretty well—not from Jacques but through trial and error with the things he liked. Last night she'd produced a good steak at last, done just right, which to Logan meant rare. Today, there'd been cowboy beans, thick ham sandwiches and creamy potato salad.

"Good lunch, Blossom."

On her knees beside him on the picnic blanket, she didn't respond. And his gut tightened. The past days had seemed idyllic, including this notion to take a break for the picnic, but now and then he caught a worried, uncertain look in her eyes again. When Logan peeked out from under the brim of his Stetson, he saw her watching a cloud on the horizon.

"What is that?" she asked.

"The herd. Probably grazing somewhere

closer to Grey's ranch. They cover a lot of ground, more than cattle do."

"I don't see much fence." They had left that behind. "They roam free here?"

He smiled. "Yeah, within certain boundaries." He gestured. "Over there is federal land. It backs up to the Circle H at this point and we have grazing rights. No fence there but they're not exactly free."

"Maybe they'd rather walk into Barren now and then."

He smiled. "I guess they might. But that won't happen." He raised himself up on one elbow to study her face. The new glow of health, the radiance in her skin made him feel even happier than he'd been before. "You worried about their not-so-solitary confinement?"

"No," she said. "Are you teasing me again?"

"Yep." He wanted to lighten that look in her eyes and reached out to touch a russet curl, then wound the silk around his finger.

Sam had wandered off toward the pond. A short distance away, Nicky was chasing butterflies, or more accurately, scaring them. The net he carried swooped in on another victim but missed.

"He's having a great time," Blossom said.

"So am I." He drew her closer. "How about you?"

"It feels good to be outdoors." Her tone seemed to say more than that.

"Nicky ate three of those quartered sandwiches you made for him. He finished all his potato salad."

"I'm glad Sam could come with us. He must miss seeing his land like this, being in charge of the Circle H."

"Not his land." Logan watched sunlight play over the red in Blossom's hair. "The ranch mostly belongs to me—and Sawyer."

"There's nothing for Sam?"

"A third portion my grandmother left him, but we hold the majority stake." He couldn't quite meet her eyes. "Sooner or later, the two of us will have to make some decision. I'm happier flying, and Sawyer—who knows what he's doing, except that he's no longer here and doesn't want to be. Sam's not getting any younger. His accident—both of them— only helped to prove that. What if he was here alone and something else happened? Years ago he'd never have risked doing what he did, getting between that cow and her calf. Or having his leg stuck in that stirrup."

"The same calf that knocked you down in the corral."

"Ouch." He winced. "At least I didn't end up in a leg cast."

"Sam's doing fine now."

He had to admit his grandfather had ridden in the Gator without incident, and as far as Logan could tell, his mind seemed clear as glass. Having abandoned the pond, he was limping across the tender green grass to reach Nicky. "Bet he'll be relieved just to get rid of that cast," Logan agreed.

"I wouldn't write him off. He may have years ahead of managing the Circle H."

He tilted his head. "And what about you, Mademoiselle Blossom?"

She raised her face to the sun. "I'm having an absolutely perfect day. That's all I want to care about." Blossom hesitated. "When I left before—when I came back for Nick's birthday party, I felt like…I was coming home."

"For as long as you want." Logan released the curl he'd been twining around his finger. Did she know how much she'd changed from the frightened woman who'd so often studied the long driveway for any sign of Ken? The vulnerable woman who hadn't trusted him at first? If only he didn't have Wichita to worry about. "We're all fine right now," he said. "Come here."

Happiness. He reached for her and, after another brief hesitation, Blossom snuggled into his arms as she had on the porch swing after Jacques left, almost purring at Logan's touch. Keeping one eye on his grandfather and Nicky, he soothed a hand over her shoulders, her back, then let it drop to her waist. "Your little one's going to be a real bruiser."

He felt her smile against his shoulder. "Maybe *he*'ll play football."

"Or win a gold buckle riding broncs."

"Or learn to fly jets—"

Logan tilted her face toward his. He angled his mouth to fit hers just so, fought back an urge to groan. He hadn't only missed her while she was gone, even for that short while. He'd realized he loved her. It was too soon to say those words, and he had to iron things out with Libby, but…

Blossom broke their kiss. "That potato salad must have gone to your head."

He'd lost his nerve. "No, I've been thinking. We need to talk. Whenever you're ready." He pulled back, too. "Something to ponder while I go catch the horses." Logan eyed the bison herd, which had been moving closer to them. It was time to go. "I promised Libby we wouldn't be long."

On his feet, he'd just tracked Sundance to a thick patch of grass not far off, the horse's reins trailing on the ground, when he heard Sam shout.

"Nick!"

And Logan's newfound happiness—tentative as it was—shattered into a million pieces.

CHAPTER TWENTY-ONE

At Sam's shout Blossom bolted upright on the picnic blanket. Sam was already thumping across the grass, but his leg cast hindered his progress. Logan was even farther away with Sundance.

Oblivious to the bison herd, which had slowly meandered toward them, munching grass along the way, Nick had wandered off with his butterfly net. He skimmed over the open pasture, sweeping it back and forth at the edge of public land. One of the cows and her calf—the young bull that had tried to hurt Logan?—were grazing less than thirty yards from Nick, but he hadn't seemed to notice.

Her heart in her throat, Blossom lurched to her feet. And ran.

At the same time the buffalo calf lifted its head. Its mother did, too, and seemed to smell danger. The little bull sniffed the air then began to lope toward Blossom, picking up speed with every stride. Did he remember her? His mother rushed forward, nosing him out of the way.

Then the cow charged. Blossom felt sure she was headed for her, but Nick was between Blossom and the cow.

Sam had come to a stop just ahead of Blossom and was panting for breath. With a growing stitch in her side, she passed him by.

The rest of the bison had picked up on the cow's change of direction. A shaggy buffalo, larger than the rest, pawed at the dirt. *These bison are unpredictable, dangerous. They don't like people much.* An hour ago they'd been far enough away to pose no threat. Now, as if they were one beast, the whole herd broke into a run, their hooves rumbling over the ground, their combined weight shaking the earth. *Stampede.*

Hampered by the baby weight she'd gained, Blossom couldn't run any faster, yet somehow she had to. She didn't think of her own well-being. Nick would get hurt, or even killed.

She was running flat out when a horse streaked past her, missing Blossom by inches. Waving his hat at the bison, yelling at the top of his lungs, Logan on Sundance thundered toward the cow.

LOGAN WASN'T SURE he was even breathing. He didn't care. In that heart-stopping instant, he didn't think of his reluctance to be on this ranch, or of Joe's warning about the future of his job. All he could see was Blossom, Nicky, Sam…in the path of the stampeding bison.

In that one second the past flashed in front of his eyes. *The lightning, the rain, the water rising, the roads closed—Nicky at the Circle H while Logan was in Wichita.* His own guilt. He'd thrown caution to the winds that night, riding cross-country in the dark and the blowing rain with Grey, but he couldn't think of that now.

If he didn't reach Nicky in time, he'd be trampled by the panicked herd, his small body ground into the chewed-up dirt by hundreds of churning hooves at a full-out run. Libby had been right after all. He should never have brought Nicky to the ranch again.

What would he tell her? She already blamed him for nearly losing their child before.

Behind him, one of the dogs barked. Then, to his horror, he saw Blossom trying to get between the calf's mother and Nicky. She was about to be overrun. So was Sam.

Logan bent low over the horse's neck. He and Sundance were one being now, like some ancient centaur, and the horse knew his job. With the lightest touch of the reins and another nudge from Logan's legs to Sundance's sides, the gelding swerved to cut the mother bison and her calf in front from the rest of the stampeding herd.

The two border collies knew their duties, too. Both barking, they raced toward the bison.

In a flash, the cow turned sharply, steered by the dogs and Sundance, with her calf back into the herd. The rest arced around with them and, to his undying gratitude, seemed to flow like a dark wave, curving as one until they, too, ran away from, not toward, Blossom and Nicky.

His breath still caught in his lungs, Logan slumped in the saddle.

IN BLOSSOM'S ARMS, Nick had buried his face in her neck. She was still giving thanks that he was alive, and unhurt, when Sundance skidded to a stop beside them. Logan slid off the horse then pulled them into a three-way hug. "You both okay?"

Blossom nodded. "I think so."

Sam hobbled over, still struggling for breath. He threw his hat on the ground with a shout. "That is one good cutting horse!"

"Believe it," Logan said. "He gets extra grain tonight, that's for sure. And treats for the dogs."

"You looked mighty good on that horse. Still think you're not a cowboy?"

Logan ran a hand over Nick's hair, and his son trembled in his embrace. So did Blossom. "All I know is, we're going home." He met her gaze. "Then I'm driving you and Nicky into Barren to see Doc. You too, Sam. That was the last chance you're taking."

Blossom managed to keep her mouth shut on the way back to the ranch. She'd put the last of her energy into packing up the picnic items, and her side still ached. At the barn Sam refused to see the doctor, and Logan ordered him to the house instead. He told Tobias to watch him and instructed Willy to make sure the herd had settled down for the night, as well as to check the cow and bull calf to make certain they weren't hurt. He didn't seem to notice that Tobias was still wearing a sling on his arm and Willy's eye was an angry-looking blue green where his bruises from Jacques were fading.

"I don't need to go into town either," Blossom tried to tell him. She'd been there only yesterday to buy new clothes that fit and some cute newborn outfits from Baby Things. She'd wanted to show the clerk and everyone in town that she was out in the open now, unafraid, although Ken was still on her mind.

"You're going," Logan said.

"Don't give me orders."

For a second, he eyed her with what she could only call respect. Something she'd never seen from Ken.

"Humor me," he finally said. "I need Doc to check Nicky anyway. You ought to be sure the baby's okay, too." He held open the passenger door of his truck and Nick hopped up onto the rear seat.

"I don't see a baby," he said.

"She's in Blossom's tummy."

At Doc's office Logan paced the floor until an older woman Blossom didn't recognize came out of the examining area behind the reception desk. He tipped his hat to her. "Afternoon, Milly. How you doing?"

"Doc fixed me up. I'll live forever."

"Glad to hear it. You take care now."

Blossom hid a smile. If Logan thought he wasn't part of this community or the Circle H, he was wrong. At the desk Doc's wife, Ida, consulted her appointment book. Doc, Logan had told her, didn't believe in computers. "Go on in. He'll see you now, Nicholas."

Blossom hung back but Logan guided her down the short hallway. The three of them crowded into the small exam room. "Like I said when I called, we had a bit of an accident, Doc. I'd have brought Sam with me but he wouldn't budge."

"I talked to him by phone after you rang on your way in." Doc motioned Logan to lift Nick onto the table. "You know Sam. He said all that was wrong with him could be cured by running the Circle H again. You want to know the truth, he sounded all jazzed up."

"His adrenaline was still flowing."

"He claims he'll talk you into staying yet. From what I heard, you're one—" he glanced at Nick "—heck of a horseman."

"I didn't have any other choice."

Doc sent Blossom a quick smile. "You handling this one okay?"

Seated on a chair, she studied her folded hands. "I try."

But she knew Logan would have plenty to say to her later.

While Doc examined Nick, and Logan roamed the tiny room as if he couldn't sit down, Doc chuckled. "Boys will be boys. You ever stop to think, Nick, that it might not be the best choice to get so near those bison?"

"They're my daddy's. And Grandpa Sam's. They wouldn't hurt me."

Doc patted Nick's scraped knee. He'd torn through the new-looking jeans Libby had dressed him in that morning. "Listen to your father. I'm kind of partial to bison myself, but I'd keep a clear distance between them and me."

"One of 'em's a baby—like in Blossom's tummy," Nick said.

Doc raised an eyebrow. "All the more reason. Mothers can be like tigers with their cubs." He looked at Logan. "I don't expect Olivia will be happy about this."

Logan frowned. "I don't expect she will."

Doc gestured for Logan to help Nick off the table. "Your boy's all right. Got a lot of spunk. Be a shame if someone else spoiled that."

"I hear you, Doc."

"Go on now, Nick. Miss Ida has a big red lollipop for you. Would that be something of interest?"

"Yes!" Nick disappeared in a flash.

Doc turned to Blossom. "Now, then, young lady. Let's take a look at you."

She didn't even try to resist. Logan was already seething inside over the stampede. She wouldn't provoke him further. Doc poked and prodded then stepped back from the exam table.

"Your little one's growing like a weed. You sure you're not carrying twins?" He winked at Logan.

"Twins run in my family, not Blossom's," Logan reminded him.

"What do you hear from Sawyer these days?"

"Nothing."

"Hmm. Well. It takes all kinds." Doc patted Blossom's arm. "Everything seems to be coming along nicely. You haven't had any pain?"

"None," she said. "I feel good. Glad to be alive," she added.

He patted her shoulder. "Thanks for coming in. I wouldn't want anyone here to worry about you—pace the floor tonight waiting for another disaster." He looked pointedly at Logan.

Blossom slid from the table without help. "You'll be the first to know if there's a problem."

As soon as Logan and Blossom stepped outside, leaving Nicky behind to say his goodbyes, Libby's car wheeled into a parking space in front of Doc's office. She shoved the gearshift into Park then burst from the driver's seat to face him.

"Nobody got hurt," Logan said. He had called her before he called Doc.

"I knew that picnic was a bad idea." Her mouth pinched, Libby eyed Blossom then him. "May I speak to you alone?"

"Sure. Let's get it over with."

He had no doubt what was coming next. Without a glance at him, Blossom got into his truck nearby then rolled up the passenger window.

"Libby, no one could know beforehand about those bison. When we got to the pond, they were grazing, almost at Grey's property line. Then Nicky decided to try his new butterfly net and didn't realize he'd gotten so far from our blanket."

"How many times should I try to trust you with him before—"

"Olivia."

"No, I'm finished, Logan."

His jaw tensed. "That's what you think. I have rights to see my son."

"Unless you agree to supervised visits somewhere of *my* choosing—not at the Circle H again—you won't! By the time you take me back to court, it won't matter. Nick will be safe."

"He's safe right now!"

Her mouth turned down. "I know that look on your face. You'd argue about this until you're blue. Instead, you should admit, at least to yourself, that Nick was in grave danger today."

Logan ran a hand over his nape. He could see the worry in her eyes.

"Yeah, he was."

"And where were you when the herd began to stampede?"

"Getting the horses ready to head home."

"Really?" She inclined her head toward Blossom in the truck.

A twinge of guilt ran through him. Libby was right. He'd gotten lost in Blossom before that, lost his head over her. He could still taste their kisses, longer and deeper than before. "I thought we'd settled that at Nicky's birthday party."

"Obviously not."

"Libby, I know you're afraid of losing him in every way—I don't blame you. But about Blossom, let it go."

"Not when Nick's welfare is at stake. If you

don't like my terms, then you won't see him again anytime soon."

"You really think that's in his best interest?" Logan threw up his hands. He had a sudden urge to throttle Olivia, but he didn't move. "Then I guess it's time to lawyer up," he said at last.

"Please do. I'll win this time, too."

Logan turned away. He sent a silent plea in Blossom's direction, but she didn't meet his gaze. Then, before he could gather himself, Nicky burst out the door from Doc's office with another red lollipop. He ran into Logan's arms.

"Thanks, Daddy! We had an exciting day."

"Yeah, buddy. We sure did."

"Nick, get in the car," Libby said.

"Not yet. I need to talk to Daddy."

"We're through talking. In the car. Now."

Nicky's face clouded up. "When will I see him?"

"We can talk about that later."

"You mean, no." With his head down, he started toward Libby's car then stopped. He turned and rocketed back to slam into Logan. Crying, he buried his face against him. Logan laid a hand on his head.

"I don't like you, Mommy. I want Daddy!

I'll go to the Circle H whenever I want! Every day to see my truck and my Blossoms."

As stiff as a post, Libby stood there, arms crossed as if she were the judge and jury. Logan steered Nicky to her car for a hug and received a sticky kiss.

"See you soon, buddy." He marched back to Olivia and stood toe-to-toe.

"One thing." It wouldn't matter if he hired the best lawyer in the Midwest—assuming he could afford one—or spent more frustrating weeks in court. "I can't keep you from denying me access to my own child right now. But I don't want to hear another word about Blossom Kennedy."

"I am *not* jealous," Libby said.

Then she got in to her car. And shut the door in his face.

HER HEART STILL feeling sore after witnessing that exchange, Blossom faced Logan across the kitchen table at the ranch. He had repeated his conversation with Olivia to her on their way home. "I know how frustrated you must feel, but you still have to try for joint custody."

Logan's cell phone rang. He checked the display then grimaced.

"I have to take this. Sorry."

She heard only his part of the conversation, enough to know his boss had called. Not a good sign right now. They needed to have that talk, but when he finally hung up, she could see the truth on his face.

"Bad timing," he said. "Bad news."

"How bad?"

"That was Joe. The big boss has been following my progress, too—or the lack of it—and he's not happy either. I wish I could have taken that last flight Joe offered me. Now there's another, more important test—a test for me, too," he added. "He suggested I find a way to get back to Wichita. By tomorrow morning. Yesterday, he said, would have been even better."

The words stuck in her throat. "Will you go?"

"It's not a redesign this time but brand-new. If I don't, Joe will give this assignment to a guy named Garvey. We've been battling it out for a promotion—the promotion I need to get Nicky back. I have more flight hours than Garvey does, but that won't matter."

"You'll lose your promotion?"

He sighed. "The paperwork's already done, ready to be sent to the higher-ups. Joe said there's nothing else he can do."

"What did you tell him?"

"I'll be there." Or else, he wouldn't have a job.

Why be surprised? Even disappointed? He was leaving, as he'd always intended to do, and after the picnic had ended in a stampede, he probably couldn't wait to put the Circle H behind him—no matter what other people thought. If Ken showed up then, she'd have to face him alone.

"Blossom, if I don't do as Joe asks this time, I won't be able to sue Libby. And, after talking with her today, I know it's going to be one whale of a fight. It's not bad enough I lost ten years off my life when I saw Nicky heading for those bison—you racing toward him with Sam in the way. Sundance and I couldn't get there fast enough."

"Yet you did."

"That hardly counts with Libby."

"What about Sam?"

"I hate leaving him here, but Tobias's arm is getting better and Willy can pick up any slack for a few days. The other men we use don't live on the ranch, but they're here during the day."

"You'd really leave the Circle H to some cowhands who—like the barn cats—might disappear tomorrow? They have no stake in this ranch, Logan."

He ran a hand through his hair. "I can't lose this last chance to prove myself with Joe and the company management. This is what I've wanted for half my life—and because of Nicky now, too. If I don't go, I'll be writing 'The End' to my career and to my son."

"You'll also be abandoning your grandfather." *And me*, though she couldn't say that. It was Blossom who'd left that message for Ken, which she hadn't told Logan about—until now. She had to. "Ken knows where I am," she said.

Shock filled his eyes. "How did he find out?"

She raised her chin. "I called him. This is my fight, Logan. Not Tammy's." *Not yours either after all.* She should have known better than to think she could—or even should—rely on him.

Logan pushed back his chair. "Blossom, I want to help. But you know what Libby said."

"Then you're as trapped by her as I've been by Ken."

CHAPTER TWENTY-TWO

LOGAN PITCHED ANOTHER forkful of straw into Sundance's empty stall. In the aisle the horse was doing a little dance that looked to him like a samba, but Logan wasn't smiling. The horse had picked up on his conflicted feelings.

The picnic with Blossom, those kisses on the blanket that had made him yearn for much more, were now a dim memory. After their quarrel, their fragile relationship seemed finished. Jealous or not, Libby had no reason to worry about Blossom.

Still, in spite of Joe and his job, he wanted to stay right here. Then Blossom wouldn't be alone when Ken came to the Circle H—because Logan had no doubt he would. Was the man as vicious as she thought? Or had he convinced her long ago she'd have no choice except to obey him or pay the price?

He hadn't been able to get through to her. Or Libby.

"Boss?"

Logan scattered straw around the clean stall. "Yeah."

Willy stood at the open door. "Got a cow down by the creek. She looks hurt, pretty bad. Want to give me a hand?"

"You'd better call the vet instead. I'm leaving in fifteen minutes." Logan had already put his packed bag in his truck. He'd avoided seeing Blossom or saying another word to her. If he did, he'd be tempted to stay, to blow his chances for shared custody. Then where would he be?

"The vet won't get here in time."

"Well, *try*," Logan growled.

He glanced up to see Willy gaping at him.

"I'm not a rancher," Logan said. He felt bad for the cow but… "Maybe it's time to put the Circle H on the market."

"Sawyer won't agree to that."

Logan scowled. This was all he needed right now: cowboy logic.

"How do you know? You've never met my brother."

"I hear tell about him from Sam."

"Yeah, well, if Sawyer cared about this place, he'd be here. Wouldn't he?"

All the frustration of the past weeks seemed to spill out of him at once. Sawyer hadn't answered his latest calls either. Willy didn't deserve his wrath, but then his go-round with Jacques and a black eye were all he really had to fret over.

"Your sour mood about Blossom?" Willy asked.

"I told you. She's off limits." Logan tossed a last forkful of straw onto the fresh bedding then stepped out into the aisle, nearly knocking Willy off his feet. He wasn't just angry—disappointed—about today. He was scared—for Blossom. Those few moments at the picnic kept running through his mind, over and over, as the memory of the flood had. Why hadn't she told him about the call to Ken? "Are you trying to make me even madder than I already am?"

But with a heavy sigh of defeat, he set the pitchfork against a wall. "Go see to that bison cow. I'll lend you whatever help I can before I go."

By the time Logan had put Sundance in the clean stall then driven a Gator down to the creek, the cow had gotten to her feet. The barbed-wire gash in her side didn't look good. "The vet can sew her up when he gets here—and bill us like usual."

Willy started to smile. "Yes, sir. Boss."

Logan realized he'd said *us*, as if he was part of the Circle H. Part of Blossom's life, too. He spun around. "One of these days, I'm going to fire you, Willy."

"Not when you need me here."

Willy, it seemed, had a greater sense of loyalty than Logan did.

He went back to the barn, then after a last check of all the horses and a pat on the neck for Cyclone—who was going to train the colt now?—he headed for his truck. *I'm not a cowboy.* He would be in Wichita tonight, in time to fly tomorrow morning. To save his job, his promotion…and regain custody of Nicky. In doing so, he'd already lost Blossom and her trust in him.

Halfway down the driveway he'd hated to even look at for the past three years, it struck him like another bolt of lightning: he was as big a coward as Libby was about Nicky's safety. Now he'd added his fears for Blossom to the mix. He was leaving her here. With Willy. To fend for herself.

Jamming on the brakes, he put the truck in Reverse, made a quick three-point turn then started back to the house. He would tell her he loved her. Now. He'd be here for her. Later, he'd worry about Wichita.

That was when he glanced in his rearview mirror and saw the car rushing along the drive behind him.

COMING FROM THE kitchen to the living room windows a moment later, Blossom watched the lone car come.

For the past hour she'd been venting her anger at Logan, her fears of Ken, on every pot in the cupboards. She'd washed them all, banging metal against the porcelain sink, running water hot enough to burn her hands.

How could Logan abandon his grandfather? Even for Nick's sake? Surely, there was another solution instead of running back to Wichita. Leaving Sam virtually alone. Leaving her.

She had to think of her baby first.

Oddly now, faced with what she'd feared most, she felt a growing sense of inner calm. She was certain it was Ken in that car. It didn't matter how he had found the Circle H itself. Unlike Logan, she wouldn't run again. She watched Ken brake at the edge of the front walk then climb out of the luxury rental she'd expected—and squared her shoulders. Strange, he didn't look nearly as tall, as solid, as menacing as she remembered. Against the vastness of the wide-open prairie, that big inverted blue bowl of Kansas sky, he looked somehow...small.

Make a stand. Shadow had said much the same. Even the stranger at the motel had said so, in his way. And all this time, she'd been afraid. Still, she had called Ken herself, tried to protect Tammy. She'd made her choice— and with their quarrel lost Logan. She had to do this. On her own.

Blossom went out to the porch. Ken stood at the foot of the steps, looking up at her now when he'd always looked down on her before, eyeing her with that smug smile she had despised, the smirk that had always frightened her. There would be no hiding her condition. She didn't want to hide.

"I'm pregnant," she said.

His brown eyes widened in obvious surprise. "When were you going to tell me?" His smile turned into a frown. "Bet that friend of yours knew. This isn't the best time for us to have a kid." Which was what he'd always told her. "But what do you know? Surprise, surprise. I'm going to be a daddy."

No, you're not. The thought hadn't left her mind before a shadowy figure suddenly appeared at the screen door holding a gun.

Sam.

SAM CRADLED THE SHOTGUN. His blood pounding hard, he pushed open the door, letting it bang back against the house. He had a pocketful of extra ammunition and wouldn't hesitate to use it. He'd seen the man barrel along the driveway, kicking up stones and raising dirt. Just before that, he'd seen Logan's truck get halfway down then turn around, flying back toward the barn ahead of the car. Where was he now?

Sam didn't hesitate to use the lie. "You're on my property. You don't want to get blasted full of lead, go."

Ken glanced up at him. "This is between me and Blossom, old man."

"No," he said. "Right now this is you and me. You heard what I said."

"Sam." Blossom held up a hand. "Let me do this."

Weaving just a little, he moved toward the steps. "Not alone," he said.

He loved Blossom like a daughter. What kind of man was he, even with a cast on his leg, if he couldn't defend an innocent woman? And this was the house, the land, where all his memories lived. Darned if he'd let them be tainted. Muriel, the boys…the plot of ground on the hill where she lay buried. Even the bison he'd raised then sold at market before his accident were still his. His hard work had built this ranch even if it wasn't truly his own. This was his *home place*.

He would defend it—Blossom and her baby—with his life.

"DON'T DO SOMETHING FOOLISH," Blossom said. "Please." Then she turned her back on Sam. She could trust him, if not Logan or… "You haven't changed at all, Ken."

He grinned. "Why would I? I'm your man. Now go get your things." He cast a glance at her sedan parked nearby. "That yours? Piece of junk. There's a new Lexus waiting for you, baby. All the bells and whistles. As soon as we get home."

Blossom wasn't fooled. So was a fist to her face or a kick to the bulge of her stomach…

"That condo is not my home. I don't want a car, or clothes, or even a cell phone that isn't really mine. I don't want anything from you."

"Since you decided to have a kid without consulting *me*, from now on I make the calls. Get moving." Before she could step back, Ken charged up the steps to grasp her arm. "You have any idea how much time and money I've spent—*wasted*—trying to find you?"

"Well, now you have." With his first words, Blossom had heard Sam lever the shotgun. Weeks ago, she would have been embarrassed, ashamed to have him witness this humiliation. Now she took comfort, and strength, from his presence. "If I'm such a waste, why do you want me back? I'm not only happier on my own. I'm safer."

He tightened his hold, turning the skin on her arm white. "Do I have to take you inside this house myself? Pack for you? How useless can you get?" He raised his other arm. "I ought to—"

He was going to hit her, as he'd done far more often than the one time she'd told Logan about. Or had she suppressed at least some of those memories until Ken had touched her again? But in touching her, he came too close to her baby.

Blossom strained against his hold. "Let me go. You're a bully—an abuser! I'm done with your moods, with everything about *you*. I'm through wondering what I did wrong every single day. I've taken all I'm going to take—"

"Why, you b—" He shoved her up against the outside wall, forcing Sam backward. He almost toppled over but still held the gun.

Blossom tried to catch her breath, but the

words came out on a gasp. "I don't need you, Ken. I don't like you. In fact, I hate you!" She shook her head. "I stayed quiet far too long. I won't bring *my* child into the world to suffer the same treatment I did. You—and my father—are cut from the same mold. I don't know what I ever saw in you."

He shook her. "You're not bringing any kid of *mine* into this world without—"

"It's not your baby."

At first Blossom didn't realize who had spoken. Then she saw Logan in her peripheral vision and took heart. He hadn't left. He shoved open the screen door onto the porch.

"Who are you?" Ken demanded.

Logan's gaze narrowed. "The owner— along with my grandfather—of this ranch. Go inside, Sam," he said without taking his eyes off Ken.

"I won't. If I have to, I'll go down right here. Beside you."

He gave Sam a measuring look, taking in his swaying stance. "I'm glad you have my back." He stepped up to Ken. "Get off the Circle H—right now—or I'll throw you off. And Sam will start shooting." He lowered his tone, yet it sounded no less deadly. "You heard Blossom. She's not going with you. Let her go."

Ken stared down at her, his grip still tight around her upper arm. And Logan surprised her all over again.

"Blossom's baby is mine," he said. "It has nothing to do with you."

Ken studied the swell of her abdomen. "Liar."

"I'm not asking you to believe me. Just get out. Like Sam told you, you're trespassing. Go, before we call the sheriff."

"Your kid? She hasn't been gone long enough," Ken said. "Even though I'm not shocked she'd take up with another man to spite me—"

Blossom's eyes filled but only for an instant. Logan would take responsibility for her baby—protect her child—when he might lose his own son to Libby? His job, his promotion, his career? She couldn't let him lie for her.

"No, Ken." She met his gaze without flinching. It was true, as Logan had said before, that she'd come a long way. She was stronger now. She would never be subjected to abuse from Ken or anyone else again. "I'm grateful Logan would offer to accept my child in order to protect me, too. But this baby is yours, Ken."

"Then that's it. Like me or don't, we're leaving. You're mine, worthless as you really are. Look at it this way. I'm doing you a favor."

Logan's fist was already cocked like Sam's shotgun, which suddenly exploded. He'd shot into the air, and as Ken reacted, Logan pulled Blossom from his grasp then hit him in the jaw. Ken's head snapped back. He howled in pain and fury.

"Blossom isn't a piece of property, yours or anyone else's." Logan shoved him toward the steps. Ken lost his balance and nearly tumbled down the short flight to the ground. His arms were still doing pinwheels when he hit the dirt at the bottom. He'd fallen into her flower bed. "Get out. Don't come back."

"Logan, wait." Blossom pushed past him down the stairs. "Ken, you can fight me about this if you like. I can't stop you. But when I left, I promised to safeguard my baby with my life, if need be. And I will. You'll never have him. Call your lawyers. All of them. I don't care."

Logan was at her back now. His arms came around her, his hands laced over her stomach as if to stake his claim. He laid his cheek against the crown of her head.

"You heard the lady. You want a fight? *We'll* give it to you."

"YOU WERE AMAZING."

Her arm still hurting where Ken had grabbed her, Blossom hurried around the kitchen, but Ken—at last—wasn't on her mind. And at first she didn't hear Logan. With all the excitement, she was already late to fix dinner, so she pulled two cans of chili from the pantry. She turned toward Logan. And beamed. "I was. Wasn't I?"

"Fierce enough to rival the best of the pioneer women who came West long ago to find a better life. They were a pretty tough bunch, too."

She set the cans on the counter. "Logan, I wasn't going back to Ken, but I'm glad you bloodied his nose for me."

"Probably the most satisfying part of my day. Except to hear you tell him off." He paused. "I called the sheriff. He has the cops in Kansas City keeping track of Ken until he's on the next plane out." He slipped his arms around her. "I figure if you could get rid of that bully, I can handle Libby in court."

Blossom smoothed his rumpled hair. "What about your job? What time is that test flight tomorrow?"

"Who cares?" His tone was light. "Sam keeps telling me I'm still a cowboy at heart—

and I guess, after the bison stampede and Ken, he's right."

Her heart turned over. "You'll lose your job. Your promotion."

He actually smiled. "Already lost it. I told Joe I'm resigning. There are other manufacturers in Wichita, some better than the smaller one I was with. Once everything settles down again, I'll look for a new job."

"And in the meantime?"

"Sam gets his cast off in a few weeks then—"

"I'll be taking over this ranch, Flyboy." Sam headed into the kitchen. He'd proved himself today. Soon he'd be zooming all over the Circle H on the Gator and eventually a horse. Sam paused. "Could still use your help."

"You've got it."

His expression fell. "Appreciate that, Logan. You're a good boy, but I know this is temporary. About any longtime plans you might have—" He cleared his throat. "If you and Sawyer sell out, you'd be selling me, too. I can't live in some nursing home in Barren or KC. That room upstairs was confinement enough. You might as well put me down like some old horse—"

Logan stared. "What are you talking about?"

"This is my home. Same as it's yours. Even if I'm not blood kin."

Looking stunned, Logan released Blossom. He walked over to his grandfather and hauled him into his arms. "You're not going anywhere. After what I saw today, you'll be back running the Circle H—with my help at least part-time—until you're a hundred years old, like Methuselah."

Sam's face brightened. "That so?"

Logan kissed the top of Sam's head. "I'd do anything for you, Grandpa. You don't think Sawyer's going to come home, do you?"

"That'll happen about the time Shadow and Grey sign a peace treaty." Sam blinked then touched Logan's shoulder before he whirled around and stumped out of the kitchen. "Sorry I interrupted something. Blossom, I hope you're staying, too."

Before she could answer, a car horn tooted near the front door. For an instant Blossom's knee-jerk reaction was *Ken*. But he wasn't here anymore. He never would be again.

Logan groaned. "It's Libby."

She had Nick with her. In the yard, where Blossom's flowers had sprouted through the warm spring earth, and a few stems now lay trampled by Ken, he stopped to scoop up his kitten. They raced off together toward the barn. "You can ride with me in my truck, Blossom!"

Libby opened the door, wearing jeans with a denim shirt and a chastened expression. Her hair was in a ponytail.

"I know I should have called first, but I couldn't. This has to be done in person." She looked back over her shoulder. "Nick couldn't wait a second longer to see that cat. He wants to go riding later—or tomorrow—with his father. And oh, that truck…"

Blossom couldn't seem to move and Logan's mouth firmed. "What's all this, Libby?"

"I was wrong, and I'm ashamed that it took Nick—our seven-year-old boy—to set me straight." Her voice quavered. "I realized after Nick cried for you in town at Doc's office. I have been overly protective—and, as you said, I've denied my little boy his daddy. Even worse, I made him dislike me."

"Aw, Libby."

"I'll never forget that night in the storm, but I'll never forget Nick saying 'I don't like you' either. That's all I can hear now." Her voice turned husky. "I can't stop remembering his tears, and after he finally stopped crying, he curled up in a ball on his bed at home, telling me to 'go away,' and I shed more than a few tears of my own." She glanced at Logan. "Hard to imagine, I know. I sat beside him anyway, knowing that in a different way I'd lost him—as I always feared." She swallowed. "About that, I can't keep Nick from being the person he can become with both of us raising him—and I shouldn't blame you for what happened three years ago."

Feeling like an intruder, Blossom stepped back. "I'll let you two—"

"No, Blossom. Stay." Libby half smiled. "I hope that's what you plan to do. You're good for Nick." She looked between them. "I think you're good for Logan."

His mouth quirked. "You okay, Libby? Grey thinks you may be sick, and after what you just said—"

He'd meant it as a joke, but for another second she hesitated. "Not...that I know of. I'm sorry, Logan. I know you did your best that night. Sam and I couldn't have done any better. I never stopped to think, but you were right. You must have been even more scared than I was. At least I was with Nick then. You didn't know what you'd find when you got here." She fussed with the strap on her handbag. "Well. I'll go now. You can bring Nick home tomorrow—I left his overnight bag on the porch—or the next day. Whenever. Just call."

"I never even thought of him staying overnight here. I was just as afraid of that as you were, Libby. But, yes. Thanks. I'll bring him home."

"I won't worry," she promised. "And by the way, another custody battle would only cost us both a lot of money. It would upset Nick even more. Instead, I think we can settle everything between us." At the door, she looked back with a genuine smile that lit her whole face. "You two make a very cute picture together."

After the door shut, Logan said, as if he couldn't quite believe it, "She actually brought Nicky here again after what she said before and ate crow. I can't believe I won't have to sue her."

"She's a good mother, Logan."

"I think she feels better knowing you're here." He paused. "You will stay? No more of this moving west into the setting sun. I didn't get to ask before."

Blossom searched in a drawer for a can opener. "I'm staying," she said, and as if that was already a done deal, she set the opener down then looped her arms around his neck. "When I first came to the Circle H, I was a… wounded woman. I wanted to be a stronger person, to rely on myself so I couldn't be hurt again." She gazed deeply into his eyes. "But today… I relied on Sam, on you. I don't think that makes me a weaker person, do you?"

"Nope. You get any stronger, you'll be running the Circle H yourself." He paused, swaying a little with her in his arms. "Blossom, we'll rely on each other. But if I get another job in Wichita, or wherever, we'll have to split our time between there and the ranch. That okay with you? You won't mind?"

"Not as long as I'm with you. I love the Circle H. I'll love wherever we are, but I don't need to keep running. Do you know how good that feels? I'm free now, Logan."

"So am I." She knew he meant from his past, as well. "I learned from that stampede that no matter how many precautions I take, sometimes things just happen anyway. The flood, too. That's all over now. I love you, Blossom Kennedy." He kissed her then raised his head. "Well?"

"I love you, Logan Hunter." Whatever he'd said or done at times, he'd done not out of control, like Ken, but out of love.

He held her close and kissed her once more. But that didn't prove to be enough for either of them, so they kissed again, lingering in the kitchen with the last light of day slanting through the windows and the open screen door. From the barn, they could hear Nick's giggles and the whinny of horses in their stalls.

"So," he said then cleared his throat. "I guess we should get married."

She laughed but with tears in her eyes. "You call that a proposal?"

"I do. That all right with you?"

Blossom pressed a hand to her stomach. "Yes. More than all right." Then she asked, "But, Logan, are you sure? You'll be raising someone else's child."

"She'll be *our* child. There'll likely be no fight with Ken for custody. I can't see him with a baby on his own. I plan to be a better father to her—and to Nicky."

"I know you will." Then Blossom frowned a little. "We'll have to make that official, though, get Ken to sign off on any claim or responsibility for the baby."

"Piece of cake. I think Sam and I put the fear of God in him today."

And Blossom smiled again. "I had no idea you two were such…cowboys."

"Well, we are. I am." Logan drew back. He picked up the can opener and put it in the drawer. He set the two cans of chili back on a pantry shelf then came out again. "Let's eat," he said. "I've got a real craving for some of your curry."

"It's only a white sauce with spices and left-over chicken. It won't take long."

Logan pulled her back into his arms to give her one more kiss. "Who knew you were such a cook?"

"You're about to find out, today and for the rest of your life," Blossom promised.

* * * * *

Don't miss the next book in Leigh Riker's
KANSAS COWBOYS miniseries,
available soon
from Harlequin Heartwarming!

LARGER-PRINT BOOKS!

GET 2 FREE LARGER-PRINT NOVELS PLUS 2 FREE MYSTERY GIFTS

Love Inspired®

Larger-print novels are now available...

YES! Please send me 2 FREE LARGER-PRINT Love Inspired® novels and my 2 FREE mystery gifts (gifts are worth about $10). After receiving them, if I don't wish to receive any more books, I can return the shipping statement marked "cancel." If I don't cancel, I will receive 6 brand-new novels every month and be billed just $5.49 per book in the U.S. or $5.99 per book in Canada. That's a savings of at least 19% off the cover price. It's quite a bargain! Shipping and handling is just 50¢ per book in the U.S. and 75¢ per book in Canada.* I understand that accepting the 2 free books and gifts places me under no obligation to buy anything. I can always return a shipment and cancel at any time. Even if I never buy another book, the two free books and gifts are mine to keep forever.

122/322 IDN GH6D

Name _____ (PLEASE PRINT)

Address _____ Apt. #

City _____ State/Prov. _____ Zip/Postal Code

Signature (if under 18, a parent or guardian must sign)

Mail to the **Reader Service:**
IN U.S.A.: P.O. Box 1867, Buffalo, NY 14240-1867
IN CANADA: P.O. Box 609, Fort Erie, Ontario L2A 5X3

**Are you a current subscriber to Love Inspired® books
and want to receive the larger-print edition?
Call 1-800-873-8635 or visit www.ReaderService.com.**

* Terms and prices subject to change without notice. Prices do not include applicable taxes. Sales tax applicable in N.Y. Canadian residents will be charged applicable taxes. Offer not valid in Quebec. This offer is limited to one order per household. Not valid to current subscribers to Love Inspired Larger-Print books. All orders subject to credit approval. Credit or debit balances in a customer's account(s) may be offset by any other outstanding balance owed by or to the customer. Please allow 4 to 6 weeks for delivery. Offer available while quantities last.

Your Privacy—The Reader Service is committed to protecting your privacy. Our Privacy Policy is available online at www.ReaderService.com or upon request from the Reader Service.

We make a portion of our mailing list available to reputable third parties that offer products we believe may interest you. If you prefer that we not exchange your name with third parties, or if you wish to clarify or modify your communication preferences, please visit us at www.ReaderService.com/consumerchoice or write to us at Reader Service Preference Service, P.O. Box 9062, Buffalo, NY 14240-9062. Include your complete name and address.

LILP15

LARGER-PRINT BOOKS!

GET 2 FREE
LARGER-PRINT NOVELS
PLUS 2 FREE
MYSTERY GIFTS

Love Inspired®

SUSPENSE
RIVETING INSPIRATIONAL ROMANCE

Larger-print novels are now available...

YES! Please send me 2 FREE LARGER-PRINT Love Inspired® Suspense novels and my 2 FREE mystery gifts (gifts are worth about $10). After receiving them, if I don't wish to receive any more books, I can return the shipping statement marked "cancel." If I don't cancel, I will receive 4 brand-new novels every month and be billed just $5.49 per book in the U.S. or $5.99 per book in Canada. That's a savings of at least 19% off the cover price. It's quite a bargain! Shipping and handling is just 50¢ per book in the U.S. and 75¢ per book in Canada.* I understand that accepting the 2 free books and gifts places me under no obligation to buy anything. I can always return a shipment and cancel at any time. Even if I never buy another book, the two free books and gifts are mine to keep forever.

110/310 IDN GH6P

Name _____ (PLEASE PRINT) _____

Address _____ Apt. # _____

City _____ State/Prov. _____ Zip/Postal Code _____

Signature (if under 18, a parent or guardian must sign)

Mail to the **Reader Service:**
IN U.S.A.: P.O. Box 1867, Buffalo, NY 14240-1867
IN CANADA: P.O. Box 609, Fort Erie, Ontario L2A 5X3

Are you a current subscriber to Love Inspired® Suspense books
and want to receive the larger-print edition?
Call 1-800-873-8635 or visit www.ReaderService.com.

* Terms and prices subject to change without notice. Prices do not include applicable taxes. Sales tax applicable in N.Y. Canadian residents will be charged applicable taxes. Offer not valid in Quebec. This offer is limited to one order per household. Not valid for current subscribers to Love Inspired Suspense larger-print books. All orders subject to credit approval. Credit or debit balances in a customer's account(s) may be offset by any other outstanding balance owed by or to the customer. Please allow 4 to 6 weeks for delivery. Offer available while quantities last.

Your Privacy—The Reader Service is committed to protecting your privacy. Our Privacy Policy is available online at www.ReaderService.com or upon request from the Reader Service.

We make a portion of our mailing list available to reputable third parties that offer products we believe may interest you. If you prefer that we not exchange your name with third parties, or if you wish to clarify or modify your communication preferences, please visit us at www.ReaderService.com/consumerchoice or write to us at Reader Service Preference Service, P.O. Box 9062, Buffalo, NY 14240-9062. Include your complete name and address.

WESTERN **WP** PROMISES

YES! Please send me **The Western Promises Collection** in Larger Print. This collection begins with 3 FREE books and 2 FREE gifts (gifts valued at approx. $14.00 retail) in the first shipment, along with the other first 4 books from the collection! If I do not cancel, I will receive 8 monthly shipments until I have the entire 51-book Western Promises collection. I will receive 2 or 3 FREE books in each shipment and I will pay just $4.99 US/ $5.89 CDN for each of the other four books in each shipment, plus $2.99 for shipping and handling per shipment. *If I decide to keep the entire collection, I'll have paid for only 32 books, because 19 books are FREE! I understand that accepting the 3 free books and gifts places me under no obligation to buy anything. I can always return a shipment and cancel at any time. My free books and gifts are mine to keep no matter what I decide.

272 HCN 3070 472 HCN 3070

Name _____ (PLEASE PRINT) _____

Address _____ Apt. #

City _____ State/Prov. _____ Zip/Postal Code

Signature (if under 18, a parent or guardian must sign)

Mail to the **Reader Service:**
IN U.S.A.: P.O. Box 1867, Buffalo, NY 14240-1867
IN CANADA: P.O. Box 609, Fort Erie, Ontario L2A 5X3

* Terms and prices subject to change without notice. Prices do not include applicable taxes. Sales tax applicable in N.Y. Canadian residents will be charged applicable taxes. This offer is limited to one order per household. All orders subject to approval. Credit or debit balances in a customer's account(s) may be offset by any other outstanding balance owed by or to the customer. Please allow 4 to 6 weeks for delivery. Offer available while quantities last. Offer not available to Quebec residents.

Your Privacy—The Reader Service is committed to protecting your privacy. Our Privacy Policy is available online at www.ReaderService.com or upon request from the Reader Service.

We make a portion of our mailing list available to reputable third parties that offer products we believe may interest you. If you prefer that we not exchange your name with third parties, or if you wish to clarify or modify your communication preferences, please visit us at www.ReaderService.com/consumerschoice or write to us at Reader Service Preference Service, P.O. Box 9062, Buffalo, NY 14240-9062. Include your complete name and address.

WPBPA16R

LARGER-PRINT BOOKS!
GET 2 FREE LARGER-PRINT NOVELS PLUS
2 FREE GIFTS!

(H) HARLEQUIN®

super romance®

More Story...More Romance

YES! Please send me 2 FREE LARGER-PRINT Harlequin® Superromance® novels and my 2 FREE gifts (gifts are worth about $10). After receiving them, if I don't wish to receive any more books, I can return the shipping statement marked "cancel." If I don't cancel, I will receive 4 brand-new novels every month and be billed just $5.94 per book in the U.S. or $6.24 per book in Canada. That's a savings of at least 12% off the cover price! It's quite a bargain! Shipping and handling is just 50¢ per book in the U.S. or 75¢ per book in Canada.* I understand that accepting the 2 free books and gifts places me under no obligation to buy anything. I can always return a shipment and cancel at any time. Even if I never buy another book, the two free books and gifts are mine to keep forever.

132/332 HDN GHVC

Name _____
(PLEASE PRINT)

Address _____ Apt. #

City _____ State/Prov. _____ Zip/Postal Code

Signature (if under 18, a parent or guardian must sign)

Mail to the **Reader Service:**
IN U.S.A.: P.O. Box 1867, Buffalo, NY 14240-1867
IN CANADA: P.O. Box 609, Fort Erie, Ontario L2A 5X3

Want to try two free books from another line?
Call 1-800-873-8635 today or visit www.ReaderService.com.

* Terms and prices subject to change without notice. Prices do not include applicable taxes. Sales tax applicable in N.Y. Canadian residents will be charged applicable taxes. Offer not valid in Quebec. This offer is limited to one order per household. Not valid for current subscribers to Harlequin Superromance Larger-Print books. All orders subject to credit approval. Credit or debit balances in a customer's account(s) may be offset by any other outstanding balance owed by or to the customer. Please allow 4 to 6 weeks for delivery. Offer available while quantities last.

Your Privacy—The Reader Service is committed to protecting your privacy. Our Privacy Policy is available online at www.ReaderService.com or upon request from the Reader Service.

We make a portion of our mailing list available to reputable third parties that offer products we believe may interest you. If you prefer that we not exchange your name with third parties, or if you wish to clarify or modify your communication preferences, please visit us at www.ReaderService.com/consumerchoice or write to us at Reader Service Preference Service, P.O. Box 9062, Buffalo, NY 14240-9062. Include your complete name and address.

READERSERVICE.COM

Manage your account online!

- Review your order history
- Manage your payments
- Update your address

> ### *We've designed the Reader Service website just for you.*

Enjoy all the features!

- Discover new series available to you, and read excerpts from any series.
- Respond to mailings and special monthly offers.
- Connect with favorite authors at the blog.
- Browse the Bonus Bucks catalog and online-only exculsives.
- Share your feedback.

Visit us at:

ReaderService.com

RS15